DISHONORED PROMISES

A Brendan O'Brian Legal Thriller

J.W. Kerwin

GREY SQUIRREL PRESS

A NOTE FROM THE AUTHOR

This is the third book in the Brendan O'Brian series. Like the previous books, it's a self-contained story that you can understand and (hopefully) enjoy without having read the earlier novels. However, reading *Slow Death in the Fast Lane* and *A Stranger In My Own Hometown* before you begin this book will enhance your reading experience by providing background information about the characters, as well as the events leading up to those that take place in this novel.

Many thanks to my advance readers: Kate, Meaghan, Pam, Jack, John, and Patrick. Their feedback was invaluable and greatly appreciated.

Book design by Maureen Cutajar
www.gopublished.com

ISBN: 978-1-7351196-0-1

1

"I promise I'll find that out for you."

Cremating a man before notifying his wife that he died is just plain wrong, and it might even be illegal.

On a sunny morning in September 1993, Ronald Anderson went to work at Consolidated TranShip Corporation a few miles from our law office in the northern New Jersey town of Troy Forge. Just after two o'clock, Anderson's wife, Edna, received a phone call informing her that her husband had died at work and his body cremated at a nearby funeral home.

A tearful Mrs. Anderson appeared at my office the following day with four children in tow. She placed a shopping bag on the chair next to her and then spent fifteen minutes providing a rambling, and at times incoherent, narrative of what had happened to her husband. Her explanation left me with more questions than answers.

When she finished, I handed her a tissue, the first of many I would dispense that morning. "Let me ask you a few questions, so I can figure out the best way to proceed." She nodded assent while wiping away the tears rolling down her cheeks. "Do you remember the name of the person you spoke to at Consolidated TranShip?"

"Mr. Antonellis," she answered, quickly adding, "I think." She dabbed at the corner of each eye with the tissue. "I'm not sure. I was so upset when he called, I'm not really sure about his name."

"Quite understandable," I said. "And this Mr. Antonellis, or whoever it was that you spoke to, did he tell you how your husband died?"

"He said it was an accident."

"What kind of accident?"

Mrs. Anderson stared off into space, as though the answer to my question could be found floating in mid-air. "I don't know," she finally said. "I asked him, of course, but he never really answered my question. He went on and on about what a nice guy Ronnie was and how everyone would miss him, but he never actually told me what happened. And every time I asked the question, he changed the subject."

I assumed that meant Ronald Anderson had died a gruesome death, and to spare his widow from seeing the horribly mangled body, the company had it cremated. Of course, there was another, more chilling, possibility. Anderson's body could have become contaminated with some type of dangerous virus or bacteria, requiring the remains to be incinerated immediately. There are dozens of pharmaceutical companies in the area, any one of which could be conducting experiments with dangerous pathogens. If Consolidated TranShip was involved in shipping or storing those substances, an accidental spill could have turned Anderson's body into a toxic time bomb.

After gathering as much information as I could from the distraught widow, I explained how I planned to proceed. "The first thing we'll do is file a worker's compensation claim on your behalf. That will provide you with money to partially replace your late husband's salary."

When I told her how much money she could expect to receive, the trickle of tears turned into a torrent. "How will I support the children on that?"

"That's just the first step," I explained in an effort to calm her down. "Next, we'll file suit against the funeral home for the infliction of emotional distress caused by the immediate cremation of your husband's body."

The mention of cremation caused Edna Anderson to wail, "I never had a chance to say goodbye." I handed her another tissue.

"We might possibly be able to sue your husband's employer as well." I added the "possibly" qualifier because under New Jersey's workers comp law, suits against an employer are barred unless the workplace injury or death was caused by an intentional act. Although I had no reason to think Anderson's death wasn't a tragic accident, there was no telling what we'd uncover once we investigated the matter. But even if Anderson's death was accidental, turning his body into a pile of ashes seemed pretty darned intentional. I made a note on my legal pad to research that angle.

"There's one other thing we could possibly do to provide you with additional funds," I told Mrs. Anderson. "We might be able to file what's called a third party action if your husband's death was caused by the negligence of someone other than Consolidated TranShip. For example, if he was operating machinery, and a defect in the machine resulted in his death, we could sue the manufacturer of the machine."

"Ronnie never mentioned operating a machine," his widow said. "But then again, Ronnie never talked much about work. All he ever told me was that he worked in a warehouse. He signed some sort of confidentiality agreement when they hired him, so he couldn't tell me what he did at work." She wiped away another tear, and I handed her yet another tissue from my rapidly dwindling supply. Then she asked the question clients always ask. "How much is all this going to cost?"

"You won't have any out of pocket costs," I assured her. "We won't charge you anything to file the workers comp claim. Everything else we'll handle on a contingent fee basis, meaning we're paid a percentage of anything we collect for you. That provides us with an incentive to get as much as we can for you." Mrs. Anderson seemed to think that was a magnanimous gesture on my part, and I didn't say anything to disabuse her of that notion. In reality, the fee we'd earn for handling the workers comp matter was a pittance compared to what I calculated we could get from suing the funeral home, Consolidated TranShip, and any other defendants we were able to uncover. I assumed both the funeral home and Anderson's employer had insurance, providing a couple of deep pockets to pay whatever judgment or settlement we eventually got.

I buzzed Carolyn, my secretary, who promptly appeared at the door to usher Mrs. Anderson and her brood out of my office. "My secretary has a few things for you to sign on your way out," I said to signal that our meeting was over.

Mrs. Anderson got up to leave, but quickly sat down again. "I was going to stop at the bank and talk to someone I know there, but as long as I'm here..." She reached into the shopping bag on the chair next to her, withdrew a stack of documents, and handed them to me. "I'm not sure how I go about cashing these in. Can you help?"

Even before I could see what was written on them, I knew the papers in her outstretched hand were very old by their yellowed appearance. I carefully unfolded the top document and placed it on my desk. It had a green certificate border and "$10,000" in a box in the upper right corner. Across the top of the certificate were the words "The Chinese Government Loan." Several inches below that was "BOND" in big, fancy, bold type with "Ten Thousand United States Dollars" underneath.

"Where did you get these?" I asked.

"Ronnie has been buying these for the past year or so." She took a deep breath, and fighting a less than successful battle to hold back tears, corrected herself. "Ronnie *had* been buying these for the past year or so. Knowing Ronnie, I assume they must be worth something, but I don't know how to cash them in."

I had no idea if the bonds had any value, much less how they could be redeemed. Based on the dollar value of each bond and how many were stacked in the shopping bag, we were looking at a small fortune if those yellowed certificates could be turned into greenbacks. "Without doing some research, I can't tell you what these are worth," I said, quickly adding "if anything" to avoid getting her hopes up. "But if they do have value, we'll get you as much as we can for them. Leave them with me and we'll do the necessary research." She seemed to hesitate, so I added, "We'll put them in the firm's fire-proof safe." I suppose I should have explained that the firm's safe was actually a fifty-dollar home security box hidden under the bed in the guest room of Carolyn's apartment, but there are some things clients don't really need to know.

Carolyn and I made eye contact, and a slight nod of her head told me she knew to add the bonds to our standard contingent fee agreement before Mrs. Anderson signed it.

"Having enough money for the children is important," she said, motioning to the four girls that it was time to leave. "But what I really want is to know what happened to my Ronnie."

"I promise I'll find that out for you," I replied, not realizing how difficult it would be to keep that promise.

2

"Why do they need
Scott's military records?"

My second appointment that day was with another grieving widow. Just before noon I arrived at The New Amsterdam Inn, a restaurant on Route 10 near the western edge of Troy Forge. The Inn is an upscale eatery that was once owned by Martin von Beaverwyck, a longtime client of Santorini, Woodson, Glickman & O'Brian, which became the law firm of Santorini & O'Brian after Scott Woodson and Avery Glickman died in the parking garage explosion at the World Trade Center.

The explosion set in motion a series of events that led up to my luncheon meeting that day with Scott Woodson's widow, Margaret. Shortly after the funerals, Margaret filed a claim with the company that had issued a life insurance policy on Scott's life. The company was a multi-billion dollar entity created when half a dozen insurers with "federal" or "American" in their name merged with a carrier that specialized in insuring international shippers. The end result was a company called Federal American International Lines Insurance. Whoever was in charge of naming the entity that emerged

6

from those mergers apparently never realized it would be referred to as FAIL Insurance by its detractors, of which there were many, including Margaret.

Shortly after submitting a claim, Margaret received a form letter demanding copies of the checks used to pay the policy premiums for the previous six years. She readily complied, assuming a check from the insurance company would soon arrive in the mail. Instead of a check, FAIL sent a second letter demanding additional information about her late husband, much of which was presumably already known to the insurance company. Once again, she complied. And once again, she waited in vain for a check. For more than a month, Margaret received a series of letters from the insurance company, each demanding still more information, which she dutifully supplied.

The company eventually sent a letter which, unlike the previous ones, was clearly not a form letter. Sent by the insurance company's "Special Investigative Unit" and signed by someone named Harry Sporn, the letter informed Margaret that she was to present herself at the company's headquarters in Newark for an examination under oath or EUO.

Margaret was already seated at a small table in the back of the restaurant when I arrived. "I just don't understand any of this," she said before I had a chance to sit down. She has waving an envelope with the FAIL logo prominently displayed in the upper left corner, and she was clearly angry and upset. "We paid the premium year after year, never missed a payment, never late. And now, instead of honoring their promise to pay, the damn insurance company sends me this." She removed a letter from the envelope and handed it to me as I took a seat to her left.

The latest letter from FAIL, which I had not yet seen, contained a list of documents that Margaret was instructed to bring to the EUO the following week. A few made sense, but most seemed to have nothing whatsoever to do with her claim.

"Why would they want a copy of my driver's license?" she asked, referring to the first item on the list.

"It's probably just to establish your identity for their records. Imagine what would happen if the insurance company gave a seven-figure check to the wrong person."

It was a plausible explanation, but based on the laundry list of other documents the insurer was demanding, I suspected it was just another delaying tactic. Margaret apparently had the same thought. She leaned over and ran her finger down the list of documents demanded until she came to one halfway down the first page. "How the hell am I supposed to get a certified copy of Scott's discharge from the army?" Before I could tell her she probably had to write to some government bureau or department, she answered her own question. "I have to fill out something called Standard Form 180 and mail or fax it to a place called the National Personnel Records Center."

"Sounds like you've done your homework," I said.

"Yes, but it took me half a day to find that out," she said between clenched teeth. "Why do they need Scott's military records? And why should I have to jump through all these hoops to get what the insurance company owes me?" Once again, she answered the question before I could respond. "I'll tell you why. Every day they hang on to those funds puts money in their pocket. That money should be sitting in my bank account, earning interest for me, not in their account earning money for them." I hadn't done the calculations, but given the size of the policy's death benefit, the interest it would generate was significant.

"Can't we just tell them to take their letter and shove it?" she asked in obvious frustration.

I laughed. "I'd love to be able to do that, but as your attorney, I have to recommend you give them what they're requesting. An insurance policy is a contract, and like any contract, both sides have to abide by the terms of the agreement." I withdrew a copy of the policy from my briefcase and flipped to a section I had highlighted. "According to your policy, after making a claim you're required to, and I quote, supply requested information and submit to one or more examinations under oath while not in the presence of another insured."

"So, I'm at their mercy and they can jerk me around for as long as they want?" Margaret was clearly annoyed, perhaps as much with the messenger as with the message. I needed to calm things down.

"No, that's not what I'm saying. Under New Jersey law, an insurance company that fails to pay a valid claim can be sued for bad faith."

"How much more valid could a claim be?" Margaret asked. "There's no question that Scott's dead. He died six months ago. His body was recovered and identified." It was the first time I had heard Margaret use the word "dead" when referring to Scott. In the past she had said he was "gone," as though there were a chance he might return. She stared into space in much the same way Edna Anderson had earlier that day in my office. But unlike Mrs. Anderson, there were no tears, just anger. "Then let's sue these bastards for bad faith."

"It may well come to that," I said. "But first you have to do all the things you're required to do under the insurance contract. And that includes attending the EUO next week."

"Fine, we'll go to their damn inquisition, but if they don't send me a check after that, I want you to promise you'll sue them for me."

"Absolutely," I said, quickly adding, "but you should know that in New Jersey, suing an insurance company for bad faith isn't as easy as you might think. A recent state supreme court case, *Pickett v. Lloyd's*, requires us to prove there are no valid reasons for delaying the processing of a claim."

"There are no valid reasons," Margaret insisted. "As you said, an insurance policy is a contract. We upheld our end of the contract by paying the premiums while Scott was alive. Now that he's gone, the insurance company has to uphold their end of the deal by paying me. The only reason they're not honoring their promise to pay is so they can hang on to the money as long as possible."

"It's tough to argue with that," I responded. "And I promise you'll get a check from the insurance company sooner rather than later." What I didn't say is that FAIL has a small army of attorneys who read every word of every insurance-related case in the state. They knew as much about *Pickett* as I did, perhaps even more. What worried me was the possibility that they knew something about Margaret's claim that I didn't know.

3

"You'll have to call
for an appointment."

After my luncheon meeting with Margaret Woodson I drove to Consolidated TranShip Corporation in an industrial park on the other side of town. Finding the place was easy, thanks to "CTSC" in big letters on the side of the building. Getting into the building was a different matter.

The sprawling concrete block structure looked like the other buildings in the Railhead Industrial Park, but was the only one with a gated entry guarded by two uniformed men with guns.

I pulled up to the guardhouse and rolled down the window of my Mustang. A big guy wearing sunglasses came out of the guardhouse. He walked to my car, leaned down, put his forearms on the door, and invaded my personal space. "Can I help you?" he asked, his face just inches from mine. It was delivered pleasantly enough, but his body language was downright intimidating.

I introduced myself and explained that I represented Edna Anderson, the widow of the employee who had died the previous week. "I'd like to speak to a Mr. Antonellis. I believe he was

Mr. Anderson's supervisor, although I'm not completely sure about that."

"No one named Antonellis works here," the guard informed me a bit too quickly. Either the company was very small – unlikely, given the size of the building – and the guard knew all the employees, or he was being less than truthful.

"That was the name of the person who called Mrs. Anderson to inform her of her husband's death. As I'm sure you can understand, she was upset by the news. Perhaps she got the name wrong." I waited for a response, or perhaps some show of sympathy, but none was forthcoming. "In any event," I continued, "I'd like to speak to Mr. Anderson's supervisor."

"I wouldn't know who that is," the guard replied.

"A minute ago, right off the top of your head, you knew there was nobody named Antonellis working here," I said, perhaps a bit too loudly. "Now you don't know who Ronald Anderson's supervisor was?" My raised voice apparently caught the attention of a second sunglass-wearing guard, who came out of the guardhouse and took up a position near the passenger's side widow of my car, his right hand resting on a holstered sidearm.

"The fact that I know there's nobody named Antonellis working here doesn't mean I know the name of every department head," the first guard said.

"But you do know who Ronald Anderson is, the guy who died here last week?"

The guard straightened up, removed his sunglasses and looked at his colleague on the other side of my car before responding. "Sorry. The guardhouse is as far as I go. I never enter the main building. The only time I see the employees is when they come through the gate."

"Fair enough," I said. "Were you on duty last week?"

My question seemed to catch him off guard. He exchanged glances with his colleague again before answering. "Yeah, I was here."

"Did you see an ambulance or a police car come through the gate?" I assumed if there had been a death on the premises, the local authorities would have responded.

"Don't recall any," the guard answered.

"How about a hearse?"

"No, don't recall a hearse either."

"Do you keep a log of vehicles that enter and leave the premises?" I assumed that was standard procedure, and that the guard would know I knew that, forcing him to answer in the affirmative lest his answer appear suspicious.

I wasn't disappointed. "Yeah, we log vehicles through the gate."

"Can I see the log from last week?" It was a long shot, but no harm in asking.

"No," came the immediate response. "That information is proprietary, and for all I know you work for a competitor."

"I don't work for a competitor. Hell, I don't even know what you do here." The guard on the passenger side of my car moved closer, his hand still resting on his holstered weapon. "I represent the widow of your fellow employee who died here last week," I said to the guard on my side of the car. "The poor woman is just trying to find out what happened to her husband. Have a little compassion and help me out here."

I waited for a response, but none was forthcoming. "Okay," I finally said. "How about letting me in to see the head of your human resources department."

"Do you have an appointment?" the guard asked.

"No, I don't have an appointment. You know I don't have an appointment." The guy was really starting to piss me off.

"You'll have to call for an appointment," the guard informed me.

I finally conceded defeat. "Okay, I'll call for an appointment. Who should I call?"

"The head of HR, I suppose," the guard replied. He was smiling as he said it. So was his buddy.

"Do you know that person's name?"

"Sorry, as I told you, I never go past the guardhouse."

"Don't you have a company directory?"

"Nope." Both guards were now smiling broadly.

At that point it was obvious that I was wasting my time. "Fine, please give me the phone number and I'll call for an appointment." Carolyn, my secretary, had tried to get a number for Consolidated TranShip shortly after Edna Anderson left my office but was unable to find one. What kind of business would have an unpublished phone number?

"Sorry," said the smiling guard who was clearly not sorry at all. "I don't know the phone number."

That was the last straw. "How the hell can you not know the phone number of the company you work for?" I yelled.

"Don't need one," the guard replied calmly. "The phone in the guardhouse is a direct line."

"Then pick up your direct line and ask whoever answers for the company's phone number."

"Sorry, I can't do that," came the immediate response.

"Why not?"

"That phone is for official business only."

"And getting a phone number so a visitor can make an appointment isn't official business?"

"Sorry," he said yet again, "but you'll have to get the number yourself."

"Consolidated TranShip doesn't have a published phone number," I replied in frustration. "What kind of company has an unlisted number?"

My question was rhetorical, but to my surprise he answered it. "The kind that doesn't have a published number, I guess."

With a shrug of his shoulders he returned to the guardhouse. His colleague took up a position in front of my car and crossed his arms, making it clear that it was time for me to leave. I slapped the Mustang's steering wheel, shifted into reverse and began to back up, narrowly missing a vehicle that was approaching the gate.

When I got back to the office, I called Tony Biffano, the firm's investigator. Biff is a former Paterson cop who's built like a small gorilla. I couldn't get past the smirking guards at Consolidated TranShip, but Biff would.

Or so I thought.

4

"That can't possibly be legal."

When I got back to the office, I found Rick, my partner, stretched out on the leather sofa that my late wife, Aimee, had bought for me when I joined the firm. I tossed my briefcase on the desk and sat down in one of the two chairs facing the sofa.

Rick opened one eye and looked at me. "I did some preliminary research on those Chinese bonds while you were out. They have an interesting history."

"Are they worth anything?" I asked.

"Maybe," he replied, sitting up and retrieving a legal pad from the table between us. "According to my research, beginning in 1913 the Republic of China issued bonds worth tens of billions of dollars to banks, insurance companies, other governments, and individual investors all over the world. They carried five percent interest and were scheduled to mature in 1960."

Anticipating where he was going, I said, "And since this is 1993, Mrs. Anderson is thirty-three years too late to collect anything."

"Don't jump the gun, my boy," Rick said with a wave of the hand. "You'll ruin my story. In theory, the bonds are still good. At least I think they are."

"In theory? You think?"

"The problem is that in 1949 the communists took over and the Republic of China became the People's Republic of China. The new government stopped making interest payments, and when the bonds matured in 1960, the PRC failed to re-pay the principal."

"That can't possibly be legal," I said. "If a change of government could cancel a country's debt, no one in his right mind would ever buy government bonds."

"My thoughts exactly," Rick said. "Of course, I'm no expert on international law, so I called a friend of mine at one of the big firms in Manhattan who is. He didn't know anything about these particular bonds, but he did tell me it's a well-settled principle of international law that successor governments are automatically responsible for sovereign debt obligations of a previous government."

"Bingo," I said, mentally calculating how much Edna Anderson stood to collect – and how much our percentage would come to. "If China is obligated to honor the bonds, but refused to pay up when they came due, I assume you found a lot of cases involving bondholders who sued China and won."

"Not a one," Rick said. "I couldn't find a single case involving these bonds in any federal or state court anywhere in the country." Rick's one of the best legal researchers I know. If he couldn't find a case, I had to assume there weren't any. And that was very odd. I said as much.

"I might have an explanation," Rick said. "In 1987 the British threatened to close their financial markets to the Chinese unless they honored the bonds held by British citizens. The Chinese paid up. Our government must have done the same thing, which explains why I couldn't find any cases of bondholders suing to collect on their bonds."

"So how do we proceed?" I asked.

"There's obviously some sort of procedure for cashing in the bonds." Rick said. "We just have to figure out what it is."

As we were discussing the logistics of making a demand for payment, Carolyn, my secretary, entered the office with letters for me to sign. She listened to the conversation for a few minutes before asking, "Do you mind if I ask a question?" In addition to being incredibly cute, Carolyn is very bright. When she begins a conversation that way, I know she has something to say that's worth hearing. I nodded for her to continue. "How did Ronald Anderson get his hands on millions of dollars in old Chinese bonds? It's not like you can buy them at the corner store."

I made a mental note to ask Mrs. Anderson that question the next time we spoke.

5

"You forgot this."

We arrived at the Newark office of Federal American International Lines Insurance promptly at nine o'clock as instructed. I checked in at the reception desk, then Margaret Woodson and I took a seat in the lavishly appointed waiting room.

After sitting in silence for several minutes, Margaret asked, "How's Rick doing?"

"The old Rick is back, sharp as ever." A few years ago, everyone at the firm thought Rick Santorini, our founding partner, was getting senile, or perhaps suffering from Alzheimer's. But as it turned out, his memory lapses and erratic behavior were the result of drug interactions. After a change in medications, the symptoms disappeared and Rick was his old self again.

"And the firm?" Margaret asked. "How's everything at the law firm of Santorini & O'Brian?"

Maybe it was just my imagination, but I sensed an undertone of bitterness the way she said "Santorini & O'Brian." I wondered if she blamed Rick and me for her husband's death. After all, it was our refusal to attend the ill-fated seminar at the World Trade

Center that resulted in Scott and Avery being there when the terrorist bomb exploded.

"Different," I eventually answered. "Very different." The deaths of Scott and Avery turned our full-service law firm into a partnership consisting of two attorneys, a secretary, and a receptionist. We really didn't need a receptionist, but Elaine, who holds that position, has the kind of job security that comes with being Rick's live-in lady friend.

Realizing that Margaret was waiting for more, I added, "With Scott gone, we don't take divorce cases anymore. And without Avery, we don't handle the complicated business deals he used to put together. We're basically a litigation firm now. And because we don't have the cash flow that Avery and Scott brought in, we have to be extra careful about the cases we take. We can't afford to finance a contingent fee case for years and then end up losing. At the moment, Rick's spending most of his time doing research on civil asset forfeiture so we can decide whether or not to take a case another firm referred to us."

"Yes, I imagine things have changed." Margaret stared off into space, no doubt thinking about her late husband. After a few moments of silence she said, "Scott always referred to you as the firm's wild child who was more interested in proving a point than making a buck. But now you seem more...." She paused, searching for the right word. I was expecting her to say "pragmatic" or perhaps "practical," but she came up with "subdued" instead.

We chatted for a few more minutes, but eventually ran out of things to say, at which point Margaret picked up a magazine from the table next to her. I found the most recent issue of *Sports Illustrated* and began to read an article about the NBA.

At nine fifteen, and again at nine thirty, I went to the reception desk to make sure the so-called Special Investigative Unit knew we were there. Each time the receptionist told me, "Please take a seat and you'll be called shortly."

Just before ten o'clock, a redheaded girl who looked like a younger version of Carolyn, my secretary, entered the waiting room carrying a stack of file folders. Halfway across the room, she stumbled and fell, causing the files to scatter across the floor. She had just started gathering up the papers when a middle-aged man appeared. "You clumsy bitch!" he bellowed. "I spent hours organizing those files, and you managed to undo all my work in less than a second."

"I'm sorry, sir," the girl said. "I'll put everything back together like it was, I promise."

"You damn well better or you'll be looking for a new job," her taskmaster said over his shoulder as he walked away.

I crossed the waiting room and bent down to help the girl gather up what had to be hundreds of sheets of paper. She looked up when she sensed my presence, and I saw that she was crying.

"Bad day, huh?"

"Around here, every day is a bad day," she whimpered, wiping away a tear with the back of her hand.

We worked in silence, collecting the papers and stacking them in a pile. I was in the process of retrieving a legal-sized page with a pie chart in the middle when a shiny, black shoe landed on it, just missing my fingers. I looked up to find the taskmaster who had castigated the girl moments earlier. Towering over me with hands on hips, his body language clearly communicated his displeasure. "What the hell do you think you're doing?" It was phrased as a question, but it sounded like an accusation.

I released the paper that was now held captive by the highly buffed wingtip, stood up, and looked the bully in the eye. "I was helping the young lady pick up the papers," I said, nodding toward the girl who was still crawling around on hands and knees.

Before I could tell FAIL's office taskmaster what I thought of his behavior, he asked, "Did it ever occur to you that these papers might contain confidential information?"

"I'm just picking them up, pal, not reading them."

"I'm not your pal," he replied, "and these papers are off limits." He looked down at the redhead who had continued to retrieve the papers while her boss and I had words. "Get these picked up, then get back to your desk."

I briefly considered telling the bastard he had violated half a dozen state and federal labor laws, but decided that escalating the confrontation would make things worse for the girl. So I returned to my seat and sat down.

"A real prince," I said to Margaret Woodson in the chair next to me as I resumed reading *Sports Illustrated*.

"You can say that again," she replied. "I'd hate to have him for a boss."

I watched as the girl continued crawling around the floor gathering up the papers she had dropped. I estimated she was in her early twenties, cute but not beautiful, with short red hair and blue eyes. After another few minutes of scrambling around the floor, she retreated to the row of cubicles behind the reception desk, the papers clutched to her chest. Before disappearing into a corporate work-cell-without-bars, she looked back in my direction, and our eyes met. She was still crying, but she managed a small smile and a nod of her head. Then she was gone.

"She's cute." I turned my head to find Margaret watching me watch the redhead. "Cute, but a bit too young for you," she added.

Before I could tell Margaret she was only half right, a tall woman in a charcoal grey, pinstriped pantsuit strode into the waiting room, pointed in our direction, and without breaking stride, commanded, "Mr. O'Brian and Mrs. Woodson, please come with me."

We followed her down a long corridor lined with cubicles on our left and offices with closed doors on our right. At the end of the corridor, she pointed to a door and walked away without uttering a word.

The waiting room bully who had terrorized the cute redhead was waiting for us inside the room, seated in a leather swivel chair at the far end of a highly polished wooden conference table. Our eyes met, and he smiled. But it wasn't a friendly smile. It was the cold, calculating smile of a natural born predator.

He motioned for us to take a seat and launched into a prepared speech even before our posteriors made contact with the hard wooden chairs. "My name is Harry Sporn. I'm the head of the company's Special Investigative Unit. You're here this morning to provide testimony in connection with a claim you recently filed." I took issue with his use of "recently," but said nothing. "You have a contractual obligation to answer every question I ask this morning." He nodded toward the video camera on a tripod in the corner of the room. "Your answers will be recorded and may be used in any further proceedings involving your claim."

I decided to interrupt his well-rehearsed monologue. "What further proceedings are you referring to?"

Instead of answering my question, Sporn looked directly at Margaret and continued his spiel. "You have the right to have an attorney with you, but your attorney may not take part in these proceedings and may not object to any questions I ask."

I objected anyway. "That's not my understanding of the law."

"Then you are misinformed," he said tersely. "If you would like to adjourn today's examination to research the law, I would be happy to accommodate you." It was clearly a delaying tactic, so I waved my hand to signal that we agreed to proceed with the EUO as scheduled.

He returned his attention to Margaret. "Did you bring the documents you were instructed to bring?" By using "instructed" rather than "requested," Sporn was trying to be as intimidating as possible. Based on his behavior in the waiting room, it seemed pretty clear that he was the kind of person who did far more instructing than requesting.

Margaret handed him the stack of documents she had brought with her. Sporn sifted through them until he came to Scott's military discharge papers. FAIL's in-house bully leaned back in his chair and held the document up to the camera positioned behind his right shoulder before sliding it down the conference table to Margaret. "Do you recognize that document?" he asked her.

"Yes," she answered, "it's my husband's military records."

"And is that document accurate?" he asked.

I recognized the question as a trap, and so did Margaret. "I didn't prepare that document, so I can't vouch for the accuracy of the information it contains. I simply brought it with me as you requested." Scott's lawyerly wariness had obviously rubbed off on his widow.

Sporn was decidedly unhappy with the answer. He picked up the document, and reading from it, asked, "But you do know your husband's name is Scott Randolph Woodson, that he's six feet tall and has blue eyes."

Margaret's answer was delivered through clenched teeth. "He *was* six feet tall and he *did* have blue eyes. But he's been dead for six months."

Instead of responding, Harry Sporn leaned back in his chair and smiled. Seconds ticked by. He said nothing; he just sat there and smiled the cold, menacing smile of a natural born predator. Eventually he got up and retrieved a bottle of water from a refrigerator concealed in a sideboard, returned to his seat at the head of the conference table, and started to drink. He didn't offer us any water.

Having quenched his thirst, the affable Mr. Sporn slowly screwed the cap back on his bottle of water and began asking a series of extremely detailed questions about the Woodson household's finances. Margaret answered most with "I don't know" or "I'm not sure of the answer to that."

After about the tenth "I don't know," Sporn said, "You have a contractual duty to fully answer all of my questions. If you fail to do so, Federal American will consider you in breach of the contract of insurance, relieving us of any obligation we might have to make payment under the terms of the policy."

Margaret was becoming angrier by the second, so before she could say anything that might damage her position, I told Harry Sporn, "If my client doesn't know the answer to a question, 'I don't know' is the only appropriate response. And I object to your reference to an obligation your company *might have* to pay Mrs. Woodson. Federal American clearly *does have* an obligation to pay her the death benefit specified in the policy."

Sporn ignored my little speech and continued the questioning. He asked about any insurance claims Scott and Margaret made in the past. She told him "none." He asked about Scott's driving record, the organizations to which he belonged, all the addresses where he had lived since leaving the military, and scores of additional questions that seemed to have no bearing at all on Margaret's claim for a death benefit under the life insurance policy.

Two hours after it began, the EUO ended with Sporn informing us, "We'll be in touch," before abruptly leaving the room. The woman in the pinstriped pantsuit who had led us to the conference room appeared and ushered us back to the waiting room where we stood in silence until the doors of the middle elevator opened.

We were about to step onto the elevator when the cute red-head who had committed the unpardonable sin of dropping Harry Sporn's files rounded the reception desk, waving the copy of *Sports Illustrated* I had been reading while waiting for the EUO to begin. "Wait up," she said as she crossed the room and handed me the magazine. "You forgot this."

"Thanks," I said, "but that's not mine. It was here."

"They won't miss it," she replied just above a whisper. "Besides, I'm sure you'll want to finish the article you were reading."

Our eyes met, and she arched an eyebrow and smiled. Then, she tucked the magazine under my arm and walked away.

It wasn't until I got back to the office that I realized what she had done.

6

"I can spot one of my own a mile away."

It was after one o'clock by the time I got back to the office and I was famished. I tossed the copy of *Sports Illustrated* on Carolyn's desk as I made my way to the inner office. "The next time you go out to the waiting room, add that to the collection – a little present from those compassionate folks at FAIL Insurance."

"How did it go?" Carolyn asked.

"They treated Margaret like a criminal instead of a woman who recently lost her husband. Give me ten minutes to eat lunch," I added over my shoulder as I entered my office, "then see if you can get Tony Biffano on the phone for me."

A few minutes later, as I was about to attack the second half of my tuna sandwich, Carolyn appeared at my door waving a document. "I found this inside that magazine you brought back from the insurance company." She laid a document on my desk, being careful to avoid the tuna salad that had oozed out from the overstuffed deli sandwich.

I picked it up and saw that it was a memo from Frankel, Baldwin & Ingram, a nationally known consulting firm, to the board of directors of Federal American International Lines Insurance. The subject line was: *Maximizing Profits By Minimizing Claims Payouts.* I flipped through pages, appalled at what I was reading. In a section dealing with EUOs, those upstanding folks at F, B & I suggested that the best way to measure the resolve of a claimant and his or her attorney was to make them as uncomfortable as possible during the examination under oath. I scanned the list of suggested tactics for doing that and realized Harry Sporn had used them all that morning. "According to this," I said to Carolyn as I read from the memo, "the insurance company's consultant is telling them the examination under oath is, and I quote, the single most important tool at your disposal to safely deny a claim or to settle it for less than its actual value."

I handed the memo to Carolyn and reached for a legal pad. I made a note to remind myself to demand all memos from outside consultants as part of the discovery process in the unlikely event we ended up in litigation with the insurance company. While I was writing, Carolyn began thumbing through the F, B & I memo. "I should be working for Federal American," she said a moment later. "According to this, they give incentive awards to people in their claims department for settling claims on the cheap. Get a claimant to accept less than half of what they're owed and you get a one-week Caribbean vacation." She handed back the document. "We should do something like that here."

"Good idea," I said. "Figure out how to cut our phone bill by fifty percent, and I'll give you a one-week vacation in beautiful downtown Newark."

The phone rang, and Carolyn picked it up. "It's Mrs. Anderson," she said, holding her hand over the mouthpiece, "and she sounds really angry."

I took the phone from Carolyn and had just enough time to say "hello" before Edna Anderson launched into a tirade. "How dare you send someone to my home without even the courtesy to tell me they were coming," she screamed. "And don't you or anyone working for you ever question my honesty."

I told her I had no idea what she was talking about. "I'm talking about those rude private investigators you sent to my home who sat there and called me a liar to my face. I'm a good Christian woman. I don't lie. Not to you, not to anyone. I have a good mind to find another attorney. And when I do, I'm going to...."

I cut her off before she could finish the sentence. "Mrs. Anderson, I never sent private investigators to your home. I don't know who showed up at your door, but they weren't sent by me."

"Well, someone from your office sent them because they said they worked for your firm." There was still indignation in her voice, but she seemed a bit hesitant.

"They may have said that, Mrs. Anderson, but I assure you that they don't. The only investigator we use is a gentleman named Tony Biffano, a retired Paterson police officer. Biff is very polite, and he works alone."

There was silence at the other end of the line. "No," Mrs. Anderson finally said, "neither of these men was named Biffano. I have their business cards right here." The anger in her voice was gone, replaced by confusion. Or perhaps it was weariness I was hearing.

I didn't bother asking the names of her visitors. Whatever names were printed on the cards probably weren't real. Instead, I asked Mrs. Anderson to tell me what the putative investigators had wanted.

"They asked where Ronnie got those Chinese bonds I left with you. I told them I didn't know. They said Ronnie had stolen them. I told them Ronnie never stole a thing in his life. That's when they accused me of lying." She paused, most likely replaying the scene in her mind. "And after having the audacity to call me a liar, they asked to see the bonds."

"Did you tell them you left the bonds with us?" I asked as a vision of the fifty dollar home security box in Carolyn's guest room popped into my head.

"No, I told them to leave," Mrs. Anderson replied. "Nobody comes into my home uninvited and calls me a liar to my face."

"As soon as we hang up," I told her, "I'm going to call our investigator, Mr. Biffano, and have him come by and speak with you. I'm going to have him bring you some of my business cards. If anyone else shows up at your house, give them one of my cards and tell them to contact me. Don't let them in, and don't talk to them." We chatted for a few minutes more. I told her Rick's research seemed to suggest the Chinese bonds might have some value, but was careful to temper her expectations of a big payday. "I promise we'll get you as much as we can for the bonds, but at this point I can't tell you how much that will be."

By the time I ended the call, Edna Anderson had calmed down. Her threat of looking for another attorney had been replaced by a sincere apology for yelling at me. I concluded the call by promising that I would find out what had happened to her husband.

I finished the last bite of my sandwich while Carolyn got Biff on the phone. "Glad you called," he said. "Saved me the trouble of calling you. I've got some interesting information about that company in the industrial park."

"Before we get to that, I've got something else for you, something I need you to take care of ASAP." I told him about Edna Anderson's encounter with the two investigators. "Swing by the office and pick up some of my business cards, then go see Mrs. Anderson. Calm her down, and find out what you can about those bonds."

"Will do," Biff said. "Now let me tell you about my visit to Consolidated TranShip Corporation. I did my usual background check but came up empty. There's virtually no information about this company anywhere. It's a corporation, so there should be articles of incorporation on file in Trenton. There aren't any. There are no business licenses, no zoning applications, no occupancy permits, no filings of any kind with a local or state agency. Nothing federal, either. It's almost as though the company doesn't exist."

"But it obviously does exist," I said, "because it's got a big building in the industrial park surrounded by a fence and protected by guards with guns."

"Yeah," Biff agreed, "and that's where things really get interesting." He paused, and the faint rustling sound I heard suggested he was consulting his notes. "When I couldn't find any records of the company, I drove over there and tried to get in."

I assumed his use of "tried" suggested he didn't get past the guards. He confirmed that a second later. "I got turned away, just like you did."

"So you didn't find anything."

"On the contrary, I found out plenty. Let's start with the chain link security fence."

"It's one of three in the industrial park," I replied, showing off my observation skills. "The electronics company and the UPS regional distribution facility are the other two places with a fence."

"True," Biff said, "but the one around the Consolidated TranShip facility is different. Let's start with the height. How tall do you think their fence is?"

"I have no idea," I said. "I didn't have my tape measure with me that day."

Biff ignored my sarcasm. "Your standard chain link security fence is eight feet tall. The one at Consolidated TranShip is ten feet tall.

Adding an extra two feet makes that fence more secure and much more expensive. And the security cameras mounted all around the perimeter are top of the line models. Again, very expensive. You don't spend that kind of money unless you really want to keep people out. And it's not just the expensive cameras and the height of the fence that caught my attention. It's the way it's designed."

It looked like every other fence to me, but I wasn't about to say that. I just waited for Biff to continue. "Unlike the other fences in the industrial park," he said, "this one has razor wire on the top. And it's the only one with a bottom rail attached to concrete every couple of feet to prevent anyone from lifting the fence and sliding underneath. And if all that weren't enough, it's the only fence that doesn't have a top rail. You only see that on a really sophisticated security setup."

"How does eliminating a top rail make a fence more secure?" I asked. "I'd think that would make it weaker."

"Nothing to grab on to if you're trying to climb the fence," Biff explained. "But the biggest difference between this fence and the others is the fact that it's electrified."

"I didn't see any signs warning that the fence is electrified."

"That's because there aren't any," Biff said.

"How can that be? I'd bet anything there has to be a state law or a local ordinance requiring signs."

"There are laws alright," Biff replied, "but these guys aren't following them."

"So you're telling me we're dealing with a non-existent corporation in a building surrounded by an illegal electric fence topped with razor wire. And, for good measure, the place is guarded by guys with guns." I thought my summary was complete, but Biff demonstrated a moment later that it wasn't.

"And then there are the guards," Biff said. "Those guys might be wearing a uniform that suggests they work for a private security company, but they're military. I served as an army MP before going on the job in Paterson, and I can spot one of my own a mile away."

"Security companies have been known to hire former military cops," I pointed out.

"True," Biff conceded, "but here's the clincher: private security companies in New Jersey are required to be licensed, and the outfit guarding this place isn't licensed. In fact, there's no record of it all. There's also no record of the trucking company I saw entering and leaving several times."

Biff spent another twenty minutes detailing what he had found during his visit to Consolidated TranShip's facility in the industrial park. The more I heard, the more convinced I became that Ronald Anderson's death wasn't your typical workplace accident. And because of his immediate cremation, I was starting to think there might be a warehouse filled with deadly toxins in our unsuspecting suburban community.

It was time to pay a visit to the last person to see Ronald Anderson before he became a pile of ashes.

7

"I don't recall anyone by that name."

For reasons I'll never understand, funeral homes are almost always the nicest buildings in a community, and Tuckerton's Funeral Home was no exception. Perched on a hill overlooking Lake Troy, it was a large structure with tall, white columns that could have been a plantation house in the Old South.

The same family has operated the funeral home since its founding back in the days when Troy Forge had more farms than strip malls. Interestingly, the people running Tuckerton are named Smith, not Tuckerton. Local legend has it that Elias Smith, the original owner, thinking Smith sounded too ordinary, named his new venture after Tuckerton, the town where Ma Bell had a switching station. Back then, local telephone numbers all began with "TU-7," the "TU" standing for Tuckerton. Perhaps old Elias thought that every time someone made a phone call they'd think of his funeral home. This ghoulish marketing scheme was apparently quite effective, allowing the Smith clan to become one of the town's most prosperous families. And that permitted them to become big financial supporters of Bob Proctor, the town's corrupt former mayor who is now on the run from the Feds.

The fact that Abraham Smith, the current proprietor, had been one of Proctor's most vocal supporters caused me to think he and I wouldn't become buddies anytime soon. That was confirmed within seconds of our meeting. After informing him that Rick and I represented Edna Anderson, he shook his head and said, "I don't know any Edna Anderson."

"You cremated her husband, Ronald, after his body was brought here by Consolidated TranShip Corporation."

"I don't recall anyone by that name," Smith said before turning his attention to paperwork on the desk before him. He looked up a few seconds later. "Are you still here?"

"Yes, and I'm staying here until you answer my questions."

"Very well," he said, shoving the papers into a file folder before leaning back in his chair and lacing his fingers together. "What is it you want to know?"

"I want to know the circumstances surrounding the death of Ronald Anderson."

"I've already told you that I don't recall anyone by that name." It was delivered with mock patience, as though he were speaking to a child.

"But you do recall receiving a body from Consolidated TranShip, don't you?"

"I have no recollection of that," Smith said.

"Come on, Mr. Smith, I'm just trying to get some answers for my client. Imagine how you'd feel if you got a phone call from your wife's employer telling you she died at work and that her body had been cremated."

"I don't have a wife," Smith said with a wave of the hand. "I'm not married."

I was tempted to tell him I wasn't surprised, but instead I said, "You don't have to be married to understand the anguish my client is feeling."

"I'm sorry for your client's loss," Smith said, almost sounding sincere, "but I don't recall anyone named Ronald Anderson."

It was time to apply a little pressure. "You do realize that the law requires you to file a death certificate for every body you handle. I can easily get a copy from the Department of Health. And if you didn't follow the law and file a death certificate for Mr. Anderson, you're in big trouble with the State of New Jersey." I didn't know what that trouble would be, but I was reasonably certain there would be a fine, at the very least, and perhaps even a suspension of his license to do business.

The threat worked – sort of. Instead of denying he handled Ronald Anderson's cremation, Smith took a different approach. "How do I know you represent this Mrs. Anderson?"

Before I could respond, a man entered the office. He had stooped shoulders, a sunken chest, thinning hair, and a sallow complexion. I thought I detected the faint odor of formaldehyde on his person. Had he been lying in a coffin, he could easily have passed for one of Tuckerton's customers or clients, or whatever the correct term is for the departed. "What do you want, Thompson?" Smith snapped. "Can't you see I'm busy?"

"Sorry, Mr. Smith," the man said just above a whisper. He placed a stack of documents on Smith's desk and quickly backpedaled out of the office, closing the door as he went. His obsequious behavior, or perhaps just his physical appearance, led me to believe he spent his days playing Bob Cratchit to Smith's Ebenezer Scrooge.

Abraham Smith returned his attention to me. "I have no way of knowing whether or not you represent Edna Anderson. And until you can provide proof of representation, I have nothing more to say to you."

"That's easy enough to do," I said, pointing to the phone on his desk. "I'll get her on the phone and she'll confirm my firm represents her."

"No dice," Smith said. "It's easy to fake a voice on the end of a phone line. I want written confirmation." He leaned back in his chair and smiled. "And I want it notarized."

I returned his smile. "When you're served with a lawsuit, you'll have your confirmation that I represent Edna Anderson." I tossed one of my business cards on his desk. "Or you can save yourself a lot of trouble, and a lot of money, by calling me."

He crumpled my business card and threw it in the trash.

8

"That's it."

The following morning, I drove to the office with the windows of my Mustang open. The air was crisp, but still warm, filled with the scent of early autumn. The trees lining the main boulevard in Mountain Springs, the upscale suburban community where I live, were just beginning their annual ritual of changing color. It was the perfect, peaceful autumn day. Then I arrived at the office, and my peaceful autumn day went south.

"You need to call Mrs. Anderson," Carolyn said as I walked through the door.

"Still angry?" I asked, remembering how our last phone call had begun.

"Scared," Carolyn answered. "Real scared. You need to call her right away."

"Get her on the phone," I said as I continued to my desk.

A minute later Carolyn arrived with a cup of coffee. "Mrs. Anderson is on line two," she said, placing the coffee on the corner of my desk.

I picked up the receiver and said, "Good morning, Mrs. Anderson. What seems to be the...."

That was as far as I got before Edna Anderson launched into a disjointed story about somebody ransacking her house while she was out. I listened patiently, asked a few questions in an effort to get a clearer picture of what had happened, and finally came to the conclusion that a phone conversation with a semi-hysterical woman wasn't going to accomplish much. I told her I'd have Tony Biffano come by as soon as possible.

I hung up and buzzed Carolyn on the intercom. "See if you can get Tony Biffano on the phone. I need to find out what the hell is going on with Mrs. Anderson."

"No need to call him," Carolyn said. "He's here."

I looked up to see Biff entering my office, carrying a small box. "I stopped by to tell you about my visit to your client with the Chinese bonds and to deliver this," he said, placing the box on my desk, "but I gather there's something else going on."

After telling him about the apparent break-in at Edna Anderson's home, I asked him to drive over and talk to her about it. "I'll do that as soon as I leave," he said. Then he told me what he had learned during his first visit to the Anderson home. According to Biff, Mr. and Mrs. Anderson were a perfectly ordinary, non-descript, suburban couple residing in a perfectly ordinary, nondescript, suburban subdivision. "Nothing out of the ordinary, nothing that would attract attention," was how he summarized his visit to the Anderson home. "I talked to the neighbors, and nobody had anything to say about your client or her late husband that sent up a red flag."

The two private investigators who had paid Mrs. Anderson a visit, on the other hand, were anything but ordinary. "I checked out the company shown on their business card," Biff told me. "And guess what, it doesn't exist. Just like the non-existent company where the husband worked, guarded by the non-existent security company guarding the place."

My run-of-the-mill workers comp case was turning out to be anything but run-of-the-mill. I just wasn't sure what it was. "How about the Chinese bonds?" I asked. "Did you find out where he got them?"

"Mrs. Anderson doesn't know," he said, quickly adding, "and I'm pretty sure she's telling the truth."

I leaned back in my chair. My disappointment was apparently obvious. "Not what you wanted to hear," Biff said. "However, the answer might be in there," he added, nodding toward the box he had placed on the corner of my desk. "I asked Mrs. Anderson how much cash her husband usually carried. It's one of the questions I always ask when I interview people. How they answer can tell me a number of things."

"Like what?" I wanted to know.

"In this case," Biff explained, "Mrs. Anderson told me her husband usually didn't carry more than twenty bucks in his wallet. He had one of those credit cards that gives you a bonus every time you use it, so he charged pretty much everything. There's a good chance he used the card to buy the Chinese bonds. That box contains all their credit card statements for the last five years. I'm betting you'll find your answer on those statements."

"Nice work," I said. "Any idea why he bought the bonds in the first place?"

"Not really," Biff said. "Mrs. Anderson said she thought she remembered her husband saying something that caused her to think the bonds were somehow connected with his job, but she couldn't remember the conversation in any detail."

"Everything seems to circle back to Consolidated TranShip Corporation," I said.

"Yeah, I agree," Biff said as he got up to leave. "I'll keep digging and let you know what I turn up."

After Biff left, I carried the box of credit card statements to Rick's office. He looked up from what he was reading when I entered. "Doing more research on civil asset forfeiture," he said. "What I'm finding is downright scary."

"Can you put that aside for the time being and help me look through these credit card bills?" I asked. After explaining what we were looking for, I divided the contents of the box into two piles, and we began our search.

"Maybe this is it," Rick said twenty minutes later. "It's a hundred dollar charge at a place called Rizzo's Ritzy Rememorables." Our eyes met and Rick shrugged. "It could just be a coincidence. Rizzo isn't an uncommon name."

"True," I replied, "but only Eddie Rizzo would come up with a name like that. Heck, I don't think 'rememorables' is even a real word."

Eddie Rizzo, known as Eddie the Skunk to northern New Jersey's less-than-solid citizens, is one of my long-time clients. Eddie owns a business in Passaic called Rizzo's Ritzy Limo Service. When I visited that company in connection with a personal injury case I had been handling for Eddie, he mentioned the limo service was just one of his investments. So, it was entirely possible Rizzo's Ritzy Rememorables was another one of his alliterative business ventures. Only Eddie would think adding 'ritzy' to a company name makes the business sound upscale.

As we combed through the credit card statements, we found scores of transactions involving Rizzo's Ritzy Rememorables.

"Brendan." I looked up to find Carolyn standing at the office door. "There's a Mr. Thompson in the waiting room who says he needs to talk to you as soon as possible. He wouldn't tell me what it's about, but the guy's a nervous wreck so I thought it might be important." She crossed the room and handed me an envelope. "And this letter from Federal American Insurance came in today's mail."

I opened the envelope and read what turned out to be a copy of a one-sentence letter to Margaret Woodson. "I'll be damned," I muttered.

"Bad news?" Rick asked.

I read him the letter. "Your claim under the above-referenced policy is hereby denied for failure to provide accurate information on the application for insurance."

"That's it?" Rick said. "No explanation of what they claim was inaccurate?"

"That's it," I said. I looked at the envelope and saw that it was postmarked the same day as the examination under oath at FAIL's office in Newark. In light of the memo that found its way into the magazine the cute redhead had given me, I suspected the decision to deny the claim had been made before the EUO had even begun.

9

"That's not what killed him."

"You probably don't remember me, but we met at Tuckerton's Funeral Home," Thompson said, quickly adding, "but, of course, we didn't actually meet." Before I could respond, he carefully laid a crumpled business card on my desk and smoothed it out so I could see it was mine. "I pulled this out of the trash when Mr. Smith wasn't looking." He almost sounded apologetic, as though he thought garbage theft was a crime in the State of New Jersey.

"Yes, I remember you," I assured him. "What can I do for you?"

Instead of answering my question, Thompson looked around my office, his gaze eventually settling on my diplomas and bar credentials hanging on the wall. I leaned back and waited. He drummed his fingers on the arm of the chair, clearly nervous, perhaps deciding how to begin, or maybe debating whether he should say anything at all. He finally took a deep breath and said, "I probably should have gone to the police, but I don't want to get Mr. Smith in trouble. And I don't want to lose my job."

The mention of the police got my attention. "Everything you tell me is confidential, protected by attorney-client privilege."

That wasn't really true. Thompson wasn't a client, so there was no privilege, but it had the intended effect. My unexpected visitor calmed down, at least a little, and started to talk.

"What we put that poor woman through is just wrong," he began. "Cremating her husband's body without her permission was unconscionable." He resumed drumming the arm of the chair. "Of course, maybe it was for the best."

I didn't ask what he meant by that, assuming I'd get the answer as the conversation progressed. "Do you know who authorized the cremation?"

"The men from the company where Mr. Anderson worked," Thompson replied. "I don't know their names. Big guys, very intimidating." He stopped talking and looked around the room, clearly nervous.

"Just tell me what happened," I prodded. "Everything you tell me is confiden tial." I hated lying to the guy, but I wanted to find out how Ronald Anderson had died, and Thompson seemed to know.

"I was in the preparation room when I heard someone pounding on the door from the parking lot behind the building. We weren't expecting a body, so I assumed it was a deliveryman who had come to the wrong door." He stopped and ran his fingers through his thinning hair before explaining, "Bodies come through the preparation room door. Regular deliveries go through another door around the side of the building, but new drivers sometimes come to the wrong door."

I wasn't particularly interested in what door was used for deliveries, but I didn't tell him that. "I assume it wasn't a delivery."

"No," Thompson said. "It was the two men from the company where Mr. Anderson worked. Of course, I didn't know that at the time."

"Can you describe the men?" I asked.

"They reminded me of soldiers. Very stiff. Very curt." I thought back to Biff's hunch that the guards at Consolidated TranShip were former military.

"So, what happened when you opened the door?"

"The men pushed me aside and wheeled a gurney into the prep room. There was a body on the gurney, covered by a sheet. They seemed to be in a hurry, as though they were afraid someone would see them." He stopped talking and adjusted his eyeglasses. "Of course, that's just speculation on my part. I don't really know. I'm just going by the way they were acting. Very rude, very brusque."

"Did they say anything when they came through the door?"

"They ordered me to get Mr. Smith. They didn't ask, they ordered," he said indignantly. Thompson paused and nervously surveyed the room again before continuing. "I had a good mind to tell them to go pound salt."

I couldn't see Thompson, who probably didn't weigh more than a hundred pounds, telling a couple of muscular military types to go pound salt. But instead of pointing that out, I asked, "Is that when you went upstairs and got Mr. Smith?"

"Actually, I called him on the intercom," Thompson said, quickly adding, "You understand, of course, at that point I didn't know who the men were or what they wanted."

"Perfectly understandable," I replied, allowing him to save face. "What happened when Smith came downstairs?"

"He went into the hallway with the two men. I could hear them arguing, but I couldn't really hear what they were saying. After a few minutes, they came back into the preparation room, the two men left, and Mr. Smith told me to prepare the body for cremation."

"I'll concede that all this seems a bit unusual, but I'm having some difficulty understanding why you think you should have gone to the police."

"Because of this," Thompson said, removing a piece of paper from his pocket, unfolding it, and placing it on my desk. It was the death certificate for Ronald Anderson.

I picked the document up and examined it. "According to this, Ronald Anderson died from a myocardial infarction, which I think is the medical term for a heart attack."

"I'm not a pathologist," Thompson said, "but I've handled a lot of bodies in my time. Mr. Anderson might have had a heart attack, but that's not what killed him. It was the bullet in his brain that killed him."

10

"They didn't provide an explanation?"

I was deciding how to tell Mrs. Anderson what I had learned about the death of her husband when Carolyn poked her head into my office. "Margaret Woodson is on line one," she said, "and she's not a happy camper."

"Fax this over to Tony Biffano," I said, waving the death certificate in the air with one hand while reaching for the phone with the other.

It immediately became apparent that Margaret was more than just unhappy; she was downright livid. "I assume you saw the copy of the letter the insurance company sent me."

"I've been in conference," I replied. It wasn't a lie, but then again it wasn't entirely truthful. It was the sort of answer attorneys give when we don't want to be blamed for not moving as quickly as clients always seem to think we should.

"They denied the claim," Margaret said. She read the one-sentence letter from FAIL Insurance.

I played dumb. "That's it? No explanation?"

"That's it," Margaret said, "So I called them and asked to speak to that charming Harry Sporn we met in Newark."

"What did he say?"

"I didn't get to speak to him. He's apparently too busy denying legitimate claims to speak to anyone. And nobody else at the damn insurance company could answer my questions. Nobody seems to know anything." Margaret spent the next ten minutes venting, in the process surprising me with the number of derogatory terms she managed to come up with for the affable Mr. Sporn. At one point in the conversation she said, "Insurance companies are happy to take your money year after year, but if you file a claim, good luck getting any of that money back."

Sensing that FAIL's refusal to make good on the life insurance policy had something to do with a previous claim, I asked Margaret about any other claims she and Scott had made, and she gave me the same answer she had given at the EUO: "none." I concluded the conversation by promising that by the end of the day I would draft a complaint to "sue the greedy bastards," to use Margaret's colorful terminology.

About an hour into the drafting process, Carolyn appeared at the door to tell me Tony Biffano was on the phone. "You're not going to believe this," were the first words out of his mouth, closely followed by, "or maybe you will, given what we've learned so far."

"Try me," I responded.

"The doctor who signed Ronald Anderson's death certificate doesn't exist."

I probably shouldn't have been surprised, but I was. "What do you mean he doesn't exist?"

"Just what I said. According to the Board of Medical Examiners, no one by that name, or a similar name, is licensed to practice medicine in the State of New Jersey."

"Maybe he's from out of state," I suggested.

"Nobody by that name is licensed to practice medicine in New York, Connecticut, or Pennsylvania either."

"That still leaves forty-six possible states," I said, "plus the District of Columbia."

"Anything's possible, but what are the chances an out-of-state doctor would appear out of nowhere to sign a death certificate?" Before I could concede he had a point, Biff said, "And there's something else you need to know. I went back over to the Anderson house like you asked. The people who ransacked the place were pros. They cleverly made it look like it was the work of kids, but, trust me, these guys were pros." I didn't bother asking how he knew that. I've worked with Biff long enough to realize the only response I'd get would be "trade secret" or "if I told you, I'd have to shoot you."

My conversation with Biff convinced me it was time to file suit and use the discovery process to find out what had happened to Ronald Anderson. I finished drafting the complaint for *Woodson v. Federal American International Lines Insurance*, and gave it to Carolyn for filing with the court. In addition to suing for breach of contract, I added a count for intentional infliction of emotional distress, and another for breach of the implied duty to deal in good faith.

Then I moved on to the Anderson complaint. The first step was figuring out who to name as defendants. There were two obvious choices: Consolidated TranShip and Tuckerton's Funeral Home. I briefly considered adding Abraham Smith and Thompson as defendants, but decided not to for tactical reasons. I did, however, add a "John Doe" defendant, the actual, but unknown, person who put the bullet in Ronald Anderson's brain.

Next, I had to decide on the causes of action – what the defendants had done that would entitle Mrs. Anderson to recover money for the death of her husband. Under the workers comp statute, she could only sue her husband's employer for an intentional wrong. A bullet through the brain seemed pretty intentional to me, but I wasn't about to tip my hand by disclosing what I had learned from my meeting with Thompson. So, the first count of the complaint simply alleged that "the intentional actions of an agent of defendant Consolidated TranShip resulted in the death of Ronald Anderson." It was as vague as FAIL's reason for refusing to make good on its life insurance policy, and it probably ran afoul of the court rule requiring a complaint to state the facts on which a demand for relief is based. But at this point, I didn't really know the facts, at least not all of them. All I really knew was that Ronald Anderson somehow ended up with a bullet in his brain, and that his body was cremated before anyone could find out what had happened.

The second count of the complaint charged both defendants with the intentional infliction of emotional distress by cremating Ronald Anderson's body without his wife's knowledge or permission. The third count was a demand for punitive damages.

It was almost five by the time I finished drafting the complaint for *Anderson v. Consolidated TranShip Corporation et al.* Before heading home, I decided to call Eddie Rizzo to confirm he was the owner of Rizzo's Ritzy Rememorables and, if so, to learn what I could about his dealings with Ronald Anderson. I began the process by calling the last phone number he had given me. As expected, I got a recording telling me that calls to that number were now being taken by a second number. When I dialed the second number a recording referred me to a third phone number. I dialed the third number in Eddie's game of telephone tag, fully expecting a gruff voice demanding to know who I was and what I wanted. That's the way things had always gone in the past, but not this time. Instead of one of Eddie's associates, I got a mechanical voice informing me that the number was no longer in service.

I had just hung up the phone when Rick appeared at my door with a piece of paper in his hand. Before he had a chance to say anything, I asked, "Want to take a trip to Rizzo's Ritzy Rememorables tomorrow?"

"Yes, but not tomorrow," he replied. "We just got a fax from someone named Wu Jin at the Chinese consulate in Manhattan. It's in response to the letter I faxed them about Mrs. Anderson's bonds. Mr. Jin, or perhaps it's Miss Jin, has had a cancellation in his or her schedule and will see us tomorrow at ten o'clock. I get the distinct impression that if we don't show up tomorrow, we might not get another appointment for a while."

11

"The needs of the many outweigh the needs of the few."

The consulate of the People's Republic of China is located between 42nd and 43rd Streets on the west side of Manhattan, a few blocks north of the Lincoln Tunnel. At first glance, it appears to be just another office tower, but look more closely and you'll see that the exterior is festooned with barely-hidden surveillance cameras and microphones.

Rick noticed them before I did. "Smile, you're on *Candid Camera*," he said, nodding toward the camera aimed at the patch of sidewalk outside the door that Wu Jin had instructed us to use.

"We're here to see Mr. Jin," I said to the uniformed guard standing in front of the door.

"I believe you may be mistaken," the guard replied.

"Perhaps it's Ms. Jin," I said. "We received a letter from him or her, but I'm not sure if Jin is a male or female name."

The guard held out his hand, and I gave him the letter. He unfolded it and looked at it just long enough to see the signature before handing it back to me. "You may go inside," he said, nodding toward the door and smiling. He seemed to find humor in the situation.

We went through the door and found ourselves in a small room with chairs along one wall and a metal detector guarding a corridor at the other end of the room. One uniformed guard was seated behind a table just inside the door, while another stood next to the metal detector.

"We're here to see Mr. Jin," I said to the guard at the table as I handed him the letter. "We have an appointment."

The guard gave me an odd look. "I think you may be mistaken," he said in heavily accented English as he examined the letter. Apparently satisfied that it was genuine, he picked up a phone and said something in Chinese. I assumed he was telling Mr. Jin, or perhaps Ms. Jin, that Rick and I had arrived. Of course, for all I know, he could have been ordering lunch. I was about to ask him why we were mistaken when he said, "Please open your briefcase." I placed it on the table and opened it. The guard spent several seconds rummaging through it before removing my cell phone and placing it in a plastic basket on the table. "We will return it when you leave," he assured me.

Satisfied that he had removed all offending items, the guard turned his attention to Rick, who wasn't carrying a briefcase. "Nothing to declare," Rick said. "I didn't even stop at the duty-free shop." Rick's lame attempt at humor was apparently lost on the guard, who pointed toward the metal detector while saying something in Chinese to his compatriot.

We passed through the metal detector and entered a long, windowless corridor illuminated by overhead florescent lights. I didn't see any security cameras, but I assumed they were there. What I did see was a very attractive young woman waiting for us at the far end of the corridor. "I will take you to see Consular

Officer Wu," she said as Rick and I approached. "He is expecting you," she added, clarifying the gender of the person we were about to meet.

The young lady led us through a maze of corridors, up a flight of stairs, and onto an elevator. When we got out of the elevator, we repeated the process on a higher floor. "I should have remembered to bring breadcrumbs," I said to Rick at one point in what was becoming an extended journey.

"Or a map," Rick replied, quickly adding, "Actually, it was white pebbles in the original Grimm story."

The young lady obviously overheard us. "We are almost there."

By the time we got to our destination I was convinced we had walked halfway to China. The office wasn't what I expected. Instead of a large room with an Oriental rug and exotic lacquered furniture, it looked more like one of the work cubicles I had seen at FAIL Insurance. Granted, it had actual walls and a door, as well as a narrow window more appropriate for a medieval castle than a Manhattan high rise, but it seemed more suitable for a clerk than a consular officer. Of course, for all I know, everyone in the building was referred to as a consular officer.

The middle-aged man seated behind a metal desk rose as we entered the room. "I am Wu Jin," he said, nodding ever so slightly in our direction. "May I offer you some refreshments?" Before we could respond, he instructed the young lady who had escorted us, "Please bring some tea for our guests."

We took seats across from him and I opened my briefcase to retrieve one of Edna Anderson's bonds, which I placed on the desk in front of our host. "Ah, yes, one of the 1913 bonds," he said, instantly recognizing the document. "It is beautiful, is it not?"

To me, it was just a legal document, but I played along. "Yes, it's very pretty, very ornate." But then I got down to business.

"It's one of the bonds owned by a client, who would like to cash them in. She retained us to determine how to do that."

Instead of explaining how to redeem the bonds, Mr. Wu said, "I understand you had some difficulty with my name. Chinese names are different than American names. In China, the name that comes first, called the zing, is the surname or family name. The second name, the ming, is the personal name, what you would call the given name. This, of course, is the opposite of how you do things in your country."

He had just finished the tutorial on Chinese names when the young lady, who I now assumed was his secretary, returned with a tray bearing a small teapot and three cups. She placed it on the desk, made a short bow, and left the room without saying a word. Mr. Wu poured three cups, handed one to Rick and one to me, then picked up the third cup and sipped the hot liquid. He nodded as if to signal approval before continuing to tell me more than I wanted to know about Chinese names. He explained that although there are thousands of family names in China, just one hundred are used by eighty-five percent of the population. Next, he explained that a woman in China doesn't take her husband's name when she marries, except perhaps in Hong Kong and Macau. By the time he got to laws regulating children's names, Rick and I had both heard enough.

Rick was the first to speak. "Mr. Wu, this is all very interesting, but I'm sure you have many things on your schedule today, and we don't want to take up more of your time than is necessary. If you could just tell us how our client can collect principal and back interest on her bonds, we'll be on our way."

"Yes, yes, I understand," Mr. Wu said. He pulled a legal pad closer and picked up a pen. "What is your client's name and address?"

I answered his question, assuming he needed that information to begin the process of getting Mrs. Anderson what she was owed.

"And how many bonds does she have?" Mr. Wu asked.

I gave him the face value of Mrs. Anderson's bonds. He was suitably impressed. "She is quite an avid collector."

"No, she's not a collector," I corrected. "She's an investor who would like to get paid."

"I am afraid I do not understand," Mr. Wu said. He looked at us as though we had asked something outrageous. "As you know, our governments have resolved this matter." No, I didn't know that, but I wasn't about to admit it to Mr. Wu. "Many people are happy with that resolution. Some are not. But the needs of the many outweigh the needs of the few." I had no idea what he was talking about. He misinterpreted my puzzled expression. "That is a memorable line from one of your movies. I must confess I am quite fond of American movies." I looked at Rick, hoping he could shed some light on what our host was talking about, but he just shrugged. Apparently, he was as much in the dark as I was.

Wu spent the next fifteen minutes telling us about his favorite American movies, his enthusiasm growing as he ticked off plot points and cast members. The guy even knew who directed each film. Wu's monologue ended with him standing up and announcing with a smile, "It has been most enjoyable speaking with you. I do not often have an opportunity to discuss American films."

That was apparently the signal that our meeting was over. The young lady who had escorted us to Wu's office appeared at the door without any obvious signal from her boss. "If you will follow me, I will show you where you can reclaim your cell phone," she said, smiling even more broadly than Cecil B. DeWu.

As I got to the office door, still trying to make sense of what had just transpired, Mr. Wu said something that sounded like *you seen onchen*.

"That is Chinese for travel safe," Mr. Wu explained with a smile. It wasn't the cold, menacing smile that Harry Sporn had displayed during the EUO at FAIL Insurance, but neither did it make me feel all warm and fuzzy.

"What just happened?" Rick asked once we were outside the building.

"My Chinese is a little rusty, but I'm reasonably certain our friendly, neighborhood Chinese consular official said 'screw you' as we were leaving."

12

"You mean he's dead?"

The following morning, Rick and I drove to Dover in search of what we assumed was Eddie Rizzo's business. We found Rizzo's Ritzy Rememorables sandwiched between a barbershop and a shoe repair business in a section of town that would never have been described as ritzy. The store had a weather-beaten wooden door flanked by display windows that looked like they hadn't been washed in years. Each contained a haphazard pile of odds and ends that had nothing in common except for the fact that they were old. In the center of the display window on the right was an American flag, folded into a triangle, in a wooden display case. Peeking out from under the American flag was a stack of documents that looked like Edna Anderson's Chinese bonds. Surrounding this incongruous pairing were rusty ice skates, stacks of old magazines, jewelry of doubtful provenance, and tools that would have been more at home in a museum than a workshop.

As we opened the door, a buzzer sounded, summoning an overweight, balding man in a Grateful Dead T-shirt who shuffled his way to the counter along the left side of the store. He nodded in our direction. "What can I do you for?"

"I'm interested in those Chinese bonds you have in the window," I said. "Do you have any more of them?"

"You're in luck," he replied. "I got a bunch of them for one of my regular customers, but I haven't seen him in a while. Besides, it's first come, first served." He rubbed his hands on his shirt before rummaging through a box on the counter.

"Is this your regular customer?" I asked, holding up a photo of Ronald Anderson that his widow had given me.

The store proprietor stopped his search and looked me up and down before turning his attention to Rick and repeating the process. "Who are you guys?" Before I could answer, he added, "You aren't cops, that's for sure."

I wasn't sure what to make of his assessment. Should I be relieved or offended? "No, we're not cops, we're attorneys. We represent the widow of the man in the photo."

"Widow? You mean he's dead?" What little semblance of friendliness he had managed up to that point disappeared. "I don't know anything about that," he added defensively.

"I'm not suggesting you do," I said. "In fact, I'm sure his death has nothing to do with you or your store. We're just trying to get some background information about the man."

"I don't know what happened to him," the clerk insisted. "In fact, I didn't even know he was dead until you told me."

Rick got involved, and together we tried to assure the clerk that we weren't trying to cause him any trouble. After ten minutes of attempting to reason with him, I finally said, "I'd like to speak to the manager."

"I am the manager," came the immediate response.

"But Eddie Rizzo is the owner, right?" I reached into my jacket pocket for a business card, and as I did, the manager's right hand disappeared below the counter, only to reappear a split second later holding a gun.

"You won't need that," I said, a bit shaken by the sudden appearance of the weapon. "I'm Eddie Rizzo's attorney." I took my hand out of my pocket with exaggerated slowness and gave him one of my cards.

He studied the card for a few seconds before reaching back under the counter with his free hand. This time he retrieved a cordless phone. He held the phone in his left hand while punching in a series of numbers with his right hand, the one holding the gun. I flinched every time he hit the keypad, afraid he might accidentally pull the trigger in the process. My anxiety must have been obvious because he said, "Relax, the safety's on," as he hit the last digit in the number he was calling.

His call went through, and he said, "It's me, Gordy," into the phone. "I got two guys here asking questions, an old guy with white hair and a younger guy whose business card says he's Brendan O'Brian."

Whoever was on the other end of the line must have asked a series of questions that the store manager answered with one-word responses like "yup" and "nope" before handing the phone to me.

I put the receiver to my ear, and heard the familiar voice of Eddie Rizzo. "Yo, counsellor, what can I do for you?"

"I'm here with Rick Santorini. We're trying to get some information about your customer who bought old Chinese bonds."

"Big, black guy," Eddie said. "Gordy told me about him. Came into the store dozens of times, always buying the same thing. Good customer. Didn't try to negotiate the price, just paid what Gordy asked."

I try to tell Eddie Rizzo as little as possible, but I decided to take a chance and tell him more than he needed to know. "Your customer turned up dead under mysterious circumstances, and his widow retained us to find out what happened."

"That I can't help you with, counsellor," Eddie said. "All I know is what Gordy told me. Your guy came into the shop and bought some old bonds. Just another collector who buys old stuff. That's all I know."

"How about the bonds?" I asked. "What can you tell me about them?"

Eddie laughed. "About a year ago, Gordy finds a stack of those bonds at a garage sale. Each one's got 'ten thousand dollars' written in big letters on it, but the seller wants five bucks for the whole stack. My stupid cousin thinks he's gonna make a fuckin' killing. After Gordy buys them, I have someone I know do some digging and we find out the whole stack is worth the five bucks Gordy paid, not ten thousand for each bond. So much for making a killing." I wanted to ask Eddie how he knew the bond's value, but decided not to interrupt his story. "Your guy comes along one day and buys the bonds for twenty bucks. Tells Gordy he wants to buy more, so Gordy starts looking around for more Chinese bonds. Your guy comes back over and over to buy the bonds Gordy finds. Gordy charges him more each time, but your guy just pays up and keeps coming back to buy more bonds. Good customer. Sorry he's dead."

"Weren't you suspicious when Mr. Anderson agreed to pay more each time?" I asked.

"Yeah, at first, but I went back to the guy who checked the bonds out for me and had him take another look. He told me those old Chinese bonds are like stock certificates of companies that went bust. They're just collectibles. People frame 'em and hang 'em on the wall. Not worth much to anybody but people who collect that stuff."

"Did he tell you why?"

"Some sort of deal the Feds made with the chinks back in the seventies."

I decided to dangle some details about Ronald Anderson's untimely demise to see how Eddie would react. "My client's late husband, your customer, went to work one morning and never came home."

"Guy must have been in a tough business," Eddie replied. It was a bit too nonchalant, but perhaps in Eddie's world, things like this were an everyday occurrence. "Where did he work?"

"Mr. Anderson worked for Consolidated TranShip Corporation in Troy Forge. Know anything about them?"

"Never heard of 'em," Eddie answered. "What did they say when you asked about the guy's death?"

"That's just it, I haven't been able to get into the place to talk to anyone. The place has more security than Fort Knox. Chain link fence topped with razor wire, armed guards, the works. I was hoping you might know something about the company."

"Sorry, counsellor, but I never heard of 'em until now," Eddie replied. "But I'll talk to some people I know and see what I can find out for you." He paused as if deciding what to say next. "This Anderson guy was a good customer. I always hate to lose a good customer."

He seemed sincere, but I couldn't help feeling Eddie knew more than he was telling me. Although Eddie has proven helpful in the past, part of me simply can't trust him.

13

"Uncle Sam never lets money slip through his fingers."

When I arrived at the office the following morning, two Troy Forge police cars were in the parking lot, the first sign that something was wrong. I found Rick, Carolyn, and Elaine in the waiting room, conversing quietly, their expressions telling me whatever was going on involved us rather than another tenant. Rick looked up when he heard me enter. "We had a break-in last night," he said. "I called the police. Then I called Tony Biffano."

"What did they take?"

"I don't know," Rick replied. "The police asked us to stay out here while they did their thing. They let Biff join them, though. Professional courtesy."

I was debating whether to take a seat or to look for Biff when two uniformed officers appeared. "You can go back now," the taller of the two said, nodding toward the door leading from the waiting room, "but you're not going to like what you find."

"Any idea what happened?" I asked.

"There are no signs of forced entry. You've got a pretty sophisticated security system, so whoever broke in knew what he was doing. Doesn't look like kids. And it's doubtful kids would have searched the place this thoroughly."

Two men in civilian clothing entered the waiting room. "Got what we need," one of them said to the uniformed cops as they passed through the room and headed for the elevator.

"The crime scene guys," the cop said, nodding toward his departing colleagues, "pulled prints from desk drawers and other places only you people would be likely to touch. But don't get your hopes up. Based on what I see here, I'm willing to bet whoever did this wore gloves. The only prints we're likely to find will belong to people in the office."

As soon as the cop and his partner were out the door, Rick, Carolyn and I headed for my office, stopping at every room in our suite on the way. All of them had been ransacked. The contents of every file cabinet and every drawer had been emptied onto the floor. Every photo and painting that had once graced our walls had been removed, including the oversized painting of the Ford Mansion that had hung in the conference room.

Tony Biffano was in my office when we arrived. He was holding what I knew from a prior incident was a gadget for locating hidden listening devices. "I checked all the rooms," he said. "Didn't find anything."

"What do you make of this?" Rick asked Tony, nodding toward the mess that used to be my office.

"A very professional job," Biff said. "Most likely the same crew that ransacked the Anderson place. They didn't find what they were looking for there, presumably those Chinese bonds, so the next logical place to search was here."

"They didn't find them here, either," I said.

"I assume that means they're at your house or Rick's house," Biff said. "I hope you guys have a top-notch alarm system, because whoever is looking for those bonds might not give up after two attempts." I didn't tell him the bonds were in Carolyn's apartment, but I did assure him that Rick and I both had alarm systems on our homes. Whether they were top-notch remained to be seen.

After Biff packed up his equipment and left, Carolyn began the cleanup process while Rick and I sat down in my office to access the situation. "Whoever is behind this is going to an awful lot of trouble to get their hands on bonds that aren't supposed to be worth much," I said to begin the conversation. "We're missing something, but what?"

"I did more research when we got back from Dover yesterday," Rick said, withdrawing a file folder from his briefcase, "and confirmed what Eddie Rizzo told us. It took a bit of digging because the answer isn't in a court case or a statute; it's in a treaty between the U.S. and China. In 1979, when we established diplomatic relations with the People's Republic of China...."

"And sold out our allies in Taiwan," I interjected.

"And ended our formal recognition of Taiwan," Rick continued, "the U.S., during the Carter administration, signed a treaty with the PRC that settled, and I quote, all property claims of U.S. nationals, real and corporate, their successors, assigns, heirs, and legal representatives, against the People's Republic of China for any nationalization, expropriation, intervention, or taking of any kind prior to the date of this agreement."

"So, you're telling me Uncle Sam signed away bondholders' right to collect the money China borrowed back in 1913?"

"Not just the 1913 bonds, but a number of other bond issues as well," Rick said. "According to some estimates, there's something like seven hundred and fifty billion dollars of Chinese bonds that were never repaid. That's billion with a 'B', not million."

"That's insane. Why would the government do that?"

"It was part of the normalization of relations with the PRC that Nixon started and Carter finalized," Rick explained. "Besides, money changed hands, so it wasn't a complete giveaway."

"You mean the bondholders got partial payment? If that's the case, maybe Mrs. Anderson's bonds are worth something less than face value." I did a quick mental calculation and realized that even at a deep discount, Edna Anderson's bonds could be worth a bundle. And if that were the case, our percentage could result in a substantial fee.

Rick dashed my hopes. "China didn't pay the bondholders. It paid the U.S. Treasury as representative for all American citizens with a claim against China."

"But the government used that money to pay individuals what they were owed by the Chinese, right?"

Rick chuckled. "Don't be naive, my boy. Uncle Sam never lets money slip through his fingers."

14

"I'm not comfortable
with what's happening here."

In New Jersey, as in other states, a civil action begins when the plaintiff files a complaint with the court. The defendant is then required to respond by filing an answer that addresses each of the allegations in the complaint. That's how things are supposed to proceed according to the Civil Practice Rules.

The attorneys for Consolidated TranShip Corporation made it clear from the outset that they had no intention of following the rules. Instead of an answer, I received a copy of a letter sent to the court by a large Manhattan law firm. The letter made the highly unusual request that the court schedule an expedited hearing "on a matter of extreme urgency." The letter provided no explanation for the supposed urgency, so I called the attorney who signed the letter, a gentleman named Carl Mercer. According to the *Martindale-Hubbell Law Directory*, Mr. Mercer was a Yale Law graduate experienced in commercial litigation and political law. He was also apparently extremely busy because he never got around to returning my calls.

The letter made its way to Ira Cohen, the judge assigned to preside over *Anderson v. Consolidated TranShip Corporation et al.* Cohen was a no-nonsense, by-the-book jurist known to local attorneys as Ice Cold Cohen. I've tried a handful of cases before Judge Cohen and I don't think I've ever seen the man smile. But what he lacked in warmth, Ice Cold made up for with ruthless efficiency. Attorneys who wasted Judge Cohen's time with frivolous motions or specious arguments could count on receiving a public scolding in his courtroom.

To my surprise, Judge Cohen granted Mercer's unorthodox request for a hearing. I was even more surprised at how things played out in the courtroom.

On the appointed day, not wanting to incur Judge Cohen's wrath by being late, Rick and I arrived ten minutes early for the ten o'clock hearing. A middle-aged man with closely cropped salt and pepper hair was already there, seated at one of the counsel tables, reading a newspaper. I approached him with outstretched hand. "Brendan O'Brian," I said by way of introduction. "Mr. Mercer, I assume. Welcome to Morristown."

"I didn't come here to socialize," he said without looking up from his newspaper. I waited, expecting something more, but when it became clear that my adversary had no intention of saying anything else, much less shaking my hand, I joined Rick at the other counsel table.

"Attorneys from big city firms are known for their warmth and friendliness," Rick said, proving that he can be even more sarcastic than me.

As soon as I sat down, a court officer knocked on the door to the judge's chambers, and a moment later Judge Cohen emerged and took the bench. "Since both parties are here, let's get started," he said, skipping the preliminaries.

Mercer stood up and addressed the judge. "I believe Your Honor will want to wait until ten o'clock to begin."

Judge Cohen was clearly incredulous. "I beg your pardon?" Mercer repeated what he had just said. "And why would I want to do that?" the judge asked in a tone of voice that mixed curiosity with barely suppressed annoyance.

Mercer never lost his composure. In fact, he was almost dismissive as he explained, "Because at five minutes before ten o'clock, you'll receive an important phone call in your chambers, and you don't want to miss that call."

"A phone call from whom?" the judge asked. "And how do you know this?"

"All I'm at liberty to say is that you're about to receive a phone call that you'll want to take." Mercer sat down and crossed his arms.

Judge Cohen leaned back in his chair, apparently deciding how to deal with the decidedly unusual situation. I took advantage of the momentary silence. "Your Honor," I said, rising to my feet. "Might I ask why the court granted Mr. Mercer's request for a hearing? I would remind the court that the defendant hasn't filed an answer to the complaint. In fact, neither has the other defendant, Tuckerton's Funeral Home."

"I'm aware of that," Ice Cold said testily. "I don't need to be reminded." He paused for a moment before continuing. "However, I believe counsel for the plaintiff has a right to know that I granted Mr. Mercer's request because I was instructed to do so by the Assignment Judge." Judge Cohen turned his attention to my adversary. "But the Assignment Judge just left for a vacation in Europe, so I doubt very much that he'll be calling me five minutes before ten, or at any other time in the foreseeable future." The judge waited for Mercer to respond, but no response was forthcoming. "Response, Mr. Mercer?" he eventually asked.

"All I can say on the record is that Your Honor is about to receive an important phone call that you really must take."

Judges don't like being told what they must do, and Ice Cold was no exception. "In my courtroom, I decide what you must do, not the other way around." Mercer didn't respond. He simply remained seated with arms crossed.

Judge Cohen looked at the clock on the courtroom wall, which was showing the time as nine fifty-four. Then he checked his wristwatch, as if to confirm the clock on the wall was correct. "Does counsel for your co-defendant know about today's hearing?" he asked Mercer.

"I don't know," Mercer replied, "but I would think not. I have no idea who is representing Tuckerton's."

The judge looked in my direction. "Do you know who's representing the funeral home?"

"No, Your Honor," I said. "I haven't received an answer to the complaint on behalf of that defendant."

The word "defendant" was barely out of my mouth when Judge Cohen's secretary entered the courtroom and hurried to the bench where she whispered something in the judge's ear. He nodded as she delivered her message, then looked at her as if to say, *Are you sure?* Turning his attention back to counsel, Judge Cohen announced, "We'll take a ten-minute recess."

As the judge exited the courtroom, Mercer calmly picked up his newspaper and continued to read. "What does he know that we don't, but should?" Rick asked, nodding toward our adversary.

"Something stinks to high heaven," I replied, "but Cohen's not the kind of judge to do anything that's not on the up and up."

Five minutes later Judge Cohen was back on the bench. "I just got off the phone with ..."

Mercer jumped to his feet before the judge could finish the sentence. "There's no reason to reveal that information in open court." It was the sort of thing that ordinarily would have caused Judge Cohen to go ballistic. But he didn't. Apparently, something he had learned during the mysterious phone call was holding him back. I avoided the temptation to point out that refusing to reveal the caller's identity gave the defense an unfair advantage. The judge must have been thinking along the same lines because he asked Mercer, "Do you know who just called me?"

"No," Mercer answered. "I was told that you would receive a phone call at exactly five minutes before ten. And although I know the substance of what you were told, I don't know any details. I also don't know the identity of the caller."

I decided it was time to get involved. "If Mr. Mercer knows the nature of that phone call, I'm entitled to know as well."

"I quite agree, Mr. O'Brian," the judge said. "For the time being, I won't reveal who just called. However, based on that conversation, I'm temporarily putting this case on hold."

"On hold?" I asked. "What exactly does 'on hold' mean?"

"It means exactly what you think it means," the judge shot back. "Neither party will file pleadings or motions, schedule depositions or conduct discovery, or take any action in connection with this case until instructed to do so by the court."

"May I know why the court is taking this highly unusual step?" I asked.

"You may not," the judge replied.

"I'm not comfortable with what's happening here," I said.

"Neither am I, Mr. O'Brian," Judge Cohen said. "Neither am I. But my hands are tied."

Mercer got to his feet. "Your Honor, with the court's permission, there's one other issue I'd like to raise, if I may." Having gotten what he had come for, Mercer was now being deferential. The judge nodded for Consolidated TranShip's attorney to proceed. "As Your Honor is well aware, Rule 4:5-2 requires a complaint to include a statement of the facts on which the claim for relief is based. The complaint filed by Mr. O'Brian in this matter fails to include such a statement of facts. It simply states that, and I quote, the intentional actions of an agent of defendant Consolidated TranShip resulted in the death of Ronald Anderson. Mr. O'Brian refers to intentional actions because he's well aware that's the only way he can sue my client under the state's worker's compensation laws. But he doesn't specify what those intentional actions are or who the agent is. There's no way my client can respond to the complaint unless we know what it is Mr. O'Brian is claiming we did."

"We would appear to have a problem here," the judge said to Mercer, who nodded his head in agreement. He stopped nodding, however, when the judge added, "Actually, we have two problems. The first is that the complaint doesn't include specific facts. The second problem is that I've just put this entire matter on hold. You can't have it both ways, Mr. Mercer. I can't put the case on hold and, at the same time, require Mr. O'Brian to amend his complaint to include specifics."

Mercer had a ready answer. "Then I would ask that the complaint be dismissed without prejudice. That would allow Mr. O'Brian to re-file at a later date and provide the statement of facts required by the Civil Practice Rules."

I got to my feet. "With the court's permission, I'd like to offer another, less radical suggestion that won't create unnecessary work for everyone and will expedite matters." As I expected, the idea of expediting matters was appealing to Judge Cohen, who nodded for me to continue. "I have depositions scheduled for the end of this week that will provide me with the details I need to amend the complaint and provide specific facts. If the court will allow those depositions to take place as scheduled, I'll file an amended complaint next week."

Judge Cohen shifted his attention to my adversary and did something I had never seen him do before. He smiled. It wasn't a friendly smile; it was an *I gotcha* smile. "There you go, Mr. Mercer," the judge said. "Problem solved. Mr. O'Brian will conduct depositions as scheduled and amend the complaint by the end of next week."

15

"We don't even know
for sure that Anderson is dead."

After the hearing, Rick and I walked across the street to the coffee shop frequented by judges and attorneys who have business at the courthouse. Rick and I made it a point not to discuss the matter in the coffee shop. You never know who's sitting at the next table, listening to your every word. More than one case has been lost because of an overheard conversation.

The drive back to the office was equally silent, each of us replaying the morning's events in an effort to make sense of them. But once we arrived, I told Carolyn to hold phone calls, and Rick and I began the process of trying to figure out what was going on with the decidedly unusual Anderson case.

"I've heard of trials being continued, carried, delayed, postponed, and rescheduled," I said to begin the conversation, "but this is the first time I've had a case put on hold after the judge receives a phone call from some unknown person."

"Actually, that person is known to someone in Mercer's firm," Rick pointed out, "even if Mercer himself doesn't, if he's to be believed. And the fact that they know and we don't might provide grounds for appeal if things don't work out the way we want in the trial court." I had an uncomfortable feeling that things definitely weren't going to work out the way we wanted, although I didn't admit that to Rick.

We spent some time trying to determine the identity of the mysterious caller, but eventually gave up. There were just too many possibilities and too many unknowns. Rick suggested that instead of trying to find out who had called the judge, it made sense to investigate the law firm representing Consolidated TranShip. "Perhaps one of their clients is in a position to exert pressure somehow." I told him I thought that was a long shot, but agreed nonetheless.

The conversation turned to the Chinese bonds. Eddie Rizzo had told us they only had modest value as collector's items, and Rick's research supported that contention. And yet someone had gone to a lot of trouble trying to find Edna Anderson's bonds, ransacking both her home and our office. Those bonds apparently had value to someone. But to whom? And why?

Before we could begin the impossible task of exploring answers to those questions, Carolyn appeared at the door with papers in her hand. "I know you didn't want to be disturbed, but I thought you'd want to see this." She crossed the room, handed the document to me, and retreated to the outer office.

A quick glance told me I was holding the insurance company's answer to the complaint I had filed in *Woodson v. Federal American International Lines Insurance*. I flipped through the pages until I came to the paragraph that contained the substance of the defendant's answer. "Get this," I said to Rick, "the insurance company is claiming the policy on Scott's life is void because, quote, the insured provided incorrect information on the application for insurance."

"What kind of incorrect information?" Rick asked.

"It doesn't say."

Rick chuckled. "There seems to be an awful lot of vagueness in filings these days." His remark was a reminder of how little we really knew about the Anderson case, and more importantly, how much additional information we needed to draft an amended complaint that would meet with Judge Cohen's approval.

"When you get right down to it," I said, "it's tough to draft a statement of facts when you don't really have any facts to go on. All we really know for sure is that Ronald Anderson died while working at Consolidated TranShip Corporation. We don't know who killed him, why he was killed, or under what circumstances."

"Actually, we don't even know for sure that Anderson is dead," Rick pointed out. "The only evidence we have is a box filled with ashes. And for all we know, those could be ashes from somebody's fireplace."

"True," I countered, "but Thompson and Smith from the funeral home told me Anderson was dead, and I'll get it on the record when we depose them on Friday. I'll also get Thompson to repeat his claim that Mr. Anderson had a bullet hole in his head."

"Let's assume you succeed in getting Thompson to say all that under oath," Rick said. "How do we know Consolidated TranShip was somehow involved, much less culpable?"

"Because Thompson told me two guys from Consolidated brought Anderson's body to the funeral home."

"How would Thompson know for sure the men who delivered the body worked for Consolidated TranShip?" Rick countered. "And even if they were Consolidated employees, that doesn't necessarily mean the company killed Mr. Anderson. In fact, it doesn't even mean he died on company property. What if Ronald Anderson committed suicide while sitting in his car outside the gatehouse and the company had his body cremated to spare his widow finding out?"

"Seriously?"

"Just playing devil's advocate," Rick responded. "When you get right down to it, there's very little we really know with any degree of certainty. You better hope the depositions on Friday provide the information you need to amend the complaint or Ira Cohen is going to be a very unhappy camper."

As it turned out, the depositions of Thompson and Smith never took place. That evening Tuckerton's Funeral Home burned to the ground. Vehicles belonging to Smith and Thompson were found in the funeral home's parking lot, suggesting both men were still in the building when the fire took place. And when neither man showed up the following day, the suggestion became a conclusion.

16

"What's in the briefcases?"

I had two motion hearings in Morristown that morning. During the first, I would ask the court to compel FAIL Insurance to provide a more detailed answer to Margaret Woodson's complaint. Ironically (or perhaps, hypocritically), during my second appearance that morning I would attempt to convince Judge Cohen that I shouldn't have to provide more details in the complaint I had filed against Consolidated TranShip Corporation.

My first hearing was before Judge Kenneth Bloomquist, the polar opposite of Judge Cohen. Ice Cold Cohen was a humorless, by-the-book jurist who moved cases through his courtroom as quickly as due process would allow. Judge Bloomquist, on the other hand, always took time to chat with attorneys, even those from outside Morris County, although it was said his best jokes were reserved for local counsel. In Judge Bloomquist's courtroom, adversaries were expected to behave like colleagues in search of the truth rather than combatants in search of victory.

FAIL Insurance was represented at the hearing by the law firm of Parker, Cole, Landy & Long. Parker Cole, as it's referred to in the legal community, is a big Newark firm known for opulent offices, well-heeled clients, and fat fees. It's said that to advance from associate to partner at Parker Cole, one has to adhere to a political philosophy favoring big business and even bigger government. I have no way of knowing whether or not that's true since Parker Cole attorneys wouldn't be caught dead fraternizing with their brethren in small firms like Santorini & O'Brian.

The attorney who handled litigation for FAIL Insurance was a former federal judge named Augustus Carter, who, after a few years on the bench, traded his robes for a Parker Cole partnership and a far bigger income. Of course, Judge Carter, as he liked to be addressed, never tried cases or appeared at motion hearings all by himself. His entourage for that morning's hearing consisted of five junior partners and associates, each no doubt billing at an hourly rate higher than mine.

Judge Bloomquist took the bench and we went through the usual procedure of entering our appearance. "Brendan O'Brian for the plaintiff, Margaret Woodson."

"Good to see you again, Mr. O'Brian," the judge replied.

My adversary got to his feet, made a show of adjusting his tie, buttoning his suit jacket, and clearing this throat before addressing the court. "Judge Augustus Carter of the law firm of Parker, Cole, Landy and Long, appearing on behalf of the defendant, Federal American International Lines Insurance Company."

Judge Bloomquist immediately made it clear that he was the only judge in his courtroom. "Good morning, Your Honor," he said to Carter. "Please refer to me throughout today's proceedings as Kenny." The attorneys waiting in the public gallery for their case to be called burst into laughter.

Carter turned bright red. "My apologies to the court. I meant no disrespect. I am a former federal court judge, and old habits die hard."

"You're not in Kansas anymore, Toto," Judge Bloomquist shot back. That elicited more laughter. Carter turned an even deeper shade of red before retaking his seat.

Since I had filed the motion that was the reason for the hearing, Judge Bloomquist began with me. "What can the Superior Court of New Jersey do for you this morning, Mr. O'Brian?"

I got to my feet, dispensed with the tie straightening, and with suit jacket unbuttoned, made my request. "I'm asking Your Honor to direct the defendant to provide a more detailed answer to the complaint. Federal American is refusing to make payment on a life insurance policy on the grounds that the insured, my late partner Scott Woodson, provided incorrect information on the application for insurance. We can't get the insurer to tell us what information is supposedly incorrect."

"I was very sorry to hear about your partners," Judge Bloomquist said. "My condolences to you and Mr. Santorini and the families of both gentlemen." He turned his attention to my adversary. "What do you have to say about this, Mr. Carter?"

Augustus Carter slowly got to his feet and once again adjusted his tie and buttoned his jacket before responding. "There are a number of irregularities in this case that we intend to address at trial."

"Such as?" the judge asked.

"I'm not at liberty to say at this time," Carter replied.

"Why can't you tell us now?" the judge wanted to know.

"We feel it would be detrimental to our case to reveal trial strategy at this time."

Judge Bloomquist nodded in my direction, seeking a response. "I'm not asking the insurance company to reveal trial strategy. I'm simply asking them to explain what they mean when they answer the complaint by saying the policy is voided by inaccurate information on the application for insurance. What information?"

"Is the information material, Mr. Carter?" Judge Bloomquist asked.

Instead of answering the judge's question, Carter said, "I would direct the court's attention to *Longobardi v. Chubb Ins. Co. of New Jersey*, which holds that an insurer has the right to rescind an insurance policy if the insured makes a misrepresentation in connection with obtaining the policy."

Carter quickly discovered that despite the judge's easygoing courtroom manner, Bloomquist was anything but a legal lightweight. "Actually, counsellor, if I remember correctly, *Longobardi* dealt with misrepresentations made by the insured during an examination under oath, not on the application for insurance. And I seem to recall a requirement that the misrepresentation has to be material. To determine if a misrepresentation is material, we have to know what that misrepresentation is."

"And we will," Carter insisted, "at trial. It's a question for the jury to decide."

"I'm not entirely sure I agree with that," the judge said. "But even if it is a question for the jury, what's the harm in telling us now? It's going to come out at trial, so why wait?"

"As I said, Your Honor," Carter replied, "it's a question of trial strategy."

"Perhaps," the judge replied, "or perhaps you're planning to spring something on Mr. O'Brian at the last minute. You haven't appeared in my courtroom before, so let me make sure you understand that in my courtroom I don't allow attorneys to conduct trial by ambush."

Judge Bloomquist looked in my direction to see if I had anything to add. "Actually, I think it's a question of stalling rather than trial strategy," I said. "This claim should have been paid months ago. The insurance company has dragged its feet right from the start. They've made multiple requests for information, which we've provided, notwithstanding the fact that they already had that information in their file. And after we provided all that information, my client was subjected to an examination under oath that was more of an inquisition than an EUO."

"Yes, I've heard that FAIL has a reputation for dragging its feet," the judge said. I made note of the fact that he referred to the company by its commonly used pejorative rather than its proper name. Judge Bloomquist gazed at the ceiling before leaning forward and delivering his ruling. "Okay, here's what we're going to do. Instead of requiring the defendant to file an amended complaint, I'm instructing counsel for the defense to reveal the information on the application for insurance that the defendant considers incorrect."

That didn't sit well with Augustus Carter. "Your Honor, I must protest. This seriously undermines our case. I would ask the court to stay this ruling until I've had time to research the matter in greater detail."

Judge Bloomquist saved me the trouble of pointing out that Carter was employing another stalling tactic on behalf of his client. "Request denied. Out with it, Mr. Carter. What information on the application is so incorrect it would permit your client to void the policy?"

Without being instructed to do so, one of Carter's minions handed him two documents. Carter held one up for the judge to see and said, "On the application for insurance Mr. Woodson represented that he was six feet, one inch tall." Carter held up the second document. "However, Mr. Woodson's military records clearly show that he was only six feet tall."

I couldn't believe what I had just heard, and jumped to my feet. The judge was equally incredulous. "I've got this, Mr. O'Brian," he said as he waved me back down to my seat. He looked directly as Augustus Carter. "Let me see if I understand you, counsellor. You're claiming the carrier has the right to void the contract of insurance, a rather large policy, because there's a one-inch discrepancy in the height of the insured?"

"As I explained earlier, this is just one of several irregularities that make this case somewhat less straightforward than Your Honor seems to realize." Carter's delivery was dripping with condescension as though he were addressing a junior associate instead of a Superior Court judge.

Judge Bloomquist responded in kind. "Then enlighten me about all of these supposed irregularities."

"I'm afraid I don't have that information with me this morning," Carter said.

Judge Bloomquist made a big show of counting the number of people sitting at the counsel table with Carter. "Let's see, including you, FAIL Insurance has sent six attorneys to a motion hearing. Quite an impressive entourage. Business must be booming." The judge did his counting routine a second time. "And I see five rather large briefcases, all bulging at the seams. And yet you don't have the information you need to answer my question. How terribly inconvenient for all of us." Carter started to respond, but the judge silenced him by holding a finger to his lips. Then he delivered the *coup de grace* in a stage whisper. "What's in the briefcases, a picnic lunch?"

17

"Maybe it's some
other type of organization."

On my way to Judge Cohen's courtroom for my second hearing of the morning, I stopped at the attorney conference room where I had left Rick, who was attempting to find out if the Troy Forge cops had any information about the funeral home fire that I could use in the hearing before Judge Cohen. "Any luck?" I asked as I poked my head into the room.

"First, they told me the detective handling that investigation was on another line, and they put me on hold. I got cut off, so I called back. Then, they told me he was in a meeting and would call back."

"And?"

"And I'm still waiting," Rick said. "How did it go with Judge Bloomquist?"

"He instructed the insurance company to file a detailed amended answer. I don't think he and FAIL's attorney are going to be golfing buddies anytime soon." I started to leave, but turned back to add, "Join me in Cohen's courtroom if you learn anything useful."

When I arrived at Judge Cohen's courtroom, I was surprised to find a court officer blocking the door. "Closed courtroom," he told me.

"I have a hearing before Judge Cohen," I explained.

He asked my name. I gave it to him, and he opened the door.

The courtroom was empty except for two court officers and Carl Mercer, who was sitting at one of the counsel tables reading a newspaper. Taking a chance that the attorney for Consolidated TranShip had become more pleasant since our last encounter, I asked, "What's with the closed courtroom? On a motion day this place is usually packed with dozens of attorneys."

"I don't make the rules," Mercer replied. "I just follow them." Then he went back to reading his copy of *The New York Times*. So much for the pleasantries.

I sat down at the other counsel table, and a moment later Judge Cohen took the bench. The first words out of his mouth were, "I have received instructions to close the courtroom for this morning's hearing."

"Who issued those instructions?" I asked, rising to my feet.

"Someone who has the authority to do so," the judge replied.

"May I know who that person is, and why this is a closed hearing?"

"You may not." It was delivered with authority, but Ice Cold Cohen looked uncomfortable nonetheless.

I wasn't about to give up. "Was it the same person who told you to put this case on hold?"

The judge ignored my question. Instead, he said, "Mr. O'Brian, the last time you were in my courtroom you were instructed to file an amended complaint setting forth the facts on which your case is the based. You have failed to do so, hence the motion by Mr. Mercer to dismiss the complaint. Care to explain why you failed to follow my order?"

"The last time we were here, you granted permission for me to conduct depositions to obtain the information that would allow me to comply with the court's instruction," I explained. "Unfortunately, the individuals I had scheduled for depositions died under suspicious circumstances before I could depose them."

"You don't know that they're dead," Mercer countered. "According to what I read in the newspaper, bodies were found but they haven't been identified yet. For all we know, those people were already dead when the fire broke out. After all, this is a funeral home we're talking about."

"Both men worked at the funeral home that burned down, their cars were found in the parking lot, and neither one has been seen since the night of the fire," I said to Mercer. Turning to Judge Cohen, I added, "Two important witnesses dying just before they're scheduled to provide critical information is highly suspicious, particularly in view of what I expected them to say."

That piqued the judge's curiosity. "And what was it you expected them to say?"

I took a deep breath and plunged ahead. "I expected Mr. Smith, the owner of Tuckerton's Funeral Home to say that Ronald Anderson's corpse was delivered to the funeral home by employees of Consolidated TranShip Corporation with orders to have the body cremated. And I expected Mr. Thompson, who prepared the body for cremation, to say under oath what he told me when I first interviewed him: Mr. Anderson died from a bullet to the head."

"That's pure speculation," Mercer said. "A mortuary technician isn't qualified to determine cause of death."

"Thompson might not have been a forensic pathologist," I replied, "but he saw enough bodies over the years to be able to tell how someone died. And whether or not a bullet to the brain was the cause of death, the real question is, how did the bullet get there?"

The judge's expression made it clear that he was troubled by what he had just heard. That provided me with the opening I needed. "However troubling that information is, there are other aspects of this case that are equally bizarre."

That had the intended effect. "Such as?"

"For starters, there's no record of Consolidated TranShip Corporation on file with the Division of Corporations. No certificate of incorporation for a domestic corporation. No authorization for a foreign corporation to do business in the state."

"Are you certain Consolidated TranShip is a corporation?" Judge Cohen asked. "Maybe it's some other type of business organization."

"There's no record of any type of business with that name," I answered. "And the sign at its facility in Troy Forge clearly identifies it as a corporation."

The judge looked in Mercer's direction. "Response?"

Mercer got to his feet. "I'm just here to argue a motion. Someone else in my firm handles corporate matters. But it seems to me, if Consolidated TranShip Corporation doesn't exist, as Mr. O'Brian claims, there's no way he can file suit against it."

"It exists, all right," I said before the judge could respond to Mercer's seemingly logical contention, "even if the paperwork doesn't. It has a facility in a Troy Forge industrial park surrounded by an electric fence topped with razor wire and guarded by men with guns. And the guys with guns, according to their uniform, work for a company that also doesn't seem to exist." Mercer tried to get a word in, but I was determined to finish. "And to top it all off, Ronald Anderson's death certificate was signed by a doctor who also doesn't seem to exist. There's no record of anyone by that name or a similar name licensed to practice medicine in New Jersey or any nearby state."

I was deciding whether or not to tell the judge about the Chinese bonds and multiple burglaries to find them when he said, "I've heard enough. I'm directing both parties to take no further action on this case until advised by the court." He banged his gavel and hurried out of the courtroom as if to put as much distance as possible between himself and the extremely strange case he had been assigned to hear.

I wasn't entirely sure what to make of the judge's non-ruling ruling, but Carl Mercer seemed satisfied – a bit too satisfied. He was still sitting at the counsel table casually reading his newspaper when I left the courtroom in search of Rick, who I found outside Judge Cohen's courtroom in a heated conversation with the court officer guarding the door."

"Never mind," Rick said to the court officer as I exited the courtroom. He fell in beside me as we made our way down the hallway.

"How did it go?" he asked.

"We're still in limbo. Get anything from the Troy Forge cops?"

"I did, indeed," Rick replied, "but I couldn't get in to tell you. The detective finally called me back. Seems the FBI appeared on the scene, told the locals to get lost, and took over the funeral home fire investigation."

18

"What does the State Department have to do with this?"

I was still in my pajamas, enjoying my second cup of coffee, when the phone rang. The caller ID showed Carolyn was calling. It's never good news when your secretary calls you early on a Saturday morning, and this call was no exception. Only Carolyn wasn't the caller.

"Is everything okay?" I asked anxiously.

"No, I'm afraid it's not," said a male voice. "This is Detective Henderson of the Troy Forge Police Department. I need you to come to Miss O'Malley's apartment right away."

"What's going on? Is Carolyn, I mean, Ms. O'Malley, okay?"

"I can't discuss this over the phone," Henderson said. "I need you here as soon as possible."

I dug in my heels. "I'm not going anywhere until you tell me what happened."

There was a long pause as though he was considering how much to reveal. "There's been a shooting," he finally said. Then he hung up.

I'm pretty certain I ran every red light between my house in Mountain Springs and Carolyn's apartment in Troy Forge, only stopping long enough to pick up Rick on the way.

When we arrived at Carolyn's garden apartment complex, the parking lot was filled with Troy Forge police cruisers, many with their lights still flashing. Although I had never been to Carolyn's apartment, it was easy to find. All we had to do was head for the crowd milling about on the sidewalk at the far end of the building. Rick and I worked our way through Carolyn's overly curious neighbors, and I identified myself to the uniformed cop posted at the door. He waved us through with instructions to "see Detective Henderson inside, not the State guy." I assumed he was referring to a state trooper. As it turned out, I was wrong.

We entered the apartment and found ourselves in a small hallway with a closet directly ahead of us, the opened door crisscrossed with yellow crime scene tape. Rick and I entered the living room to our right. It was filled with a small army of uniformed cops and their counterparts in civilian clothing. A middle-aged man with close cropped graying hair, dressed in a blue suit, crossed the room to meet us. "One of you O'Brian?" he asked.

"That would be me," I responded. "Rick Santorini, my partner," I added, nodding in Rick's direction.

"Henderson," he said. "We spoke on the phone."

"Is Carolyn – Ms. O'Malley – okay?" I asked.

"She's fine," Henderson said. "In fact, she's the one who asked me to call you."

"What happened?" Rick asked.

Henderson withdrew a small notebook from his jacket pocket and began to read from his notes. "Miss O'Malley claims she went out for her morning run. When she came back, she heard what she took to be someone in the apartment. So, she got a handgun out of the hall closet." He pointed to the closet criss-crossed with yellow tape. "She then entered the living room and ascertained that the sounds she was hearing were coming from one of the bedrooms." He nodded in the direction of a hallway leading off the living room. "When she entered the guest bed-room, she saw a man going through the dresser. She aimed the gun at him and ordered him to stop. As he turned around, he reached under his jacket and withdrew a gun. She then fired her weapon in self-defense." Henderson put the notebook back in his pocket. "She's a good aim. The guy's dead."

"You obviously questioned Ms. O'Malley after she requested an attorney," I pointed out, my first thought being to protect Carolyn in case she was facing charges in connection with the shooting.

"As a matter of fact, nobody questioned Miss O'Malley," Henderson said. "She volunteered that information to the first officer on the scene and then repeated it to me when I arrived. She's been completely cooperative the whole time."

"But she did ask for her attorney," I pressed.

"Relax, counsellor," Henderson said. "Based on what we know at this point, I don't think Miss O'Malley is going to be charged with anything. We found a gun near the body of the in-truder, which would seem to back up her version of events." Henderson paused and once again looked in the direction of the hallway that apparently led to the bedroom where the shooting had taken place. "If the guy from the State Department hadn't shown up, I'm guessing Miss O'Malley probably wouldn't have wanted me to call you at all."

I was relieved to hear that Carolyn was apparently in the clear, but confused about Henderson's reference to the State De-partment. "What does the State Department have to do with this?"

"That's what I'd like to know," the detective said. "Which is why I was more than happy to call you. I'm hoping you can tell me."

"I don't have a clue," I said. I looked at Rick to see if he had any ideas, but he just shrugged his shoulders. "Last I checked, the State Department doesn't investigate attempted burglaries."

"Exactly," Henderson said. "And the guy from State isn't offering any explanations. He's talking to Miss O'Malley in the guest room right now, and I was politely informed that my presence wasn't required." From the way he said it, it was pretty clear that Henderson had been instructed, not requested, to leave while the federal agent talked to Carolyn. "Of course, as her attorneys, you gentlemen can insist that you be present while she's being questioned. He looked right at me and arched an eyebrow. "And since I don't want you two tampering with my crime scene, I'll have to accompany you."

I got the message. "Yes, we demand to be present while our client is being questioned."

"Thought you might." Henderson smiled, then led us down the hallway, knocked on the first closed door, and without waiting for a response, entered what turned out to be a bedroom. Rick and I followed. There was a body lying on the floor, covered with a sheet. Carolyn was sitting on the bed a few feet away, with a very large, very muscular man towering over her. He was a bit too close, like the guard at Consolidated TranShip who had leaned into my car and invaded my personal space.

The man looked in our direction as we entered the room, and his piercing, blue eyes seemed to drill right through us like a pair of lasers. He looked vaguely familiar, but I was pretty certain we had never met before. I would have remembered those eyes. "I thought I told you to wait outside," Laser Eyes said to Henderson. "And who the hell are these two?"

I answered his question before Henderson could respond. "We're Ms. O'Malley's attorneys and we demand to be present when you speak to our client."

That elicited an immediate, and entirely too forceful, response. "I don't respond to demands."

"Then consider it a request, young man," Rick said as he crossed the room and put a grandfatherly hand on Carolyn's shoulder. "Are you okay?" he asked her gently.

"A bit shaken up, but I'm okay," she replied.

As Rick and Carolyn conversed in hushed tones, I asked Laser Eyes for identification. He complied by showing me credentials identifying him as Donald Helms, an agent of the State Department's Bureau of Diplomatic Security. "Since when does the Bureau of Diplomatic Security investigate burglaries?" I asked.

"When the person shot is a foreign diplomat," he answered. Helms leaned down and uncovered the face of the person under the sheet.

It was Wu Jin from the Chinese consulate.

Although I never said a word, my reaction gave me away.

"You know this guy?" Helms asked.

I stalled for time by answering his question with one of my own. "Should I?"

"I don't know. Should you?" He waited for a response, but I wasn't about to admit knowing the victim until I could figure out what was going on. "Hey, you know what they say: to Caucasians, Asians all look alike, and vice versa." I'm not sure that's true, but it was a convenient way to avoid answering his question.

"I'll note in my report that the shooter's smart aleck attorney wouldn't answer my question," Helms said.

"I have a better idea," I responded. "Note in your report that I'm reasonably certain the dead man wasn't one of our clients, but I'm not about to make any definitive statement to a federal official in case it turns out that I'm mistaken."

"Fair enough," he said after considering my answer for a few seconds. I wasn't sure whether he was satisfied with my response or simply chose not to pursue the matter.

Helms returned his attention to Carolyn. "Now that your attorneys are here, will you answer my questions?"

Before Carolyn could respond, I said, "Not until she's been able to confer with her attorneys." I nodded toward the door. "In private."

Helms glared at me with those laser eyes. "Five minutes," he said before leaving the room. I asked Detective Henderson to leave as well, but I was considerably more polite, a decision that was to pay dividends at a later date.

When we were alone, I asked Carolyn what had happened. She repeated the story Henderson had recounted, adding a handful of details. "I assumed this is somehow connected with the break-ins at Mrs. Anderson's home and the office, so I asked Detective Henderson to call you. I didn't want to say anything until we had a chance to talk."

"Good thinking," Rick said.

True to his word, Helms gave us exactly five minutes of private discussion before returning. Rick and I used that time to prepare Carolyn for what we assumed would be a routine questioning, but which turned out to be an aggressive interrogation. He began by uncovering the body on the floor and asking Carolyn, "Do you know him?"

"I've never seen him before," she answered, following our advice not to tell an outright lie, but to avoid revealing what we knew about the Chinese consular officer.

"Do you know why he was here?" he asked next.

"I assume he was here to rob me. When I entered the room, he was rummaging through the drawers," she said, nodding toward the dresser. Again, it was a truthful statement, but avoided any mention of the Chinese bonds.

But then Helms asked, "What was he looking for?"

Before Carolyn could respond, I answered for her. "How would she know that? She's got a lot of skills, but reading minds isn't one of them."

"I'm not asking her to read minds," Helms said to me, "but she must have some idea what the intruder was looking for."

Again following the advice we had given her during our five-minute discussion, Carolyn avoided saying anything untruthful, answering the question with one of her own. "What do burglars usually look for: jewelry, money, anything they think is valuable?" Instead of stopping there, she turned the tables on Laser Eyes. "You seem to know what he was looking for, so why don't you tell me."

Helms clearly wasn't expecting that response, but his surprise quickly gave way to anger. "I'm asking the questions, not you. And the sooner you answer my questions, the sooner we can wrap things up." He spent the next twenty minutes asking questions, many of which seemed to have nothing to do with the attempted burglary or the shooting of a supposed diplomat. I intervened to point that out several times, but each time Helms responded with, "Counsellor, please let me do my job." As the session progressed, the questions came faster, and Helms pressed harder for answers. When Carolyn provided a response he didn't like, Helms reminded her that lying to a federal official was a crime. The third time he pulled that routine I told him the interview was over. That elicited a vehement response from Laser Eyes. "Then perhaps I'll just arrest your client for killing a diplomat in cold blood."

"Not your call." I turned to find Detective Henderson standing by the door. "This is our investigation," he told Helms, "and if anyone is going to be arrested, we'll handle it."

Henderson and Helms conducted a staring contest, which the Troy Forge detective eventually won. Helms stormed out of the room with Henderson on his heels, the two exchanging angry words as they made their way down the hallway to the living room.

Carolyn looked as though she were on the verge of tears. I wanted to wrap my arms around her and tell her everything was going to be okay. But I didn't. I couldn't. Regardless of whatever feelings I might have toward her, she was an employee and that sort of thing could be misinterpreted.

Rick apparently didn't feel constrained. He bent down and put his hand on her shoulder. "I think you should take some time off and visit your sister in Georgia." The suggestion took me by surprise, not because Rick was giving grandfatherly advice, but because I didn't know Carolyn's sister lived in Georgia. In fact, I hadn't even known my long-time secretary had a sister. My ex-girlfriend, Stacey, told me shortly before we broke up that I was, to use her exact words, absolutely clueless when it came to people. At the time, I thought it was a silly comment, made in anger, but perhaps she had a point.

Carolyn objected to Rick's suggestion, arguing that she was needed at the office. Although I agreed with that assessment, I said nothing. She eventually relented after Rick pointed out the advantages of having her, and the Chinese bonds, out of harm's way in a small Georgia town where nobody was likely to find her. "The police can't question you if they can't find you," he told her. "And Brendan and I won't have to hire a bodyguard to protect you." She reluctantly packed a suitcase, and Rick and I escorted her to her car while Henderson was engaged in conversation with one of his colleagues.

We stood in the parking lot as Carolyn drove away to ensure she wasn't followed. Laser Eyes, who was sitting behind the wheel of a dark sedan, speaking on a cell phone, didn't seem to notice her departure. As Helms concluded the conversation, he slipped on a pair of mirrored sunglasses and began backing out of the parking space. That's when I realized why he had looked familiar. Laser Eyes was the second guard at Consolidated Tran-Ship, the one who had stepped in front of my car to emphasize I wasn't welcome at that mysterious facility.

19

"The federal government can do whatever it wants."

The following Monday, Detective Henderson arrived at our office, as we assumed he would. And as expected, he was more than a little upset by the fact that we had spirited Carolyn away while he wasn't looking. A split second after taking a seat on the sofa in my office, he said, "I get the Feds off your secretary's back and you repay me by hiding a key witness?"

"Protecting, not hiding," I replied. "There's more going on than you realize."

"Then enlighten me," Henderson said.

After leaving Carolyn's apartment on Saturday, I had called Sean McDermott, my high school buddy who's now a member of the Troy Forge police department. Sean assured me that Henderson was a straight shooter who could be trusted to do the right thing. Based on that assessment, Rick and I had decided to tell him about the mysterious death of Ronald Anderson, the Chinese bonds, and the burglaries at Edna Anderson's house and at our office.

"So, you're telling me the break-in at your secretary's apartment was another attempt to find these bonds?" Henderson asked after I had finished outlining what had happened. "Seems pretty far-fetched if the bonds are worthless, as you claim."

"I would agree," I replied, "except for the fact that we know the person who broke into Ms. O'Malley's apartment."

"You know the victim?" I wasn't sure if Henderson was more surprised or angry.

"I also know the State Department guy, Helms or whatever his real name is, although I didn't realize who he was until later when I saw him outside wearing sunglasses."

Henderson crossed his arms, and looked first at Rick and then at me. "You two have a lot of explaining to do."

"And we will," I told him, "but first you have to assure us that Ms. O'Malley isn't going to be charged with anything."

Henderson leaned forward in his chair, and glared at me. "I don't *have* to do anything." The staring contest only lasted a few seconds before the detective leaned back and said, "As I told you on Saturday, it would appear that Miss O'Malley acted in self-defense. The victim's fingerprints were on the weapon your secretary claims he pulled on her, as well as on the bullets in the gun. The gun fits the holster the victim was wearing, further supporting her version of events. So, based on what we know at this point, it looks like Miss O'Malley is in the clear. Ordinarily, we'd treat this as a garden-variety burglary that ended badly for the burglar. But when the State Department shows up, and then you two make the shooter disappear, I have to dig deeper. And based on what you've told me this morning, I think I have to dig a whole lot deeper. So, now it's time for you to tell me what you know. Let's start with the man your secretary shot."

"His name is Wu Jin. Rick and I met him at the Chinese consulate in New York."

Rick handed Henderson the letter we had received from Mr. Wu, and the detective scanned it before asking, "Why a meeting? If the bonds are worthless, why not just say that in the letter?"

"We didn't realize it at the time, but the meeting was a fishing expedition," Rick replied. "Wu began the meeting by asking for the name and address of our client. Then he asked how many bonds she owned. Brendan gave him that information, obviously thinking it was needed to prepare the appropriate paperwork to collect on the bonds. But once Wu had that information, he told us the bonds were worthless without ever explaining why."

"Exactly how many bonds does you client have?" Henderson wanted to know.

"Her bonds would be worth millions," I answered, "if the Chinese were obligated to honor the debt. But as Rick discovered after our meeting with Wu, Uncle Sam signed a treaty with the Chinese in 1979 that extinguished China's debts to individual U.S. citizens in exchange for a payment to the Treasury Department as representative for all American citizens with a claim against the Chinese government."

"And our government used the money to pay individual bond owners?" Henderson asked.

"No, Uncle Sam kept it," I replied.

The detective was surprised by that answer. "Wait a minute. I'm not a lawyer, but that doesn't seem legal. How can the federal government do that?"

I laughed. "The federal government can do whatever it wants. Who's going to stop it?"

"How much money are we talking about?" Henderson asked.

"Something like seven hundred and fifty billion dollars of Chinese bonds were never repaid," Rick said. "Of course, there were bondholders all over the world, so the amount owed to U.S.

citizens is less than that. But we're still talking about a considerable amount of money."

"Why would the government make that kind of deal with the Chinese?" Henderson asked.

"It was part of the so-called normalization with the People's Republic of China that Nixon started and Carter finalized," Rick explained.

"Fucking politicians," Henderson muttered, shaking his head in apparent disbelief. "How about Helms, the State Department guy? How do you know him?"

I related my story of how Helms and one of his fellow goons wouldn't let me through the gate when I tried to get in to Consolidated TranShip.

The detective began tapping his notebook with the pen as he processed what we had told him. "None of this makes sense," he eventually said. "If these bonds are worthless, why would anyone want to steal them? And why would an agent from the State Department's Bureau of Diplomatic Security be working as a guard at a private company?"

"Maybe he's not from the State Department," Rick suggested.

"His credentials sure looked legit," Henderson said.

"Probably were," I said. "But that doesn't necessarily mean Helms works for the Bureau of Diplomatic Security." In response to Henderson's quizzical look, I added, "Remember, the federal government can do pretty much whatever it wants, including handing out official government credentials to private contractors, assuming that's what Helms is."

"Son of a ...," Henderson muttered, apparently realizing that Helms might very well have deceived him at Carolyn's apartment.

It was the opening I needed. "Consolidated TranShip is the key to everything. I'm certain Helms, or whatever his real name might be, was working there as a guard. It was where Ronald Anderson turned up dead. If you want to get to the bottom of three murders, that's the place to look for answers."

"Three murders?" Henderson asked.

"Three murders, all here in Troy Forge, your jurisdiction. Ronald Anderson goes to work at Consolidated TranShip and never comes home. Instead, his body arrives at Tuckerton's Funeral Home with a bullet hole in the head. Shortly thereafter, the funeral home's owner and the employee who told me about the bullet hole in Anderson's head end up dead just before their scheduled depositions." I held up three fingers. "Three murders."

"Three deaths," Henderson responded, "but not necessarily three murders. For all you know, these could all have been nothing more than tragic accidents."

"Then why can't I get anyone from Consolidated TranShip to talk to me? And why is the FBI investigating the funeral home fire instead of your department?"

Henderson began the pen tapping again. "Maybe you're right," he eventually said. "Maybe a visit to Consolidated TranShip is in order."

"Rick and I would like to go with you."

"Not gonna happen," came the immediate reply. "This is police business."

"It's also our chance to help Anderson's widow find out what happened to her husband. Put yourself in her shoes. Her husband leaves for work in the morning, and the next time she sees him he's a pile of ashes in a cardboard box. Don't you think she deserves to know what happened?"

"I'm not unsympathetic, O'Brian," Henderson said, "but I do things by the book, and having civilians tag along isn't by the book."

Rick and I spent the next fifteen minutes pleading our case, pointing out all the ways we could be helpful. At one point in the conversation I said, "Remember, I'm the one who identified Helms. Who knows what else I saw during my first visit to the place that might be helpful." Henderson eventually agreed to allow us to accompany him, but only after imposing all sorts of restrictions, including a requirement that we only speak to him and not communicate with anyone from Consolidated TranShip. As it turned out, that wasn't a problem.

20

"That's no ordinary electric fence."

Three days later, Rick and I arrived at Consolidated TranShip Corporation fifteen minutes early, just in case Henderson decided to proceed without us. We needn't have bothered. The detective's reputation for honesty was apparently well deserved. He was waiting for us outside the main gate, leaning against a white Ford sedan and drinking a cup of coffee. Three uniformed officers from the Troy Forge police department stood nearby in a tight circle, also drinking coffee.

After a brief exchange of pleasantries, Henderson and I walked to the gatehouse. As we approached, a uniformed guard came out to meet us. "Good morning," Henderson said to the guard, a tall, muscular guy in his late twenties with a boot camp haircut. The detective held up his credentials for the guard to see. "Would you please open the gate so we can get in?"

"Do you have an appointment?" the guard asked in an equally congenial tone of voice.

"No, but I do have a search warrant," Henderson said, withdrawing a document from the pocket of his sports coat and handing it to the guard.

"One moment, please," the guard said politely before retreating to the gatehouse where he picked up a phone and began what turned out to be a lengthy conversation. At one point he appeared to be reading the search warrant to whomever was on the other end of the call.

"Have any trouble getting the warrant?" I asked Henderson while we waited for the guard to complete his phone call.

"I have friends in the County Prosecutor's office, and they have a friendly Superior Court judge who's not inclined to be a stickler for details."

The guard ended his telephone conversation with a vigorous nod of the head. Then he returned to where we were standing. "I'm sorry, sir" he said to Henderson, "but my orders are to deny entry."

"I don't think you understand," Henderson said to the younger man. "You don't really have that option. This is a search warrant issued by a Superior Court judge. You're legally obligated to comply. Now, please open the gate."

"I'm sorry, sir," the guard said. "I'm just following orders."

"Let me talk to your superior," Henderson said.

"I'm sorry, sir. I can't do that."

"Why not?"

"Orders, sir."

Henderson pointed to the gatehouse. "The person you just spoke to on that phone told you not to let me speak to him or her?"

"Not exactly, sir," the guard answered politely.

"Well, what exactly did he say?"

"He told me to get rid of you, and to not call back because he was busy."

"Did you tell him I'm a police detective with a search warrant issued by a judge?"

"Yes, sir."

Henderson looked back at the three Troy Forge cops. That must have been a pre-arranged signal because they ended their conversation, opened the trunk of the unmarked sedan and withdrew what I assumed were bulletproof vests, which they quickly donned. Each cop then retrieved a shotgun, and the trio began walking toward where Henderson and I were standing. I noticed that one of the cops was carrying what looked like an oversized bolt cutter. Rick, who had been chatting with the cops, having neither a weapon nor a bulletproof vest, remained with the unmarked police car. It was at that point that I realized Henderson was also wearing a bulletproof vest ... but I wasn't.

When the three cops reached the gate, they fanned out behind Henderson and me. "Now, son," Henderson said with mock politeness, "I'm going to ask you one last time to please open the gate so I can execute the lawfully issued search warrant I showed you."

"Yes, sir," the guard said deferentially before returning to the gatehouse. Once inside the structure, he reached for what I assumed were the controls to open the gate and the fence beyond it. But a moment later his hand reappeared holding a telephone. The guard began a conversation, all the while looking directly at us. When the guard concluded his phone conversation, he closed the door to the gatehouse, crossed his arms, and stood there as though waiting for something to happen.

"Does the person he called open the gate?" one of the uniformed cops asked.

"That wouldn't make sense," a second cop answered.

Henderson was infuriated. "Enough of this nonsense," he said, motioning to the cop holding the oversized bolt cutter, who ducked under the gate and approached the fence ten feet beyond it.

"That fence is electrified," I told Henderson.

"The bolt cutters are insulated," he responded.

Out of the corner of my eye I saw the guard pound on the guardhouse window to get our attention. When I looked in his direction, he began frantically waving his arms. He was clearly issuing a warning.

"Are you sure your guy isn't going to fry himself when he cuts that fence?" I asked Henderson.

Before the detective had a chance to respond, the cop with the bolt cutters went flying backward as though pushed by a giant, unseen hand, landing unceremoniously on the seat of his pants. He seemed stunned, but otherwise unhurt. The two other cops rushed forward to help him up.

"That's no ordinary electric fence," Henderson said.

I turned to face the guard, whose sheepish look I interpreted to mean, *I tried to warn you.* I was about to ask Henderson what he planned to do next when a vehicle appeared from behind Consolidated TranShip's building and accelerated toward us. The camouflage paint job and machine gun on the roof identified it as a military vehicle. It came to a sudden stop on the other side of the fence with the machine gun pointing right at us.

I don't think any of us expected Consolidated TranShip's private army to open fire on four police officers and an unarmed civilian. But neither did we think a mere search warrant was going to get us into the facility. "Let's get out of here," Henderson said. The cop with the bolt cutters was the first to leave, with the rest of us not far behind.

"Did you happen to see who was sitting in that vehicle?" I asked Henderson when we had retreated to our cars.

"No," he answered, "I guess I was too focused on the machine gun pointed at me to notice."

"It was Helms, your buddy from the State Department."

21

"This case is troubling on so many levels."

I was the first person to arrive at the office the Monday following our attempted visit to Consolidated TranShip. The phone started ringing as I punched in the code to disarm the alarm system. I picked up the receiver on Elaine's desk in the waiting room, and a woman who identified herself as Judge Cohen's secretary informed me that Rick and I were expected in the judge's chambers immediately, if not sooner.

When Rick arrived ten minutes later, we drove to Morristown and wove through the assembled throng of attorneys and litigants to the chambers of Ice Cold Cohen. His secretary stopped typing as we entered her office and, without saying a single word, pointed to the door leading to the judge's inner sanctum.

Judge Cohen was standing at the window, his back to us as we entered. "I instructed you to take no action in the Consolidated TranShip case until further notice, didn't I?" The judge didn't wait for an answer. "Now I hear that you two paid a visit to the company last week." The judge turned around and walked toward us, adding, "And you nearly got shot in the process."

"We were there with a detective who was attempting to execute a search warrant," I explained. "He took us along because I convinced him that my previous experience might come in handy."

"I don't care why you were there," Ice Cold said. "I gave explicit instructions that you were not to take any action on that case until I directed you to." The judge walked to his desk and sat down, motioning us to the chairs across from him.

"I interpreted your instructions to mean we couldn't schedule depositions, serve interrogatories, file motions, or take an interlocutory appeal. I didn't think you meant we couldn't continue our investigation." That wasn't entirely true, but it was certainly a plausible interpretation of the judge's instructions.

"So, let me be clear," the judge began. "You are to do nothing involving this case until I tell you otherwise. That includes going to Consolidated TranShip."

Rick joined the conversation. "With all due respect, I'm not sure Your Honor has the authority to tell us what we can and can't do outside your courtroom."

Judge Cohen stood up and slapped both hands on his desk before returning to the spot by the window he had been occupying when we first arrived. I assumed Ice Cold was preparing to tell Rick that a Superior Court judge has the power to do pretty much whatever he pleases, and attorneys who appear before him had better just accept that reality. But to my surprise, Judge Cohen turned to face us, and in a surprisingly soft tone of voice said, "You don't understand what you're dealing with. The people behind Consolidated TranShip are the kind of people you don't want to antagonize. And showing up with local cops waving a search warrant is clearly antagonizing them."

"Who are those people?" Rick asked.

"I don't know, the judge replied. "I just know you need to stay away from that place."

Judge Cohen returned to his desk chair, sat down, and stared off into space as though deciding what to say next. "This case is troubling on so many levels," he eventually said. "We have a man who dies under mysterious circumstances, a company that, according to you, doesn't officially exist, two witnesses who die in a fire before they can be deposed, and phone calls from politicians who think they have the right to tell me how to run my courtroom."

"So, it was a politician who told you to put the case on hold." I phrased it as a statement, but intended it as a question.

"Politicians, plural," the judge replied.

"I don't suppose you'd care to tell us who you're referring to," I prompted.

Ice Cold Cohen actually smiled. "You'd suppose correctly. But I'll tell you this, they both made it clear, in no uncertain terms, that you're to stay away from Consolidated TranShip."

"Anything else you'd care to share?" I asked, hoping, but not expecting, that the judge would inadvertently reveal something useful.

"I'm not authorized to tell you anything more." Judge Cohen shook his head and laughed. "Hell, the senator from Georgia had such a thick accent I'm not sure I understood half of what she said. She did, however, manage to make it clear that showing up at Consolidated TranShip again could be detrimental to your health. So, stay away from the place." He opened one of the files on his desk and began reading. Rick and I waited patiently, assuming that file was somehow connected to our case. Eventually, Ice Cold Cohen looked up. "Are you two still here?" He waved us toward the door. "Get out of here. I have work to do."

"That was bizarre," I said to Rick as soon as we were outside the courthouse.

"You do realize the judge just tossed us a bone, don't you? He went out of his way to tell us one of the people pressuring him is a female senator from Georgia. I've known Ira Cohen for years, and I can guarantee that wasn't a slip of the tongue."

On the ride back to the office we played "name that senator," and decided Elizabeth Scott must be the female senator pressuring Judge Cohen. How or why she was doing that, however, was a mystery.

"I'll call Carolyn when we get back to the office," Rick said, "and have her do some research. Maybe she can find someone there in Georgia who knows the senator and can provide us with useful information."

"I have a feeling Judge Cohen isn't really serious about us staying away from Consolidated TranShip," I said to Rick as we pulled into the parking lot of our office building, "I think he's just following orders to deliver a message. My gut tells me he's as curious about that place as we are."

"I'm not so sure about that," Rick replied. "He seemed pretty serious to me."

Detective Henderson was waiting for us when we entered our office suite. "I just had an interesting meeting," he said as we walked through the door. "The mayor and the chief of police told me in no uncertain terms that if I want to keep my job and my pension, Consolidated TranShip Corporation is off limits. I get the distinct impression they're getting heat from someone higher up the political food chain."

22

"I don't think a motion hearing is the place to pursue this."

I spent many hours the following week thinking of ways to get into Consolidated TranShip Corporation. Unfortunately, everything I came up with would have been far too outlandish for *Mission Impossible*, not to mention far too rigorous for my abilities.

My planning was interrupted mid-week when the amended answer in the *Woodson* case arrived. Despite Judge Bloomquist's instructions to file a comprehensive amended answer, Augustus Carter's handiwork simply stated that the cause of Scott Woodson's death was "one of several policy exclusions," thereby absolving FAIL Insurance from writing a seven-figure check to Margaret Woodson.

I immediately filed a motion to compel the insurance company to, once again, provide a more detailed answer. And as long as I was filing a motion, I decided to tack on a request for an order directing FAIL to answer the interrogatories I had sent them and to produce documents that were essential to preparing the case for trial. Interrogatories, the legal term for a list of questions, are customarily the first step in what's called the discovery process, the pre-trial maneuvering whereby each side obtains information about the other party's case. And once each side knows what the other has in the way of evidence, the parties usually settle to avoid the time and expense of a trial. Of course, in the Woodson case, the insurance company seemed intent on dragging things out as long as possible, hoping Margaret would eventually accept less than what she was owed.

The next day, Judge Bloomquist's secretary called to inform me that the judge had scheduled an expedited hearing for the following Monday. "I think Bloomquist is even more annoyed with Carter than I am," I said to Rick later that day.

The judge's annoyance became obvious at the outset of Monday's motion hearing. As soon as Augustus Cater and I entered our appearance, Judge Bloomquist told my adversary, "Mr. Carter, I'm quite certain the last time you were in my courtroom, I instructed you to file an amended answer that set forth all of your reasons for denying this claim."

"That is correct," Augustus Carter answered.

"But you haven't done that, have you?"

"Respectfully, I believe we have. The insured ...."

"Mr. Woodson," the judge interjected. "The insured has a name: Scott Woodson."

"My apology," Carter said. "I meant no disrespect," he added, nodding in my direction. He adjusted his tie before continuing. "The cause of Mr. Woodson's death was one of several policy exclusions, as we stated in our amended answer."

"What are the policy exclusions you're referring to?" the judge asked.

"I would rather not reveal that information at this time, but will, of course, do so at trial."

"No, you'll do so now," Judge Bloomquist shot back.

"That would compromise our trial strategy," Carter said.

"If there are specific policy exclusions that would eliminate your client's obligation to pay this claim, that's an affirmative defense," the judge explained. "Rule 4:5-4 of the Rules of Civil Procedure states, and I quote, a responsive pleading shall set forth specifically and separately a statement of facts constituting an avoidance or affirmative defense."

"And that's what we've done," Carter insisted. "We've stated that Mr. Woodson's death was caused by something that's specifically excluded from coverage under the policy."

"But you haven't told the plaintiff what that 'something' is," the judge replied. "How can Mr. O'Brian possibly prepare his case for trial if he doesn't know what it is you claim excuses the insurance company from paying this claim?"

"That's not my problem," Carter said.

"Actually, it is your problem," Judge Bloomquist replied, "because I'm ordering you to identify the policy exclusions you claim apply in this case. And if you don't, I'm going to bar you from raising them at trial."

"In federal court ..." Carter began.

That's as far as my adversary got before Judge Bloomquist shut him down. "You're not in federal court. You're in my courtroom, and I'm instructing you to specify the policy exclusions you claim apply to this case."

Augustus Carter nodded toward one of the six associates who had accompanied him that morning, a young lady with the same severe look of the woman who had escorted Margaret Woodson and me to the room where Harry Sporn conducted the examination under oath. She withdrew a document from her briefcase and handed it to Carter.

"There are three policy exclusions that apply in this case," Carter said. "The first involves death arising out of the commission of a criminal act."

I jumped to my feet to object, but before I could respond, Judge Bloomquist said, "That provision refers to illegal acts committed by the insured, not by third parties."

"Perhaps," Carter responded, "but the policy doesn't specify that. It's a question for the jury to decide."

"No," Judge Bloomquist said, "that's not a jury question. That exclusion is a standard provision in every policy written in this state. It's designed to prevent an insured's beneficiary from profiting from a crime committed by the insured. It doesn't apply to a crime committed by a third party. No reasonable jury could decide otherwise. It's public policy, not a jury question."

"I disagree," Carter said, perhaps a bit too forcefully.

"Then, by all means, see if you can convince the Appellate Division," Bloomquist replied. "But I don't think you'll have much success."

Another member of Carter's team handed him a document, which he scanned before saying, "Mr. Woodson's policy also specifically states that Federal American is not obligated to pay if the insured's death is caused by smoke inhalation."

"But it wasn't," I said. "Mr. Woodson was crushed to death when a section of the parking garage collapsed in the explosion."

"Yes, that's my understanding," the judge agreed. "Is the insurance carrier disputing the cause of death?" he asked my adversary.

"I'm not sure anyone will ever really know with certainty what caused Mr. Woodson's death," Augustus Carter answered. "We do, however, know that the explosion resulted in a cloud of particulate matter in the air and that Mr. Woodson inhaled some of that material. At the very least it was a contributing factor to his death."

"Smoke and particulates are two different things," the judge pointed out.

Augustus Carter and his team were obviously expecting that response. "On the contrary," my adversary said as one of his assistants handed him a document. Reading from the document, he continued, "Smoke is defined as a visible suspension of carbon or other particulates in air. Smoke can be a suspension of any type of particle, including the concrete dust that was present in the immediate aftermath of the explosion."

It had been apparent since entering the courtroom that Judge Bloomquist was somewhat less than happy with the insurance company's legal team. So, rather than contest Carter's definition, I waited to see how the judge would respond. I wasn't disappointed.

"That might be the dictionary definition of smoke," Judge Bloomquist said, "but that's not the way the average person would define it. As I'm sure counsel is aware, here in New Jersey we have the reasonable expectation rule. Words in insurance policies are given the meaning that a policyholder would reasonably expect them to have. And I'm quite certain that most people would expect smoke to mean something created by a fire, not dust caused by a collapsing building."

"I believe that is a question for the jury to decide," Augustus Carter said.

Judge Bloomquist shook his head. "No, it's not a jury question. As a matter of law, no reasonable jury could decide smoke is the same thing as concrete dust."

Carter wasn't about to give up. "Thirdly, the policy of insurance specifically states that there is no coverage in the event the insured dies as a result of an act of war. Clearly, the bombing of the World Trade Center was an act of war, and as such, my client is not obligated to pay the policy proceeds to Mr. O'Brian's client."

The judge looked in my direction for a response. "The reasonable expectation rule would apply here as well. The average person would think a war is a declared war between countries, not a bombing conducted by terrorists. I would direct the Court's

attention to *Pan American World Airways, Inc. v. Aetna Casualty &
Surety Company*, a 2nd Circuit case decided in 1974 involving the
hijacking of a plane by terrorists. The court held that the act of
war exclusion in the insurance policy only applies to hostilities
by entities that have significant attributes of sovereignty. It concluded that the hijackers were agents of a radical political group
and not a sovereign government. That's exactly the situation in
his case."

"Mr. Carter," Judge Bloomquist said, nodding toward my adversary. "Response?"

"I would direct the court's attention to *New York Life Insurance Company v. Bennion*, a 1946 case decided by the 10th Circuit
which established the principle that war need not be officially
declared for an insurer to invoke the war exclusion. As in this
case, there is no officially declared war, but as Mr. O'Brian
pointed out just months ago, right here in this building in a case
before Judge McAndrew, we are nonetheless at war with an ide-
ology that seeks our defeat through any means necessary." He
turned to face me, and with mock congeniality said, "And I agree
with him completely."

He was obviously referring to *CIRR v. McCain*, the case in
which I defended my former girlfriend, a newspaper reporter,
who was sued for defaming Islam. I couldn't recall whether or
not I had actually said those words, but there was a very good
chance that I had, or at least something pretty close. "Mr. Carter
is taking my words out of context," I said to the judge. "And even
if he's quoting me accurately, my statement would be inadmissible as hearsay."

"I would tend to agree," Judge Bloomquist said. "Mr. Carter,
I'm instructing you not to mention Mr. O'Brian's statement at
trial." The judge leaned back in his chair, crossed his arms and
looked toward the ceiling, apparently considering the arguments

we each had made. Having reached a decision, the judge leaned forward and said, "In support of his argument, Mr. Carter relies on a very old case decided by the 2nd Circuit, which covers appeals from federal courts in New York, Connecticut and Vermont. Mr. O'Brian cites a more recent case from the 10th Circuit, which handles appeals from courts in western states like Colorado and New Mexico. Neither of you cites a case decided here in New Jersey, which is understandable because the question has not been addressed by a New Jersey court. Given all that's going on in the world, I have a terrible feeling that we're going to see more and more tragic events like the one that took the life of Mr. Woodson. So I think we need to resolve this issue sooner rather than later. I'm going to allow Mr. Carter to raise the act of war exclusion as an affirmative defense at trial. We'll let the jury decide if the bombing of the World Trade Center was an act of war. My secretary will be in touch to schedule a trial date."

The judge was about to gavel the hearing to a conclusion when I reminded him there was another issue to be resolved. "The interrogatories, Your Honor? The deadline for answering interrogatories has expired. We've answered the defendant's, but they haven't answered ours. They also haven't produced the documents I requested."

Judge Bloomquist nodded toward my adversary. "Mr. Carter, is there some reason for the delay?"

Carter adjusted his tie before extending his right arm. One of the attorneys accompanying him that day placed a file folder in his hand. "Mr. O'Brian has asked for, among many, many other things," he began, reading from something in the folder, "a list of beneficiaries who settled for less than the policy amount during the two previous years, as well as all manuals, memoranda or other writings relating to the defendant's policies, official or unofficial, regarding the payment, negotiation, or denial of claims." He closed the file folder and handed it back to the other attorney. "As I'm sure Your Honor can appreciate, it takes time to respond to such a wide-ranging request. However, my staff has been working with people at Federal American to compile that information, and we're almost finished. We're planning to bring it to Mr. O'Brian's office when we go there for the deposition of one of Federal American's employees."

"Excellent idea. That will save your client the cost of postage," Judge Bloomquist said sarcastically as he made a show of counting the attorneys sitting at the counsel table with Carter.

The judge gaveled the hearing to a conclusion, and a smiling Augustus Carter and his small army of insurance company attorneys filed out of the courtroom. As he passed where I was sitting, my adversary looked right at me and winked.

23

"You can't forget
something you never knew."

I called Margaret Woodson as soon as I returned to the office. It was a call I had an obligation to make, but not one I was looking forward to. I had promised her that FAIL Insurance would soon be sending her a check, a promise that I really shouldn't have made, and one that I had failed to keep.

"Any idea how long it will take to get a trial date?" she asked after I explained what had happened at the hearing.

I told her I wouldn't know until the judge's secretary called, and that I had no way of knowing how long I'd have to wait for that call. "But," I added hopefully, "the judge does seem annoyed with the insurance company's delaying tactics, so there's a good chance he'll set this down for trial sooner rather than later. But we have a lot to do before we go to court. I'm still waiting for answers to the interrogatories I served on the insurance company. No telling what those will reveal. We also have Harry Sporn's deposition, our chance to do to him what he did to you during the examination under oath."

Margaret's response was emphatic. "Promise me you'll rake the bastard over the coals."

"I promise," I replied.

"When we do eventually get to trial, what are our chances?" she asked next.

"Better than 50-50," I answered. When she didn't respond after several seconds, I added, "Much better than 50-50. We thought they might raise the act of war exclusion, so Rick researched that angle and I was prepared. It's not a particularly strong position, but it's the only defense they've got."

"Yes, but the judge ruled that the jury gets to decide if Rick's death was caused by an act of war. And if they do, the insurance company doesn't have to pay me a dime. You and I both know that juries can be unpredictable."

She had a point. Seasoned trial attorneys know cases that should be an easy win can be lost simply because juries sometimes make bad decisions. That's especially true in cases involving complex legal or technical issues that the jurors don't really understand. And although Margaret's case didn't involve anything overly complicated, it was still a crap shoot. But we did have one important advantage: the sympathy factor. As I explained to Margaret, "When the jury has to choose between a grieving widow or an insurance company that's collected premiums for decades and now refuses to make good on its policy, who do you think they're going to side with?"

"I hope you're right," she said barely above a whisper.

We spoke for a few minutes more. I got the impression she was reluctant to hang up, as though a conversation with me was a link to Scott, a link that she didn't want to break. But eventually, it became clear that there was nothing more to discuss. "I'll get back to you after Sporn's deposition," I said to conclude the conversation." But before she could reply, Elaine entered the office, put a document on my desk and left.

"I'll be damned," I muttered, scanning the document.

"What?" Margaret asked.

"Elaine just brought me a fax from Augustus Carter. That pompous twit filed a motion for summary judgment on the grounds that our complaint fails to state a viable claim."

"But you were just in court," Margaret said.

"These kinds of motions are fairly routine, but filing one just a few hours after a judge tells you he's going to set a case down for trial is a dumb move. Particularly when the judge is already annoyed with you."

"Why would he do it?" Margaret asked.

"Two reasons," I answered. "First, it's one more thing we have to deal with, one more delay they hope will soften us up and make it more likely that we'll accept a lowball offer to settle the case."

"Which we won't," Margaret said defiantly. "That's right, isn't it, Brendan?"

"I'm in this case to the end," I assured her. It wasn't actually a commitment to not accept a settlement, but she took it that way.

"You said there were two reasons. What's the second?"

"Money," I said. "Carter's firm is no doubt charging the insurance company on an hourly basis. So, the more hours they spend on the case, the more they get paid."

"Speaking of money," Margaret said, "you and I need to come to an understanding about what I'm paying you."

"You're not paying us anything. I told you that right from the start. After all that Scott did for this firm, there's no way we're going to charge you anything."

"That's sweet of you," Margaret replied, "but that was when we both thought this was going to be over quickly. This case is eating up a lot of your time. You and Rick have bills to pay. I can't ask you to work for free."

"I'll tell you what," I replied, "I'll treat it like a contingent fee case. Rick and I will take a third of any punitive damage award." I didn't tell her that collecting punitive damages wouldn't be easy because of *Pickett v. Lloyd's*, the case we talked about when we met for lunch at the New Amsterdam Inn. Margaret must have forgotten about that conversation because she agreed to my proposal and we concluded the conversation.

Seconds after I hung up the phone, Elaine reappeared at my door. "Edna Anderson on the other line," she said, pointing toward the phone I had just hung up. Having spoken to Mrs. Anderson a few days earlier, I was surprised by her call.

"Is there a problem?" I asked, thinking perhaps she had received a return visit from the men who had interrogated her about the Chinese bonds.

"No, no problem," she replied, "but I had a thought that might help you find out what happened to Ronnie. Thinking back, I realize I never told you that Ronnie was a pretty hard negotiator. In fact, I stopped going with him when we went to the flea market or a car dealer because I was embarrassed by his wheeling and dealing. He was always trying to get a better price."

"Interesting," I said, "but I'm not sure what that has to do with your case."

"Well, last night as I kissed his photo on my nightstand – something I do every night before going to sleep – it occurred to me that maybe the person who sold him those bonds killed him because Ronnie negotiated a deal that turned out to be too good. Those bonds are obviously worth something or we wouldn't have people breaking into my house and your office to find them."

I decided I had better dampen her expectations. "Our research suggests those bonds might have some value to collectors, but can't be cashed in the way you'd cash in U.S. savings bonds. At this point we don't know what they're worth, but I promise we'll get you as much as we can for them." Like my promise to Margaret Woodson of a quick check from FAIL Insurance, it was a promise I shouldn't have made.

If Eddie Rizzo could be believed, Ronald Anderson happily paid an increasingly higher price for each batch of Chinese bonds he purchased from Rizzo's Ritzy Rememorables. I doubted that Edna Anderson's information about her late husband's negotiating skills had much value, but I thanked her and concluded the call.

"Got a minute?" I looked up to find Rick standing in the doorway.

"For you, I've got two minutes. What's up?"

"I spoke to Carolyn earlier today. She's located someone who knows Elizabeth Scott, the Georgia senator who's apparently responsible for the Anderson case to be put on hold. Carolyn wanted to know if you could come to Georgia to interview this person. I suggested a conference call, but Carolyn was quite insistent that you come to Georgia."

"Fine," I told Rick. "Could Elaine make the arrangements for me? I have to spend my time drafting a response to Augustus Carter's latest delaying tactic."

"Already done," Rick said. "She has you on a flight to Atlanta the day after tomorrow. She booked you a rental car and after considerable effort managed to get you a hotel reservation in Dahlonega."

"Dahlonega?"

"The town where Carolyn's sister lives."

"Yes, of course; I forgot the name," I lied. You can't forget something you never knew.

24

"Can I call you Dancing Squirrel?"

The sun had just set as I approached Dahlonega, the little town northeast of Atlanta where Carolyn was staying with her sister. It was a beautiful late October evening, the temperature about seventy degrees, so I was taken aback to see what appeared to be snow by the side of the road. Lampposts decorated to look like giant candy canes added to my confusion.

The hotel Elaine had booked me into was, according to her printed directions, halfway around the public square in the center of town. Unfortunately, before I got to the square, I was stopped by a sheriff's deputy who motioned me to turn onto a side road. Being unfamiliar with the area, I rolled the window all the way down to ask for directions. It was then that I realized that the roadside snow was actually giant swaths of cottony material.

"I'm trying to get to the hotel on the public square," I said.

"Which hotel?" the deputy asked.

I hadn't realized there was more than one hotel. Elaine's description of what she referred to as "a cute little town" made Dahlonega sound like a one-hotel burg. As I discovered during my brief but eventful stay, Dahlonega is actually a popular destination for history buffs because of its role in an early American gold rush. I gave the deputy the name of the hotel, and he responded with a set of directions that he assured me would get me there in five minutes. "What's with the fake snow and giant candy canes?" I asked him before setting out on my five-minute drive.

"They're filming a Christmas movie for television. That's why you have to take the long way to your hotel."

As it turned out, the five minute drive was actually fifty-five minutes because of streets closed off for filming or blocked by large trucks loading and unloading props and equipment. Exhausted from a day of travel, I fell into bed and slept soundly.

The following morning, I had breakfast at the second-floor restaurant overlooking the town square where I could watch the film crew in action. Carolyn had arranged an eleven o'clock meeting with a woman named Anita who, according to Carolyn, had some important information about Senator Elizabeth Scott. So, with several hours to kill, I walked around town, looking into store windows, eventually ending up at the gold museum housed in the historic courthouse in the center of the town square. Constructed in 1836, it's reputed to be the oldest surviving county courthouse in Georgia.

I was in the process of reading about the Georgia gold rush, which I was surprised to discover pre-dated its much more famous California counterpart, when a middle-aged man with a goatee appeared at my side. "Fascinating, isn't it?"

"It is, indeed," I agreed. "I always thought America's first gold rush was in California, not Georgia."

"Actually, America's first gold rush was in North Carolina, starting about 1804. Gold mining in Georgia didn't start until 1828 or '29." He smiled sheepishly. "Sorry, didn't mean to sound like a college history professor." He extended his right hand, "Tom Albright. I'm with the company filming a movie here in town."

"Actor?" I asked. The goatee made him look like a character actor who specialized in playing villains.

Albright laughed. "With this mug?" he asked, pointing at his face. "Not a chance. They don't let me anywhere near a camera. I'm stuck in a back room doing research and arranging filming locations. The only reason I'm in town is because one of the creative geniuses decided at the last minute that he needed another filming location, and I'm here to negotiate with a local land owner."

We talked about the television business for a few minutes, agreed that the autumn weather in Georgia was quite pleasant, and then parted company. It was a short conversation, but a pleasant one. Albright struck me as a decent guy.

I finished my tour of the courthouse and made my way to a coffee shop on the south side of the town square where I was scheduled to meet Anita, the woman who Carolyn insisted I needed to speak with in person. It was a bit early for lunch, so only a few of the coffee shop's tables were occupied. A particularly attractive woman at a corner table immediately caught my eye. She had the type of complexion I associate with Mediterranean countries, but her eyes looked almost Asian. As I entered the coffee shop, she glanced at the document she was holding, then waved me over to where she was sitting.

When I got to the table, I realized the document in her hand was actually a photo of Carolyn and me that Rick had taken at a firm get-together. The last time I had seen that photo it was taped to the computer monitor on Carolyn's desk. "You must be Anita," I said to the woman, who was even more striking up close.

"Actually, it's Ayita," she responded, "Ayita Salolee."

"Interesting name," I said as we shook hands.

"Ayita is a Cherokee name meaning first to dance. But feel free to call me Anita, everyone does. I've gotten used to it."

"No, no," I protested. "If Ayita is your name, I'll call you Ayita. It's a very pretty name." I thought about adding "for a very pretty woman," but decided that might seem too forward. "I assume Salolee is also a Cherokee name."

"It is," she confirmed. "It means squirrel."

"So, can I call you Dancing Squirrel?" I asked playfully.

"Only if you want to be scalped, paleface," she replied with a smile. It was a dazzling smile that made her beautiful, exotic features even more alluring.

"I have to confess that I don't know very much about the Cherokee," I said. "In fact, everything I know about Native Americans I learned from watching the Lone Ranger on television as a kid. Apparently, Indians named Tonto are good guys, and the rest attack wagon trains and scalp people."

Ayita rolled her eyes and shook her head. "Carolyn warned me you had an oddball sense of humor."

"I'm afraid you have me at a disadvantage," I replied. "Carolyn apparently told you about me, but all I know about you is that you have some important information about Senator Scott."

"It's really not that important," Ayita said. "I would have been happy to talk to you on the phone and save you a trip to Georgia."

Her comment caught me by surprise. I was under the impression Carolyn wanted me to interview this woman in person. Either Rick had misunderstood Carolyn, or I had misunderstood Rick. I made a mental note to pursue this with Carolyn when we had lunch at noon.

We spent the next half hour talking about the Cherokee tribe and its connection to Georgia. According to Ayita, the Cherokee lived in Georgia and other southern states for generations before the arrival of European settlers. In 1830, Congress passed the Indian Removal Act, which lead to the forcible relocation of the Cherokee to federal reservations west of the Mississippi River. Ayita concluded her impromptu history lesson by explaining, "It was this forced removal from our ancestral lands, commonly referred to as the Trail of Tears, that connects Senator Scott to the Cherokee, but not in the way she'd like people to believe." She paused, seemingly reluctant to continue. "Look," she finally said, "I don't like to badmouth people, particularly someone like Lizzie Scott who, in my opinion, is a patriotic American. I was a volunteer in her campaign when she ran for Congress and then for the Senate, so I'd like to think I know her better than most people."

"I'm not asking you to badmouth Senator Scott," I said. "My secretary was under the impression that you had important information about the senator, and I'm just trying to find out what that is."

"Okay," she said, "but you're going to be disappointed. I met Carolyn at a party at her sister's house and we struck up a conversation. At some point I said something to the effect that it annoys me that Senator Scott claims to be part Cherokee, but doesn't really have a single drop of Cherokee blood. In fact, ironically, one of her ancestors was in charge of moving my ancestors off our tribal lands."

"That's it?" I asked.

"That's it," she assured me. "As I said, I admire the way Senator Scott always puts America first. She's been a very vocal opponent of appeasing the Russians or doing business with communist China. So, however annoyed I might be at her claiming Cherokee ancestry to advance her career, I'm willing to overlook it if it puts her in a position to do some good for the country."

"In that case," I said, slipping the legal pad into my briefcase, "I must have misunderstood my secretary's message." I didn't really believe that, but it seemed like a good way to end our meeting. "Let me atone for taking up your time by buying you dinner this evening." I made it sound like I had just come up with the idea, rather than something I had been planning since first laying eyes on her.

She smiled. "That's very kind of you, but I don't think my boyfriend would approve." She patted me on the arm as she came around the table and headed for the exit. I was disappointed, but not surprised. It was unlikely a woman as beautiful as Ayita would be unattached.

Checking my watch, I saw that it was almost noon. I moved around the table to where Ayita had been sitting so I would be able to see Carolyn when she entered the coffee shop. Noon came and went, and Carolyn hadn't arrived. By 12:30, Carolyn still hadn't arrived and I was getting hungry. I considered ordering a tuna on rye, but settled for another cup of coffee. At 12:45, Carolyn appeared at the door carrying an expanding file folder under her arm. She was accompanied by a tall, thin – almost gaunt – man dressed in jeans and a tweed sport coat with elbow patches. I pegged him as a college professor who taught something esoteric, perhaps Medieval poetry.

Carolyn smiled when she saw me, and she and the man accompanying her headed toward where I was sitting. "Brendan, it's good to see you," she said when she got to the table, quickly adding, "I'd like you to meet my fiancé, Chad."

I was more than a little surprised – and hurt – but I wasn't about to show it. I stood up, thrust out my hand in Chad's direction, and said in as jovial a voice as I could muster, "Glad to meet you at last. Carolyn's told me so much about you. I'm fascinated by Medieval poetry." I probably shouldn't have done it, but I couldn't help myself.

Chad was understandably confused. "Medieval poetry?"

"Carolyn told me you taught Medieval poetry at the college."

"No, I teach biology," Chad said.

"Oh, I'm sorry," I said. "How embarrassing. I'm confusing you with the other Chad."

Carolyn tried hard not to laugh. "He's yanking your chain," she said to Chad, who couldn't decide whether to be angry or amused. Carolyn didn't give him time to decide. "Why don't you wait for me outside. I'll only be a minute."

Professor Chad obediently retreated to the exit, and Carolyn and I sat down.

"No lunch?" I asked.

"No lunch," Carolyn confirmed. She put the bulging file folder on the table. "You have a knack for making me laugh just as I'm about to get angry with you."

"One of my many underappreciated skills." I pointed to the folder. "What's that, my invitation to the wedding?"

"Mrs. Anderson's Chinese bonds," Carolyn replied. "I'm not coming back to New Jersey. My time here in Dahlonega has given me a new perspective on everything. I've decided it's time for a change."

"Yes," I agreed, "marrying a guy you've only known for a short time would certainly be a change."

"Chad is wonderful," Carolyn said. "He reminds me a lot of you."

"I've never taught biology."

She laughed. "No, but you and he both have a quirky sense of humor."

"Do you love him?" I asked.

She didn't answer my question. Instead, she said, "Chad's a great guy. We'll have a good life together – a quiet life in a peaceful, little town." She stood up, reached across the table and patted my arm the same way Ayita had a few minutes earlier. "Besides, a girl can't wait forever."

I watched as she left the coffee shop and walked away holding hands with Chad. Then I ordered a tuna on rye.

25

"No, you do it."

Rick and Elaine were waiting for me when my plane from Georgia landed at Newark Airport. "How was your flight?" Rick asked as I approached them in the terminal.

I answered his question with one of my own. "Did you know about Carolyn?"

"Yes," he admitted, "but she wanted to tell you in person. And I guess I was hoping you'd talk her out of it, or at least convince her to put things on hold." Elaine nodded in agreement.

In retrospect, I probably should have asked why they thought I could make Carolyn change her mind. But I was tired from travelling and annoyed at everything that had happened, so instead, I asked, "What do you know about this Chad character?"

"Not much," Rick replied, "only that he teaches at the college with Carolyn's sister."

"She doesn't love him," I said. Rick and Elaine exchanged glances, but neither responded to my observation.

After I paid a small ransom to get my car out of the airport parking lot, the three of us headed home. Shortly after we got on Interstate 78, I told Rick what I had learned about Senator Scott.

"Interesting," Rick said. "The phony ancestry claim, if true, could turn out to be important. Senator Scott has the backing of some powerful party leaders who are eyeing her as a future presidential candidate. But if it turns out she's lying about being part Cherokee, instead of becoming America's first Native American president, her political opponents could expose her as just another scheming politician willing to do anything to win an election."

"Yes, interesting," I agreed, "but it doesn't explain how or why she pulled strings to get the Anderson case put on indefinite hold. And we still have no idea who the other politician was who called Judge Cohen."

"That I can't tell you," Rick said, "but I did learn something about the attorney for Consolidated TranShip. Turns out that Carl Mercer's firm has something in common with Parker, Cole, Landy & Long, Augustus Carter's firm.

"They both bill at outrageous hourly rates?"

"Besides that."

"I give up."

"Both firms do a lot of work for a certain political party."

"Don't tell me," I said. "Let me guess. The big government party?"

"No, the bigger government party, Senator Scott's party."

"What kind of work?"

"You name it, they do it," Rick answered. "In fact, a lot of what they do is more political than legal. Opposition research. Planting stories with friendly journalists. Stuff like that. According to a friend at one of the big New York firms, this political work is worth millions each year."

We drove in silence for several minutes before I asked, "All this is interesting, but how does it help us?"

"I'm not sure it does," Rick answered.

Just before the intersection with Route 24, while we were driving in the right lane on I-78, a black Lincoln pulled alongside. Instead of passing, the other vehicle kept pace with us. "I hate it when people do this," I muttered. "If you're going to pass, go ahead and pass. Don't just hang there."

I waited for the Lincoln to either pass or drop back, but it just stayed in the left lane, keeping pace with my Mustang. I'm not the most patient driver in the best of circumstances. And when I'm tired, as I was after my flight from Georgia, I tend to be even less patient. So instead of ignoring the Lincoln, I rolled down the window, stuck my hand out the car, extended my middle finger and gave the other driver the international sign of goodwill and friendship. The passenger in the Lincoln responded by rolling down his window. I found myself face to face with an Asian man who I assumed was about to return my salute. But instead, he smiled. It wasn't a friendly smile, but a predator's smile like the one Harry Sporn had displayed during Margaret Woodson's examination under oath at FAIL Insurance.

The driver of the Lincoln tapped Smiley on the shoulder before pointing with his thumb toward the back of the car. Smiley turned and looked out the car's rear window, then began frantically gesturing to the driver to go faster. I checked my sideview mirror to see what had caused his concern. Another vehicle was rapidly bearing down on Smiley's car in what could have been an attempt to ram it.

The driver of Smiley's car didn't hang around to find out. He accelerated and sped off with the second vehicle in pursuit. As the pursuing car passed us, I got a fleeting glimpse of the person in the passenger's seat. The goatee made him look a lot like Tom Albright, the man I had met in the museum in Dahlonega.

I rolled up the Mustang's window a bit too forcefully, breaking the mechanism in the process. That left two inches of open space that turned my classic 1965 Mustang into a makeshift musical instrument that whistled high C.

Other than an unwanted single-note concert, the rest of the drive was uneventful, except for the silver Porsche 968 that appeared to be following us. However, I eventually concluded the Porsche was simply heading in the same direction when it disappeared shortly before we reached Rick's house. I dropped Rick and Elaine off, drove to my house in Mountain Springs, and collapsed into bed.

I tossed and turned for most of the night, my head filled with questions I couldn't answer. What did Carolyn mean when she said that a girl couldn't wait forever? What was so special about Edna Anderson's bonds that a Chinese consular official would break in to Carolyn's apartment to get them? Was he the same person who had broken into our office and Mrs. Anderson's home? Why was the FBI, rather than the local police department, investigating the funeral home fire? Why was Senator Scott pressuring Ice Cold Cohen to put the Anderson case on hold? Who were the people in the cars that seemed to be following us on the way home from the airport? Were the deaths of Thompson and Smith, two potentially crucial witnesses in Mrs. Anderson's case, an accident, or were they killed to prevent them from giving testimony at the depositions I had scheduled? I felt particularly bad about Thompson, who had gone out of his way to reveal what had really happened to Ronald Anderson. Had I gotten him killed by attempting to depose him?

Shortly before daybreak the questioning stopped, I finally fell asleep, and the dream began. I found myself standing in front of Tuckerton's Funeral Home. There were several people standing next to me, but I couldn't see who they were.

"Are we sure Anderson's inside?" a male voice said. It sounded like Eddie Rizzo.

"Yeah, he's there, and he's toxic as hell," another voice said. That one sounded a lot like Laser Eyes.

"Then do it," a female voice instructed. "A girl can't wait forever." I immediately recognized it as Carolyn's voice.

One of the figures emerged out of the darkness and doused the funeral home's stately columned porch with gasoline. Another one of my dream companions tossed a lighted match onto the porch, which promptly burst into flames. Fire danced across the porch and up the wall of the building, engulfing the structure in a rainbow of reds and oranges.

At that point my dream became unnervingly realistic. I could hear the distinctive crackling sound the fire made as it consumed the building. And I could smell the smoke as it swirled in the chill night sky.

I awoke with a start, sitting up in bed and sniffing the air. The smell of smoke wasn't part of my dream. It was real.

26

"You mean he's alive?"

My first instinct was to pick up the phone on the nightstand and call the fire department. But for some reason I don't really understand, I threw on my bathrobe and charged downstairs instead. Perhaps I was being heroic, planning to use the fire extinguisher in the kitchen to put out the blaze. Or perhaps, too tired to think clearly, I was just doing something stupid.

I swung around the newel post at the bottom of the staircase, and ran toward the kitchen in the back of the house, passing one of two entrances to the living room on my left. Out of the corner of my eye, I saw the fire ... in the fireplace.

"I started a fire to take the chill off," a vaguely familiar voice said from the darkened room. "Hope you don't mind."

In the dim light of the dancing flames I could make out a human form seated in one of two wing chairs near the fireplace. "Who's there?" I demanded.

"It's Reynaldo Renoir, Brendan. Sit down; we need to talk."

I first met Reynaldo about five years ago when Eddie Rizzo hired him, through an intermediary, to protect me from what turned out to be a non-existent threat. He resurfaced during the defamation case that the Council for Islamic Religious Respect filed against my ex-girlfriend. Having been legally declared dead, Reynaldo, a former navy SEAL, is able to do things unofficially that can't be done officially. Although Reynaldo describes himself as a freelance problem solver, I tend to think of him as a freelance gun for hire – though, admittedly, I've never actually seen him shoot someone. I was initially suspicious of Reynaldo, but I eventually came to trust him, or at least as much as it's possible to trust someone in his line of work.

"Who are you working for now?" I asked, settling into the chair across from Renaldo. "FBI? CIA? YMCA?"

"Always the funny man," Reynaldo said. "Actually, I'm working for the Juvenal Bureau, which is part of the Treasury Department."

"So, what, you chase after juvenile delinquents who don't file their tax return on time?"

Reynaldo laughed. "Juvenal as in the Roman poet, not juvenile as in a minor. Juvenal is best known for the phrase *quis custodiet ipsos custodies,* a line from his *Satires* that means 'who will guard the guards?' Our job is to keep an eye on other government agencies to make sure they don't do things they're not supposed to do."

"Like spend a thousand dollars for a hammer they could get at the local hardware store for twenty bucks?"

"We started out as a financial watchdog, but our role expanded to investigating any type of malfeasance or illegality, including things like the unexplained death and immediate cremation of a civilian worker at a government facility."

"So, you know about Ronald Anderson?"

"We know there's a paper trail showing he got a regular paycheck from Uncle Sam and that he's no longer among the living. When we started looking into that, we discovered he had a hobby of collecting seemingly worthless Chinese bonds."

"You apparently know more about the bonds than I do, so explain why they got Anderson killed, if, in fact, they did. And why was he collecting them? People collect things like stamps, coins, even baseball cards, but who collects old Chinese bonds?"

"Those old bonds have been popular with collectors for years," Reynaldo replied, "probably because the Chinese writing makes them look exotic. But in the last year or so, the bonds have been disappearing. You could usually count on finding a bunch of them at flea markets or swap meets. But now, whoever is buying the bonds is hanging on to them."

I thought back to what Eddie Rizzo had told me. "Maybe collectors are framing them and hanging them on the wall like stock certificates of companies that went bankrupt."

"That might account for some of it," Reynaldo conceded, "but something else is happening. Too many of these bonds are disappearing."

"Why don't you just ask these bond collectors?"

"Because finding these people isn't easy. Most of these sales take place at flea markets and garage sales, which means there are no records that would allow us to track down the buyers and interview them. And in cases where the sale was made by a business that does keep records, the buyers are using fictitious names. That's what caught our attention and, presumably also caused Wu Jin's people to get involved."

"Wu Jin, the consular officer Rick and I met in New York?"

"No, Wu Jin, the Chinese intelligence officer who pretended to be a consular officer," Reynaldo corrected.

The mention of Wu Jin conjured up a mental image of the two Asian men I encountered on my drive home from the airport. I asked Reynaldo about them and the car that appeared to be following them. "Probably Wu Jin's people, he said. "We're pretty certain they've been keeping tabs on you after they discovered you represent someone who owns a bunch of these bonds."

"And your people were in the other car." I framed it as a statement rather than a question.

"Most likely people connected to Consolidated TranShip."

"Ah, yes, Consolidated TranShip. A very mysterious place. What do you know about it?"

"Not nearly as much as I'd like," Reynaldo said. "The paper trail that alerted us to Anderson's death proves it's a front for some type of government operation. Probably CIA, but we don't know that for sure."

"I thought the CIA wasn't supposed to operate domestically." I must have sounded hopelessly naïve because Reynaldo laughed – more of a snort, actually. "Based on truck traffic entering and leaving, we think it's being used as a warehouse."

"Why would the CIA need a warehouse? What's stored there?"

"No idea," Reynaldo answered. "But given the security setup, we assume it's something valuable, or perhaps something very sensitive that they don't want anyone to see."

"So, you haven't been able to get inside?"

"We haven't tried," Reynaldo said. "At least not yet. As soon as we show up, whatever agency is operating there will know we're investigating them. So that comes later." I wondered if the so-called Juvenal Bureau would have more success getting through the gates than the local police had. As if reading my mind, he added, "Hopefully we'll have more success than you and the Troy Forge cops had. In theory, we can go anywhere and ask anybody in government anything. Of course, theory and reality aren't always the same thing, particularly when you're dealing with one of the agencies whose employees carry guns."

I took the conversation in a new direction. "How does Senator Scott from Georgia fit in with all this?"

Reynaldo wasn't expecting that. "So, you do know something we don't know. Tell me more."

I told him about Judge Cohen putting the Anderson case on hold after a phone call from a female senator from Georgia. "We knew the case was in limbo," Reynaldo said, "but we didn't know Lizzie Scott was involved." Next, I told him about my trip to Dahlonega, meeting Ayita, my chance encounter at the museum, and seeing what I thought was the same man on the drive home from the airport. When I finished, Reynaldo said, "We thought you made that trip to collect the Chinese bonds after your secretary decided to get married and stay in Georgia." Apparently, everyone but me knew about Carolyn's impending marriage.

We spoke for another half hour, during which I learned that despite having considerably more resources, Reynaldo didn't know much more than Rick and I did about Consolidated Tran-Ship, Ronald Anderson's death, or the Chinese bonds. At one point in the conversation, I asked if he thought the Chinese killed Ronald Anderson to get their hands on his collection of bonds.

"Maybe," Renaldo said, "but we don't think so. We think his body was delivered to the funeral home by Consolidated Tran-Ship's people. That suggests he was shot by someone at their facility. And given the security at that place, it's unlikely a Chinese agent could have gotten in."

"Wait a minute," I said. "How do you know Ronald Anderson was shot? That's not what the death certificate says." I knew Anderson's death certificate was phony, but did Reynaldo know that?

Apparently, he did. "That death certificate is as phony as the doctor who supposedly signed it. And I know Anderson was shot because Thompson, the guy from the funeral home, told us that. We picked him up when he got out of his car at the funeral home the night it burned down. Lucky guy. If he hadn't been with us, he might have been inside when the place went up in flames."

"You mean he's alive?!"

"Alive and well where nobody will find him. He'll be a witness when we figure out who put the bullet in Ronald Anderson's skull." Reynaldo checked his watch. "I have to run." He got up and headed for the front door.

"Wait a minute," I said, chasing after him. "I need Thompson to testify in Mrs. Anderson's civil case, assuming Judge Cohen finally lets us go to trial."

"We'll cross that bridge if and when we come to it," Reynaldo said over his shoulder as he opened the door and stepped out onto the front porch.

I followed him outside, instantly regretting I hadn't taken the time to put on my slippers. "How will I get in touch with you?" He handed me a business card. "According to this," I said, reading from the card, "your name is Ron Reynolds and you're vice president of Axberg Novelty Products."

"If Chinese intelligence or the people running Consolidated TranShip manage to get your wallet, we don't want them to find a business card from the Juvenal Bureau," he said before getting into a silver Porsche 968 and disappearing into the night.

27

"Your firm has offered you up as a sacrificial lamb."

On Monday morning, Rick walked into my office carrying a cup of coffee. "Learn anything else during your trip to Georgia?" he asked.

"No, I think we covered everything on the drive back from the airport."

He waited, perhaps hoping I would elaborate on my meeting with Carolyn. When I didn't, he changed the subject. "Over the weekend, I spoke with a friend who has contacts with the D.C. bar association. According to him, Augustus Carter's firm and the one representing Consolidated TranShip are both registered lobbyists, and both are paid millions by Senator Scott's political party each year."

"Interesting," I replied, "but as we discussed in the car on Friday, I'm not sure that information helps us."

"Agreed," Rick said as he turned to leave. "Speaking of your car, you're going to want to get that window fixed sooner rather than later. It's almost winter. You'll freeze your ass off every time you drive someplace." He reconsidered. "Well, maybe not your ass, but your left ear for sure."

"On my list of things to do," I assured him.

"Which means you won't get around to it until February," he muttered as he disappeared into the outer office where Carolyn used to sit.

As soon as Rick left, I began to draft a particularly strident response to the motion to dismiss that Augustus Carter had filed the previous Monday. I was putting the finishing touches on my masterpiece when Elaine buzzed me on the intercom to report that Judge Bloomquist's secretary was on line two.

"Good morning," I said as I picked up the phone. That was as far as I got before the judge's secretary informed me that I was to appear in his courtroom at two that afternoon. Interestingly, she added that it would be unnecessary for me to prepare a written response to Carter's motion.

"I think we're going to see some fireworks," Rick said when I told him about the call. "I think I'll tag along, if you don't mind. I'll sit in the back of the courtroom and see what I see."

"Good idea," I said. "You can keep track of the number of people Carter brings with him this time, each one billing at an hourly rate that's probably higher than yours or mine."

"We're just a couple of country lawyers," Rick said in his best imitation of a southern drawl. "Not like them highfalutin city slicker attorneys."

Just before two o'clock that afternoon, Rick and I entered Judge Bloomquist's courtroom to find a familiar face on the far side of the public gallery, and an unfamiliar one at the defendant's counsel table. "The suit in the back row is Harry Sporn," I whispered to Rick. "Keep an eye on him."

I made my way to the empty counsel table. The baby-faced young man at the other table looked in my direction and nodded, but no words were exchanged. He was apparently the attorney *du jour* for FAIL Insurance, but not one of the brief-case-toting lawyers who had accompanied Augustus Carter to previous hearings.

Judge Bloomquist entered the courtroom a moment later and took the bench. "Where is Mr. Carter?" he asked even before he was fully seated. "I gave explicit instructions I wanted him here at two o'clock." The judge was obviously annoyed.

The attorney for FAIL Insurance got to his feet. "Mr. Carter is unavailable today, Your Honor."

"Why?" the judge wanted to know. "Where is he?"

"I don't know. I was instructed to appear here at two o'clock for a hearing on our motion to dismiss. That's all I was told."

Part of me felt bad for the young attorney who, if he were to be believed, had been put in an awkward position. Of course, given all that had happened, I wasn't inclined to accept anything involving FAIL Insurance at face value. The judge wasn't either. "I'm having some trouble believing that," Judge Bloomquist said, "but I'll give you the benefit of the doubt." He rapped his gavel on the bench. "Counsel, enter your appearance."

Without the elaborate ritual of adjusting his tie, buttoning his suit jacket, or clearing his throat the way Carter had done at previous hearings, the attorney identified himself as Harold Lamb.

I couldn't help myself. I started to laugh.

The judge gave me a look that made it clear he was annoyed by my laughter, but instead of admonishing me for my breach of decorum, he said, "Let the record show that Mr. O'Brian is appearing for the plaintiff." Then he addressed my adversary. "Mr. Lamb, are you familiar with the history of this case?"

"No, Your Honor," Lamb admitted.

"Do you know why Mr. Carter had you appear to argue this motion instead of doing it himself?"

"No," Lamb answered. "All I know is when I got to the office this morning, Mr. Tyler, the partner I report to, told me I had to go to Morristown to argue a motion to dismiss."

Judge Bloomquist leaned back in his chair, looked at the ceiling and shook his head. Then he leaned forward and said to the young attorney in a surprisingly gentle voice, "Young man, allow me to provide you with some background. The last time Mr. Carter was before me, I told him I was going to set this case down for trial on the affirmative defense he raised, the act of war exclusion. Two hours after his appearance in my courtroom, Mr. Carter filed a completely frivolous motion to dismiss. Knowing I would be exceedingly annoyed with him, he sent you instead of appearing himself. In short, Mr. Lamb, your firm has offered you up as a sacrificial lamb, hence Mr. O'Brian's earlier laughter."

"For which I apologize," I interjected, "to both Mr. Lamb and the court."

That was Lamb's cue to issue his own apology for wasting the judge's time and to beat a hasty retreat. But, instead, he said, "It's standard practice at Parker Cole to file a motion to dismiss in every case involving an insurance claim."

I made eye contact with Judge Bloomquist. He obviously realized Lamb's statement could be helpful to my case, but instead of pointing that out to my adversary, he said, "That might very well be, but filing such a motion just two hours after I've announced the case is going to trial strikes me as a waste of everyone's time. And Mr. Carter's failure to appear before me today, sending an associate who's completely unfamiliar with the case, makes things worse." Judge Bloomquist tapped the bench with a pen as he appeared to consider what to say next. The tapping stopped a few seconds later, and instead of asking Lamb to argue in support of his motion, the judge said, "The defendant's motion to dismiss is denied. The court finds that motion to be a frivolous filing. Accordingly, the defendant is ordered to pay the plaintiff's attorney one thousand dollars for the time he was forced to spend responding to this motion."

Judge Bloomquist was about to gavel the proceedings to a conclusion when I said, "One more thing, Your Honor, if I may."

"Mr. O'Brian?"

"The last time we were here, Mr. Carter promised that the overdue answers to interrogatories would be provided at the deposition scheduled for later this week. Would the court please order Mr. Lamb to remind Mr. Carter to follow through on that promise?"

"So ordered," the judge said, getting up from the bench and heading for the door to his chambers.

As I turned to face the back of the courtroom where Rick was sitting, I caught sight of Harry Sporn hurrying to the exit.

"Interesting hearing," Rick said as we left the courtroom at a more leisurely pace. "The newbie's comment about filing a motion to dismiss in every insurance case might be useful at trial if you can get it into evidence."

"I almost feel sorry for the kid," I replied. "Augustus Carter hung him out to dry just so he could run the meter and bill a few extra hours."

"And waste more of your time," Rick added. "But at least you picked up a thousand bucks."

"Which I'll probably never collect."

We walked in silence through the courthouse, lest our conversation be overheard. When we got to the parking lot, I asked Rick, "What did you see?"

"Sporn was obviously there to observe, but I'm not sure whether he was keeping an eye on Lamb or watching you in action to prepare for the deposition."

28

"Oh, stuff like flying saucers."

Rick, Elaine and I spent the better part of an hour preparing the conference room for the deposition of Harry Sporn scheduled for four o'clock that afternoon. Our goal was to make the head of FAIL Insurance's so-called Special Investigative Unit as uncomfortable as possible. We had plenty of guidance, thanks to the memo the cute redhead had slipped into a copy of *Sports Illustrated* the day Margaret Woodson and I had our first encounter with Sporn.

"So, according to this," Rick said, reading from that memo, "we should put him in an uncomfortable chair."

"One uncomfortable chair coming up," I replied as I removed the plastic leveler from one leg of the hard, wooden chair I was holding. I put the chair back down and rocked it back and forth. "Perfect."

I put the makeshift rocking chair at the end of the conference table facing the window on the west side of the room. Next, we removed the blinds from that window so Sporn would be forced to squint while looking toward the late afternoon sun. And to ensure he wouldn't try to sit elsewhere, we set up the video camera so it pointed directly at that chair.

After making a few other modifications to the room, Rick and I took our seats at the conference table, and to kill time while we waited, I started going through my list of ideas for getting into Consolidated TranShip's facility where the late Ronald Anderson had worked. Each of my scenarios was met with "unrealistic" or "couldn't possibly work" from Rick.

Just before four o'clock, Elaine buzzed us on the intercom to tell us that the court reporter who would make a transcript of the deposition had arrived. I told Elaine to make the reporter comfortable in the waiting room so I could continue telling Rick my ideas for getting into Consolidated TranShip. That conversation came to an abrupt halt moments later when Rick asked, "You do realize the reason they call it *Mission Impossible* is because the stuff they do on that show really is impossible, don't you?"

We sat in silence after that. Four o'clock came and went. No Harry Sporn. Then four-fifteen and four-thirty. "Either he ran into traffic or he's playing games with us," Rick said.

"Maybe his car collided with a cement truck." I must have sounded a bit too hopeful because my comment elicited an arched eyebrow from Rick.

Just before five o'clock, I called FAIL Insurance and was told by Sporn's secretary that he was on his way. "Just be patient," she added condescendingly before hanging up.

Less than a minute later, the intercom buzzed. I assumed Elaine was letting us know Sporn had finally arrived. "Send him in," I said before she had a chance to say anything.

"Tough to do when he's in Rockaway," Elaine replied.

"What the heck is Harry Sporn doing in Rockaway?"

"Who said anything about Harry Sporn? Tony Biffano is on line two, calling you from a bar in Rockaway. Says he has news about Ronald Anderson and those Chinese bonds."

I punched the button for line two and then put the call on speaker. "Tony, you're on speaker. Rick's with me. What's up?"

"I just talked to a guy at a place Anderson used to stop at for a beer on his way home from work. One day this guy is telling Anderson how he needs money, and Anderson tells him about the bonds. Says something to the effect that they're not worth much now, but will soon be worth plenty."

"Why did he think they were about to become valuable?"

"That I don't know. The guy I talked to didn't know either, except, get this, he seemed to think it had something to do with what Anderson learned at the place where he worked."

"How does he think Consolidated TranShip is involved?" Rick asked.

"I don't think Anderson ever mentioned Consolidated Tran-Ship by name," Tony said, "and I don't think he gave his drinking buddy any details."

"Did he say anything else?" Rick asked.

"Oh, yeah, he had a lot more to say, none of it useful." Tony laughed. "I had to buy him a few beers to get him talking. But by the time his tongue was at maximum looseness, his brain was at maximum mushiness. Toward the end of the conversation, he was babbling about all sorts of crazy stuff."

"Like what?" I wanted to know.

"Oh, stuff like flying saucers."

"Great," I muttered. "I'm not sure we can trust anything the guy told you."

"The bonds came up pretty early in the conversation, before he became totally shitfaced," Tony said. "So, that information could be reliable. The rest of the stuff, not so much. I gotta go. He just staggered out of the men's room, and I told him I'd give him a ride home. Hopefully, he's sober enough to remember where he lives."

The line went dead. "And to think we're paying Tony for that," Rick said. Our late partner, Avery, had a running battle with Tony over his bills. I just tell Elaine to pay them. Tony's services don't come cheap, but in my opinion, he's worth every penny.

The intercom buzzed. This time Elaine informed me that Harry Sporn was in the waiting room. I told her to show Sporn and the court reporter in.

The great man arrived a moment later, stood in the doorway surveying the room, and without saying a word, laid his briefcase on the conference table and sat in the chair we had prepared for him. Then, he did something completely unexpected. He nonchalantly reached into his jacket pocket, pulled out a pair of sunglasses, and put them on. He was most likely expecting me to object, but I didn't.

The court reporter took her seat, and after we went through the formalities, I began the deposition by asking Sporn, "Are you represented by counsel at the deposition that's about to begin?"

"I don't need an attorney," Sporn responded. "I am an attorney." I knew from our research that Sporn had been a particularly tough prosecutor in Hudson County before joining FAIL Insurance, but I was still surprised. Augustus Carter had led me to believe he would be attending the deposition.

"Did you bring the answers to the interrogatories I served on the defendant?" I asked next.

"I did."

I waited for more, but Sporn just sat there. "Would you mind giving them to me?"

"They're in your waiting room," Sporn said. "My people can bring them in whenever you want."

Sporn's use of "people" was the tipoff that the insurance company was going to play the bury-them-in-paperwork game. The answers to my questions should have required a few dozen pages. But FAIL was about to waste my time by delivering a dozen boxes of documents, only some small percentage of which would be responsive to my actual questions.

As it turned out, I ended up not with a dozen boxes, but with thirty-five, each with a large number printed on its side. Sporn smiled his predator's smile as his crew piled the cardboard containers in a corner of the conference room. Rather than give him the satisfaction of thinking I was annoyed by this gamesmanship, I said, "I'm pleased to see you finally provided answers to my interrogatories." Sporn nodded. "But," I continued, "did you bring the four items I requested you to bring with you?" I consulted the list I had made on a legal pad. "The list of beneficiaries who settled for less than the policy's death benefit during the two previous years?"

"Yes," Sporn answered, patting his briefcase on the conference table.

"A copy of your company's claims manual?"

"Yes." Another pat of the briefcase.

"Memos or other writings from outside consultants relating to your company's policies, official or unofficial, regarding the payment, negotiation, or denial of claims?"

"Yes."

"Internally generated memos or other writings relating to your company's policies, official or unofficial, regarding the payment, negotiation, or denial of claims?"

"Yes," Sporn answered, once again patting his briefcase.

I waited for Sporn to hand me the documents, but he just sat there. "Well?"

"Well, what?" Sporn replied.

"Hand me the documents."

He responded by pointing to the boxes piled in the corner of the conference room. "Everything you asked for is there."

"That's not the way it works," I said. "Under Rule 4:18-1, the production of documents is a separate form of discovery. You're required to produce the documents I requested, not hide them in boxes containing answers to interrogatories."

"No one is hiding anything," Sporn said. "You asked for a lot of information, and we provided it. We put everything you asked for in boxes to make it easier to transport. Each box is numbered, and in box number one you'll find an inventory of every document." The transcript and video recording of the deposition would make it appear as though FAIL Insurance had gone to great lengths to carefully organize the unspeakably huge amount of information I had demanded. I was reasonably certain that wasn't the case, but rather than take the time to inspect the contents of the boxes, I began the deposition.

For the next hour Sporn provided clipped answers to routine questions, but evasive responses to more detailed inquiries. He readily admitted that he was the company's vice president in charge of the so-called Special Investigative Unit. But when I asked him to explain the purpose of that unit, he said, "to conduct special investigations." Additional questions brought out the fact that the SIU, as he called it, handled claims that were "complex or questionable." That was the last real answer he gave. As I continued to probe for details, "I don't know" became the most common answer to my questions, with "I'm not sure" coming in a close second. I'd like to think I'm a skilled questioner, but Sporn was equally skilled at providing answers that weren't really answers.

Margaret Woodson called me at home that evening to ask if I had done to Sporn what he had done to her during the examination under oath in Newark.

I couldn't bring myself to tell her the truth.

29

"Chicken tetrazzini, pizza, and bread pudding."

The following morning, Rick and I began looking though the supposedly well-organized treasure trove of information Harry Sporn had brought us. When we opened the box with a large number "1" printed on it, we found the interrogatories I had served on FAIL Insurance lying on top of dozens of file folders.

At first glance, it appeared as though FAIL had followed the Civil Practice Rules by neatly typing an answer in the space I had left after each question. But when I looked more closely, I discovered that each response was anything but a straightforward answer. "Unbelievable," I muttered as I read the answer to my first question, which asked for the names of the company's executive officers. The response was "see documents 13, 47, 72, 114, and 227 provided herewith." I removed the first file folder in the box, assuming it would contain those five documents. It didn't. Instead, it contained an array of paperwork that not only wasn't responsive to my question, but didn't appear to have anything to do with the case at all. I let out a string of expletives.

"Maybe start at the back?" Rick suggested.

I pulled the last file folder in the box and opened it. "You were right," I told Rick. "The names of the company's executive officers are chicken tetrazzini, pizza, and bread pudding." In response to Rick's *What the hell are you talking about?* expression, I handed him a copy of a lunch menu from the FAIL Insurance employee cafeteria. "Let's see what other wonderfully enlightening information Carter's people have provided," I said as I leafed through the other documents in the file folder. "An announcement that a departmental softball game is cancelled, an invitation to a seminar on employee benefits, and a memo about a retirement party. But, hey, at least each one is numbered."

"Unbelievable," Rick said.

"I've seen the bury-them-in-paperwork tactic countless times," I replied, "but FAIL has taken it to the next level. Augustus Carter isn't even making an effort to make it look like he's responding to my questions. It's as though he's deliberately trying to provoke me."

"I think he's succeeding," Rick said. "Calm down. You're too young to have a heart attack." He began looking though the box. "I seem to recall Sporn mentioning a document inventory in box number one."

Several minutes passed as Rick checked each file folder. Then he removed all the folders, laid them on the conference table, and looked inside the box. "If there's some sort of inventory sheet, it must be invisible."

I picked up the phone on the conference table, consulted my file for the number, and called the opulent Newark office of Parker, Cole, Landy & Long. I asked for Augustus Carter, but was told he was unavailable. I asked his secretary about the document inventory, but she politely informed me that she knew nothing about it. She did, however, promise to speak with Mr. Carter when he returned to the office. "Someone will get back to you," she said before hanging up.

Rick and I waited all day for that "someone" to get back to us. The following morning, I faxed a letter to Augustus Carter confirming my phone conversation with his secretary and politely asking him to fax me the inventory sheet Harry Sporn had mentioned. Without waiting for a response, we began combing through the thirty-five boxes. When we found something that was actually responsive to the interrogatories I had served on FAIL Insurance, we made a photocopy and placed the original back in the box, keeping everything in the same order. Rick asked why we were doing that since it made a time-consuming job even more tedious. "Preserving evidence," I answered. "I'm not sure at this point how we're going to use all this stuff at trial, so I want to keep things intact."

The so-called inventory sheet still hadn't arrived two days after I had faxed a letter to Carter. Fortunately, late that afternoon we found, quite by accident, what I considered the most important document: the list of beneficiaries who had settled for less than the policy's death benefit. There were one hundred and ninety-seven names on the list. I asked Elaine to make a copy and get it to Tony Biffano with instructions to interview the people who lived in the tri-state area. I added all one hundred and ninety-seven names to my list of proposed witnesses, even though I really only planned to have a handful testify at trial. "Let Carter figure out who I'm going to call to testify," I told Rick.

30

"It seemed like a reasonable request."

November is a gray, dismal month in New Jersey, the colorful leaves of autumn having fallen, and the glistening white snow of winter not yet making its first appearance. We spent most of that bleak month going through the thirty-five boxes that Harry Sporn had delivered the day of the deposition. In fairness, Rick and Elaine did most of the work because I spent much of my time responding to a series of pre-trial motions filed by Augustus Carter on behalf of FAIL Insurance.

The first motion came just days after the deposition of Harry Sporn. It asked the court to compel Margaret Woodson to provide "complete and correct" answers to the insurance company's interrogatories, something I thought we had already done. When I received Augustus Carter's moving papers, I faxed him a letter asking what information he was missing, but I never got a response. It wasn't until we were before Judge Bloomquist that Carter revealed our glaring omission. Apparently, Margaret had failed to reveal a minor claim for damage to a car windshield that she and Scott had filed almost ten years earlier with their auto insurance carrier. I explained to the judge that we hadn't disclosed the claim because Margaret had apparently forgotten about it. When I raised the question of why that information was relevant to a life insurance claim, Augustus Carter informed the court that "all claims are relevant." Judge Bloomquist thought otherwise, pointing out that the insurance company obviously already knew about the incident, and a simple phone call to me would most likely have provided whatever additional information was needed.

Carter's next motion sought summary judgment in favor of the defendant on the grounds that no reasonable jury could find for the plaintiff based on the evidence obtained during discovery. I reminded the judge that my adversary had previously sent the clueless Harold Lamb to argue a motion to dismiss. Carter justified this new motion by pointing out that a motion for summary judgment and a motion to dismiss aren't the same thing. He was in the process of reading from a case that made that distinction when Judge Bloomquist cut him off. "Mr. Carter," the judge said, "technically you're right, but you and I both know that I'm not going to grant your motion, so why waste everyone's time?" Everyone in the courtroom knew the answer. Carter had filed the motion so he and the five associates who accompanied him that day could bill the insurance company for their time at a hefty hourly rate. And if this latest motion helped convince Margaret to settle the case for less than the policy amount, so much the better. Carter's firm might even receive a bonus for negotiating such a settlement. Of course, Augustus Carter would never admit his actions were financially motivated. Instead, he piously told the judge, "I have an ethical obligation to my client to pursue every avenue." The court reporter's record of the motion hearing would show that Judge Bloomquist didn't respond to Carter's explanation. But those of us who were in the court-room saw the judge roll his eyes.

My adversary didn't get the summary judgment he sought, nor did he prevail on a subsequent motion for a change of venue. During that motion hearing he advanced a novel public policy argument. Carter tried to convince the judge that the case should be moved to Essex County where the offices of Parker, Cole, Landy & Long are located so FAIL Insurance could save money on legal fees, thus allowing it to keep a lid on insurance premiums. Judge Bloomquist didn't roll his eyes in response to that argument, but he did shake his head in disbelief before telling Carter, "First of all, there's no guarantee that reducing legal expenses would lower insurance premiums. And secondly, if you want to help your client reduce legal expenses, don't bring a small army of attorneys to a straightforward motion hearing." Before gaveling the hearing to a conclusion, the judge announced that he had scheduled a trial for the second week of December. "If you have any more pre-trial motions, you better file them quickly."

As it turned out, Augustus Carter did have one final pre-trial maneuver, which started out as a motion to exclude the testimony of people who had settled with FAIL Insurance for less than the policy amount. He argued vehemently that such evidence was immaterial and prejudicial. I was equally passionate that the evidence would show a pattern of conduct that amounted to bad faith, a key requirement to collect punitive damages. For most of the back and forth argument, things seemed to be going my way. But then, Carter told the judge, "If the court won't exclude this evidence, I would ask that Your Honor at least limit the number of witnesses or we'll be here until spring. Mr. O'Brian's witness list contains about two hundred names."

"How many witnesses do you plan to call on this issue?" the judge asked me.

"I haven't determined that yet," I replied. "The defendant was late in providing those names so we're still interviewing potential witnesses. Until we're finished, we won't know how many will testify."

"Two hundred is a lot of witnesses," Judge Bloomquist observed. He was right, of course, and I wasn't really planning to call all of them. But I wanted to keep Carter guessing. The judge leaned back in his chair and began tapping his pen on the bench. The tapping stopped a moment later, and the judge announced his decision. "Mr. O'Brian, I'm going to limit you to four witnesses to testify about their dealings with the defendant." I started to respond, but the judge silenced me by holding up his hand. "But I'll allow you to tell the jury that these four people are representative of a larger group."

Carter objected to that arrangement, arguing that my four witnesses might not be representative. "You'll have an opportunity to cross examine them," Judge Bloomquist responded, "and call rebuttal witnesses if necessary."

My adversary wasn't about to give up. "Allow me to respectfully remind the court that during an earlier motion hearing, Your Honor forced me to provide information to Mr. O'Brian, rather than waiting for it to be disclosed at trial. I believe Your Honor's exact words were something to the effect that in your courtroom there is no trial by ambush. That being the case, I would ask that Mr. O'Brian provide me with the names of those four witnesses so that I can prepare my cross-examination and arrange for any necessary rebuttal witnesses."

It seemed like a reasonable request, so I wasn't surprised that the judge granted it.

31

"Not to worry."

"I've found the perfect witness for your case against the insurance company," Tony Biffano said during one of our regular phone conversations. "Three of the witnesses I located are pretty good, but the fourth, a woman named Marie Callahan, will win the case for you."

I interviewed Tony's "perfect" witness two days later, and within five minutes concluded that he wasn't exaggerating. Marie Callahan was, indeed, the perfect witness. She was attractive, articulate, believable, sympathetic, and had a story that would resonate with jurors. Her late husband, like Scott Woodson, was a big believer in life insurance. Five years before his untimely demise from cancer, leaving behind a thirty-nine-year-old widow and four small children, he had purchased a two-million-dollar term life policy. Like Scott, the late Mr. Callahan had paid the premiums when due, never missing a payment. But when he died, FAIL Insurance had balked at paying his widow the death benefit.

"It's too late for me," Marie Callahan said to start the conversation, "but if I can prevent that insurance company from doing to your client what it did to me, I'm happy to help. I should have come to you guys instead of Shiff," she added, referring to the now-disbarred attorney who had represented her in her dealings with FAIL Insurance.

"Shiff happens," I said, eliciting a laugh from Mrs. Callahan and an arched eyebrow from Rick, who I had asked to sit in on the interview. Shiff was known to, and despised by, virtually every attorney and judge in Morris County. The man was a notorious liar. If he told you it was raining, you could be sure the sun was shining. Shiff was the kind of person who told a lie even if telling the truth would be more advantageous.

"At our first meeting, Mr. Shiff promised me that Federal American would send me a check as soon as they knew he was representing me because he had prior dealings with them and they knew not to screw around with his clients."

"Let me guess," I said, "that turned out to be somewhat less than completely accurate."

"On both counts," Mrs. Callahan replied. "When the insurance company got his letter, instead of sending me a check, they made me come to their office in Newark for what they called an examination under oath. And when we got there, they made Mr. Shiff sit in the waiting room while some guy named Sporn gave me the third degree. So much for not screwing with his clients."

"Before we get to the examination under oath," Rick said, "tell us what happened before that."

"About a week after my husband died, I sent the insurance company a certified letter informing them of his death and providing them with a copy of the death certificate. Then I sat and waited, assuming they would mail me a check."

"But they didn't," I suggested.

"No, they didn't"

Marie Callahan spent the next forty-five minutes outlining in detail everything that had happened after she notified FAIL

Insurance of her husband's death. Her experience with the company was remarkably similar to Margaret Woodson's. First came numerous letters demanding additional information and documents that she had already provided or that seemed to have nothing to do with her claim for the death benefit. Then, FAIL subjected Mrs. Callahan to an intrusive, and sometimes embarrassing, EUO. "Two months later" she concluded, "I got this letter denying my claim." She withdrew a letter from a folder on her lap and handed it to me. I read the insurance company's reason for denying her claim and burst out laughing.

I handed the letter to Rick. "Unbelievable," he said before returning it to Marie Callahan.

"Mr. Shiff negotiated with the insurance company, or at least he told me he did," Mrs. Callahan said. "A month went by, and then a second. By that time I had pretty much drained our savings. My mother moved in to help with the children so I could go back to work."

"What kind of work do you do?" I asked.

"I'm a nurse," she answered. I made a note on my legal pad to ask her that when she testified. Juries tend to like nurses. "Six months after Don's death, the insurance company offered to pay me half of the death benefit to settle my claim. I didn't think that was right, but Mr. Shiff convinced me a million dollars was a lot of money, and if I went to court I might end up with less, or even nothing at all."

Rick and I exchanged glances. We were both thinking the same thing. Shiff had sold out his client for a settlement that would generate a hefty fee without having to actually try the case. As if to confirm our suspicion, Mrs. Callahan added, "Of course, after paying Mr. Shiff, I ended up with less than a million dollars. A lot less, actually."

Marie Callahan leaned back in her chair, took a deep breath, and looked at the ceiling, fighting back tears. I waited. She eventually looked right at me. "If testifying will prevent this company from doing to your client what they did to me, I'll be happy to help." I assured her that her testimony was essential to our case, thanked her for her time, and told her Tony Biffano would stay in touch with her and drive her to the courthouse when the time came to testify.

"Tony was right," Rick said after Mrs. Callahan had left, "She'll be a great witness, particularly since her experience with the insurance company was so similar to Margaret's. We should have her testify right after Margaret so the jury can see Margaret's experience isn't unique."

"No, I have a better idea," I said. "Marie Callahan and Margaret are our two strongest witnesses, so we'll sandwich the three other witnesses between them. And having her testify just before Sporn will make him appear even more arrogant by comparison."

"How about your two expert witnesses?" Rick asked, referring to a couple of high-priced university professors I had lined up to testify that the average person would interpret the policy's act of war exclusion to mean an actual, declared war, not a terrorist bombing like the one that took Scott Woodson's life.

"I'll wait and use them as rebuttal witnesses after Augustus Carter finishes his case. Hopefully their testimony, combined with the judge's instruction to the jury regarding the reasonable expectation rule, will neutralize Carter's affirmative defense."

"Assuming Judge Bloomquist gives the jury instruction you want," Rick said.

"The reasonable expectation rule is settled law in New Jersey. Not telling that to the jury would be reversible error. Besides, I don't think Judge Bloomquist is a big fan of FAIL Insurance or Augustus Carter."

I swiveled my chair and looked out the window behind my desk. A telephone lineman was climbing a pole near the parking lot exit. I watched as he inched his way up the pole, digging into the wood with spikes protruding from his shoes while leaning back against a belt at his waist connecting him to the pole. Exhausted just by watching his arduous climb, I turned back to Rick. "You and Elaine have everything ready on your end?"

"We finally finished going through the thirty-five boxes of mostly useless paperwork that Harry Sporn brought with him to the deposition," Rick said. "I think we found everything you'll need in court."

"Anything jump out at you?"

"No smoking gun," Rick said, "but then again, we didn't think there would be. They wouldn't be stupid enough to put anything questionable in writing. We found the company claims manual, as well as three internal memos about claims procedures. All standard stuff, nothing incriminating."

"Except for that memo from Frankel, Baldwin & Ingram," I said. "That document is as incriminating as hell."

"Yeah, about that memo," Rick began. "We know it exists because the young lady at the insurance company slipped you a copy when you were there with Margaret for the EUO. Unfortunately, those honest folks at FAIL neglected to provide a copy in response to your request for documents."

"Why am I not surprised?"

"Not to worry," Rick replied. "I fixed their oversight by putting our copy in box number eighteen. It's right in front so you'll be able to find it quickly at trial."

32

"It was easier to buy them than steal them."

The following day I began reviewing the documents I planned to use in the Woodson trial, which was scheduled to start the following week. I had just finished snickering over a section of the FAIL Insurance claims manual informing employees that they were required to deal with claimants in a "fair and ethical manner" when Rick appeared at my office door.

"Good time for a firm meeting?" he asked, taking a seat across from me at my desk. Before Scott and Avery died in the World Trade Center bombing, we had formal meetings on a regular basis. But now that it's just Rick and me, meetings tend to be spur of the moment affairs, usually involving our financial situation.

"Money troubles?" I asked.

"I wouldn't call it troubles," Rick replied, "but Elaine and I just finished paying bills, and once again last month we made more money as landlords than attorneys." A couple years ago, at Avery Glickman's suggestion, we had purchased the building in which our offices are located, giving us a reliable cash flow from rents. In those days, we had a variety of cases, all generating a consistent income stream. Now that our two-man shop is a litigation practice, we only get paid when we win or settle a case. Although the fees we collect can be many times what Avery's business transactions or Scott's divorce cases produced, we can go months between paydays.

"I've been talking to some of my old contacts in the real estate business," Rick continued, "from back when I did a lot of planning work for developers. I'm pretty sure I can get them to send us a regular stream of real estate closings."

"Real estate closings? Seriously?"

"I realize they're not as exciting or as profitable as trial work, but they'd generate a nice, steady cash flow." Rick hesitated, and I sensed there was another reason for his suggestion. What he said next confirmed that. "Besides, I don't feel as though I'm carrying my weight. It's your trial work that generates the money around here. It's as though I'm just along for the ride."

"Nonsense," I said. "Research is the key to winning in court, and you're the best legal researcher I know. Besides, I like having you sit second chair. Two sets of eyes and ears are better than one." I made a mental note to figure out a way to get Rick more involved with actual courtroom work.

We talked for another ten minutes about the pros and cons of adding real estate closings to the services we offered. That conversation came to a halt when Elaine buzzed me from the reception area. "There's someone here to see you. He didn't give me his name, but he says it's about Mrs. Anderson's bonds, and it's important." Elaine paused momentarily before continuing in a whisper. "He looks Chinese."

I told Elaine to escort the unexpected visitor to my office. She appeared a moment later with a man in a blue suit. He looked to be in his mid-thirties, a bit shorter than me, and obviously Asian, although I couldn't be sure he was Chinese. His most distinguishing characteristic was a nasty scar across his left cheek.

He tossed his overcoat on the sofa and crossed the room to my desk with hand extended. "Good morning, Mr. O'Brian. My name is Jeremy Lin." We shook hands. I introduced Rick and motioned Mr. Lin to the empty chair next to him. "Thank you for seeing me without an appointment," Lin said as he sat down.

"Have we met?" I asked. "You look familiar?" That wasn't really true. But I was hoping the question might elicit something useful from our visitor.

It didn't. "I don't believe so," he said, "but I suppose it's possible. I've lived in the area for a while. Our paths might have crossed at some point." I noted that he spoke perfect English, without any trace of an accent or the somewhat stilted style that Mr. Wu had exhibited during our visit to the Chinese consulate in New York. "I know you gentlemen are busy, so I'll cut to the chase. I represent a buyer who is interested in purchasing the Chinese bonds owned by your client, Edna Anderson."

"Who's your buyer?" Rick asked.

"I'm afraid his identity must remain confidential," Lin responded, "but I assure you he is a serious buyer with the financial wherewithal to complete the transaction." He withdrew an envelope from his pocket, placed it on my desk, and slid it toward me. Nodding toward the envelope, he said, "He is prepared to pay what I think both you and your client will agree is a very generous price."

I opened the envelope and withdrew the single sheet of paper it contained. On the paper, neatly typed, were two numbers. One was a phone number. The second was a number preceded by a dollar sign. I handed the paper to Rick, who arched an eyebrow as he read it.

"I realize you have to discuss this with your client," Lin said. I was expecting him to ask me to call Mrs. Anderson right then and there, but instead, he got up from his chair, retrieved his overcoat and headed for the door. He turned when he got to the doorway. "Payment will be made in the form of a certified check made payable to your escrow account. Or, if you prefer, in the form of cash. Should you and Mrs. Anderson accept our offer, please call the phone number I gave you. You may speak with whomever answers."

"What do you make of that?" Rick asked as soon as our visitor had left.

"I think whoever is after the bonds decided it was easier to buy them than steal them."

33

"Your job is getting out."

Rick and I talked about Jeremy Lin's offer for the better part of an hour. We were both leery of doing business with an unknown buyer, but the amount Lin was offering – assuming the offer was genuine – was significant. We both realized we had an ethical obligation to convey the offer to Mrs. Anderson, but we couldn't agree on whether or not we should express an opinion about the advisability of accepting it. Rick was in favor of trying to talk her out of doing business with Lin's unknown buyer. "Something doesn't smell right," he said over and over during our conversation. "There's no way we can trust these people given all that's happened." Using his fingers, Rick counted off the events he considered warning signs. "The way Wu at the Chinese consulate tricked us into giving him Mrs. Anderson's name and address. The break-in at Mrs. Anderson's home. The break-in at our office. The break-in at Carolyn's apartment. The car that pulled up next to us on the way back from the airport. With all that's happened, why would you even consider this?" And then he added the *coup d'grace*. "And since when do we do business with someone who offers to pay that much money in cash? That sounds like something the mob would do."

I had to admit that Rick's argument was persuasive, but the money, assuming we actually received it, would make a significant difference in Edna Anderson's life. It wouldn't bring her husband back, but it would ease the financial burden his untimely death had caused his family. And our percentage would be a welcome boost to the firm's cash flow.

I called Edna Anderson a number of times throughout the day, finally reaching her just after five o'clock. She was beyond ecstatic when I told her about her forthcoming bounty. "Thank you, Lord!" she repeated over and over for what felt like an eternity. When she finished thanking the Almighty, she began to thank me. At some point the display of gratitude stopped, either because she assumed both the Almighty and I were sufficiently thanked or because she interpreted my silence as a sign that I had reservations about the proposed transaction.

"You don't seem to share in my happiness," she said.

"No, I'm very happy for you," I replied, "assuming you actually end up with the money."

"Why wouldn't I?"

I went through the problems that Rick had highlighted earlier that afternoon, including his observation that an offer to pay in cash seemed a bit fishy. "But here's what bothers me the most. These bonds have been repudiated by China, and only have nominal value as collectors' items. We've done the research and we're sure of that. So, why would someone be willing to pay that much for them?"

"Yes, I see your point," she said. "That is strange." There was a long silence as she considered the matter. "I wish Ronnie was here," she said. "He'd know what do." It sounded as though she was about to cry. "Let me pray on it, and I'll get back to you."

Rick appeared at my office door just as I was hanging up the phone. I told him about my conversation with Mrs. Anderson.

"Let's wait and see what she decides," was his response. He pointed toward my office window. "The snow's getting worse. Elaine and I are heading out. You might want to as well."

I took his advice and headed home twenty minutes later. It was one of those dreary December afternoons that I detest, made even gloomier by low-hanging steel gray clouds and swirling snow.

As I turned right out of our parking lot onto Route 46, my Mustang fishtailed on the slick pavement and momentarily encroached on the left lane. The driver of the red Honda in that lane, who was driving much too fast for the road conditions, acknowledged my trespass with a blast of his horn, followed by a one-finger salute as he sped by. I reciprocated with a gesture of my own, but he was moving too fast to see my response.

I inched along in traffic, joining other commuters trying to get home before the snow accumulated. Traffic slowed even more as I approached the western edge of town where the highway steepens. Halfway up the hill, traffic in the right lane had come to a standstill, blocked by a Volkswagen that spent more time sliding sideways than moving forward. I carefully eased my Mustang into the left lane and passed the line of cars and the stranded Bug. The black Lincoln that had been behind me followed suit, dropping in behind me as I returned to the right lane. It was a perfectly normal maneuver, but given all that had happened recently, I began to suspect the Lincoln was tailing me. I tried to catch a glimpse of the driver, but the swirling snow, combined with the movement of the Lincoln's windshield wipers, prevented me from seeing anything but a vague outline. "You're getting paranoid," I said to the empty car. "Just another motorist trying to get home."

The Lincoln followed close behind me until I got to the main boulevard leading into Mountain Springs. I put on my turn signal, half expecting the Lincoln to do likewise. But to my relief, the other car continued its slow westward trek on Route 46. "Just another motorist trying to get home," I told myself again.

An hour after leaving the office – twice the time it should have taken – I arrived home, parked my Mustang in the circular driveway in front of the house and went inside.

The phone was ringing as I entered the house. I crossed the foyer, tracking snow as I went, and lifted the receiver.

"Yo, counsellor!" I knew the caller was Eddie Rizzo even before he identified himself. "It's me," Eddie," he continued, incorrectly assuming that he and I were on a first name basis. "You still interested in finding out what happened to the guy who was buying those Chinese bonds?" He didn't wait for an answer. "I figured out a way to get into that place where he worked. I don't know what happened to the guy, but whatever it was, I'm betting it happened there. That place is weird."

This was one of the rare occasions when Eddie and I were in total agreement. Reynaldo Renoir had confirmed that Consolidated TranShip was most likely a government facility operated by the CIA, but that's all I knew, having obeyed Judge Cohen's instructions to stay clear of the place. But Eddie hadn't been constrained by Ice Cold Cohen's order.

"I had some people I know check out the place," Eddie said. "They got an electric fence, barbed wire, cameras, the whole bit. And, get this, the place is guarded by guys working for a phony security company."

"How do you know it's a phony security company?"

"I know every security company in this part of Jersey," Eddie said, "cause I own one."

The thought of Eddie the Skunk owning a security company was inconceivable, but instead of saying that, I asked, "So if this place has such great security, how do you plan to get in?"

"Oh, I don't plan to get in," Eddie said. "But I got a way for you to get in."

As I assumed it would, Eddie's plan began with "I know a guy who owes me a favor" and concluded with "of course, I don't guarantee it will work."

After listening to Eddie's proposed plan, I realized why it didn't come with a guarantee. "I see two problems," I said. "First, if that door is locked, then what?"

"Then the plan don't work," Eddie replied, his tone of voice adding an unspoken "Duh" at the beginning of his response.

"The second problem is that if I don't move fast enough, I can't get out."

"Hey, counsellor," Eddie said, "My job is getting you in. Your job is getting out."

"Let me think about it," I told Eddie.

"Don't think too long," Eddie replied. "My guy's contract is up for renewal at the end of the year, and if he don't re-up, there goes my plan."

I wanted to conclude the call by asking Eddie how he had gotten my home phone number, but decided that would make me sound ungrateful. After all, Eddie had gone out of his way to do me a favor, even if the favor was a screwball plan that made some of my *Mission Impossible* scenarios seem tame by comparison. Of course, that didn't mean it wouldn't work.

34

"Do you need all that in the courtroom?"

The jury trial of *Woodson v. Federal American International Lines Insurance Company* began on a cold Monday morning two weeks before Christmas at the Morris County Courthouse, the Honorable Kenneth Bloomquist presiding.

When Rick, Margaret Woodson, and I arrived, Augustus Carter was already seated at the defendant's counsel table. He was accompanied by six associates, four men and two women. Harold Lamb, the novice attorney who represented FAIL at the motion hearing that resulted in the insurance company owing me the still-unpaid thousand dollars, wasn't part of the entourage. Carter glanced in our direction as we sat down, but he didn't bother to acknowledge our presence or exchange pleasantries. We didn't either.

Tony Biffano arrived a few minutes later, accompanied by the two witnesses scheduled to testify after Margaret that day. Once he had them seated in the public gallery, he met me at the railing separating the gallery from the well of the court. "Everything ready?" I asked.

"They're just outside the courtroom," Tony answered. "But are you sure you want to do this? Even for you, this is pretty outrageous. Judge Bloomquist isn't going to be happy with you."

"Trust me, this will pay off in the long run."

Tony shrugged. "You're the boss."

Judge Bloomquist entered the courtroom and took the bench moments later. He had just finished welcoming the jurors we had selected the previous Friday when Tony Biffano entered the courtroom followed by seven men in coveralls, each pushing a hand cart stacked with five boxes. They proceeded down the center aisle and stopped at the railing.

"What's going on here?" Judge Bloomquist wanted to know.

"This is the material Mr. Carter provided in response to my interrogatories," I answered, holding up the interrogatories. The judge looked at the couple dozen pages I was holding, then to the boxes, then back to the interrogatories. He made a show of counting the boxes in the same way he had counted the number of attorneys who had accompanied Carter to the first motion hearing in the case.

"All that," he asked, pointing to the thirty-five boxes, "in response to interrogatories?"

"Yes, Your Honor, all that."

He shook his head in apparent disbelief. "Do you need all that in the courtroom?"

"I'm not sure, Your Honor, but I want to have it available in case I do."

"Very well, put it over there," the judge said, pointing to the side of the courtroom across from the jury.

Tony and his crew stacked the boxes, being careful to arrange them so the numbers were clearly visible to the jurors. Their task completed, they exited the courtroom, and the trial got underway.

I began my opening statement to the jury by telling them they were about to decide a very simple, straightforward case that would allow them to finish jury duty quickly and get on with preparations for the upcoming holiday. "Years ago, my client's late husband, Scott Woodson, purchased a life insurance policy from the defendant, Federal American International Lines Insurance Company. Mr. Woodson dutifully paid the insurance premium every year, expecting that when he died, his widow would receive the policy's death benefit. In February of this year, Mr. Woodson was killed when a terrorist bomb collapsed a portion of the World Trade Center. Since then, the insurance company has used a series of excuses, each one more absurd than the last, to avoid paying my client the death benefit she's entitled to under that policy. And when the insurance company ran out of delaying tactics, they suddenly discovered a policy provision that they contend allows them to collect premiums for decades, but pay nothing to Mr. Woodson's widow, the policy beneficiary. As you'll discover, their contention is based on re-defining a common term, the meaning of which is well known to all of us. The company's actions are all the more disturbing because Mrs. Woodson's case isn't an isolated incident. The evidence I'll present will show that Margaret Woodson was just one of many people who were dealt with in bad faith by the defendant."

My opening statement, short and to the point, seemed to go over well with the jury. Some jurors leaned forward when I said Margaret's case wasn't an isolated incident. An older woman sitting in the back row frowned while looking toward Augustus Carter and his small army of well-dressed attorneys, hopefully thinking that money spent on high-priced attorneys could have been better spent to pay claims.

"Good start," Rick whispered as I returned to my seat. "Looks like you've got a sympathetic jury."

Augustus Carter got to his feet, adjusted his tie, buttoned his impeccably tailored suit jacket and told the jury, "Mr. O'Brian says this is a simple case. And he's right, but not for the reason he would like you to believe. An insurance policy is a contract. And each party to the contract, the insured, Mr. Woodson in this case, and the insurer, my client, has an obligation to honor the terms of that contract. And that's exactly what my client has done. You see, the insurance policy Mr. Woodson purchased specifically provides that no death benefit is payable if death is caused by an act of war. And the actions that led to the untimely death of Scott Woodson were an act of war." Carter looked in my direction and pointed at me, before adding, "Mr. O'Brian has previously admitted that fact right here in this courthouse."

I jumped to my feet to object, but before I could say a word, Judge Bloomquist banged his gavel multiple times and bellowed, "Counsel, approach."

Judge Bloomquist is among the more easy-going members of the judiciary I've appeared before, but he was clearly angry. As soon as we arrived at the bench, he told my adversary through clenched teeth, "You knew what Mr. O'Brian said in another case was inadmissible, but you deliberately mentioned it in your opening statement."

"I'm terribly sorry, Your Honor," Augustus Carter replied, "but I don't recall you ever ruling that Mr. O'Brian's statement was inadmissible."

It was a blatant lie and Judge Bloomquist certainly knew that, but instead of admonishing my adversary, the judge turned toward the jurors and announced, "Ladies and gentlemen of the jury, due to a legal technicality, your services will no longer be required. You are dismissed with the court's thanks for your service. Merry Christmas."

The judge watched as the jury filed out of the courtroom before turning back to Carter and me. "Mr. Carter, you've tried my

patience once too often. I have a good mind to dismiss your affirmative defense and enter a directed verdict for the plaintiff."
I turned to see if Margaret heard what the judge had said. Her smile told me she had.

Carter started to respond to Judge Bloomquist, but the judge silenced him by holding up his hand. The judge began tapping his pen on the bench, apparently deciding whether or not to make good on his threat. When the tapping stopped, the judge leaned forward and looked first at me and then at my adversary. "Personally, I think the insurer has played games from the outset, and I'm sorely tempted to enter judgment for the plaintiff. But I suspect that would simply result in an appeal to the Appellate Division, and drag this case out even longer. And given all that's going on in the world, the issues involved need to be resolved sooner rather than later. So we're going to select a new jury and start this trial over right after the first of the year. And, fair warning, Mr. Carter, if you pull a stunt like this again, you'll regret ever setting foot in my courtroom."

As I returned to the counsel table where Margaret Woodson waited, I could see that she was visibly upset. Augustus Carter, on the other hand, could barely suppress a smile.

35

"I don't want blood money."

Edna Anderson called the following afternoon. Rick was with me in my office, trying to convince me we should expand our practice to include real estate closings, so I put Mrs. Anderson on speaker.

"I've given the matter a lot of thought," she began. "And I've prayed for guidance." She paused, apparently deciding how to announce her decision. "The children and I certainly could use the money. Lord knows that's a lot of money. But no amount of money will bring my Ronnie back." She was clearly choking back tears. "But I don't want blood money, Mr. O'Brian. When we first met, you promised me you'd find out what happened to my husband. That's what I really want."

"Are you telling us you don't want the money?" I asked. "That's a lot of money to walk away from."

"I'm telling you I don't want dirty money, blood money" she replied. "I'm a good Christian woman. I couldn't live with myself if I thought I was accepting money from anyone who had something to do with Ronnie's death."

Rick entered the conversation. "We don't know who the buyer is, Mrs. Anderson. He could be someone from the company where your husband worked trying to make things right."

She responded by asking the obvious question. "If that's the case, why wouldn't the company just say so?"

Because the company your husband worked for was probably the CIA, and government spooks would never admit shooting a civilian employee through the head for no apparent reason and then cremating the body to hide the evidence. Of course, I wasn't really sure of that, or anything else involving Mr. Anderson and his mysterious workplace. So instead of telling her that, I said, "I'm not sure we'll ever know who this buyer is, or why he's interested in buying your Chinese bonds. It's possible this person has nothing to do with your husband's company at all. We really have no idea. All we really know is that this person has offered to buy the bonds for considerably more than what we think they're worth."

That's when she asked another obvious question. "Can't you find out who his buyer is? That investigator you sent to my house..." She paused, apparently searching for a name.

"Tony Biffano," I prompted.

"Yes, Mr. Biffano. He mentioned he used to be a police detective. I'm sure he could find out who this person is."

I wasn't sure I agreed with her, nor did I want to pay Tony's hourly rate to find out if she was right. Of course, I couldn't tell her that. So, instead, I said, "Let us look into it and I'll get back to you." Mrs. Anderson thanked me and ended the call, apparently unaware that looking into something is lawyer talk for *I don't really plan to do that.*

As soon as I hung up the phone, Rick said, "Instead of paying Tony, why don't you just call Jeremy Lin and ask him who the buyer is? The worst that can happen is he refuses to tell you. And, who knows, if Lin's buyer is anxious enough to buy these bonds, Lin might give you something you can take back to Mrs. Anderson."

"Good point," I said, reaching for the phone on my desk. Before I could pick it up, Elaine appeared at my office door waving a piece of paper.

"This fax just came in and I knew you'd want to see it right away." She put the paper on my desk, smiled at Rick and left the office.

The fax was a letter from Augustus Carter offering to settle Margaret Woodson's case for approximately half of the insurance policy's death benefit, plus a sizable five-digit fee to the law firm of Santorini & O'Brian.

Rick took the letter from me, scanned it and shook his head. "I'm not sure how Margaret is going to react when she learns about this."

"Only one way to find out." I picked up the phone and dialed Margaret Woodson's number.

Margaret answered on the third ring and we exchanged pleasantries before I put the call on speaker so Rick could take part in the conversation. I read her Carter's letter, which resulted in an emphatic response. "Those bastards. After all they put me through, they have the gall to make an offer like that." She continued in a similar vein for several minutes, expanding my lexicon of off-color words in the process, before breaking down in tears.

I waited for the sobbing to stop. "I know how you must feel," I began.

My attempt at sympathy backfired. "No, you don't, Brendan. Until you lose someone close to you, you don't understand. Not really." She was clearly angry, perhaps at FAIL Insurance for making the offer, me for conveying it, or maybe at the miscreants who had taken her husband away from her. Or perhaps, deep down, she was angry that Scott and Avery had gone to the seminar at the World Trade Center that day because Rick and I had refused to go.

"I'm sorry. I didn't intend to suggest I could understand your loss. I just meant that I could understand how offensive an offer like this is, given all that's happened."

There was an awkward silence, which Margaret finally filled by asking, "You're not seriously suggesting I consider this offer, are you?"

Rick joined the conversation. "Brendan's just doing what he has an ethical obligation to do, informing you of a settlement offer. He isn't suggesting anything, just conveying their offer."

"What do you recommend?" Margaret asked. The fact that she asked the question meant Carter's letter had achieved it's intended purpose. By dangling the prospect of an immediate seven-figure, tax-free payday in Margaret's face, he had caused her to question the wisdom of continuing her case against his client.

"If you accept their offer, you end up with a bundle of money and get to put all of this behind you. That's the easy way to end all this, which is exactly what the insurance company is trying to get you to do. But if you settle, you don't get what Scott paid for when he bought that insurance policy. If you try the case and win, you get everything you should have gotten months ago, plus interest from when the insurance company should have paid you."

"And what are my chances of winning?" Margaret asked.

"I think you have a very good chance of forcing the insurance company to pay the death benefit, but I'm not sure you'll collect punitive damages. To collect punitive damages in New Jersey, you have to prove the insurance company acted in bad faith, which is tough to do because of *Pickett v. Lloyd's*, the supreme court case we talked about when we had lunch at the New Amsterdam Inn."

"So, you don't think the jury will buy the company's act of war defense?"

I didn't actually answer her question. "I think the jury will decide that the insurance company tried to rip you off and needs to finally pay up to make things right."

We spoke for another fifteen minutes or so, and at the end of the conversation, Margaret decided not to accept Carter's settlement offer, although at one point she almost convinced herself that she should.

After I hung up the phone, Rick got up and started to pace around the office, thumbs hooked into the pockets of his vest. He eventually ended up staring out the window behind my desk. I've seen him do this before, and the routine usually ends with an insight that helps solve whatever legal problem we're dealing with at the time. I assumed he was going to comment on the Woodson case or perhaps return to his argument that we should begin handling real estate closings. But instead, he nodded toward the window and said, "I'd hate to have his job." I joined him at the window to see who he was talking about. A phone company lineman, perched near the top of the pole by our parking lot, was being buffeted by the wind. "Guy must be freezing his ass off," Rick said as he resumed his pacing around my office.

The pacing eventually stopped. "We know that boosting profits was apparently a concern at FAIL Insurance because the Frankel, Baldwin & Ingram memo talks about increasing profits by reducing claims payouts." Rick pointed at me. "Imagine you're the guy tasked with doing that. How would you go about it?" Rick answered his own question. "You'd concentrate your efforts on people like Marie Callahan and Margaret Woodson. If you can get someone with a two million dollar claim to accept a million dollars, you've saved the company a million dollars."

I saw where he was going. "And those people are more likely to settle because they still walk away with a million tax-free dollars. But if they go to court and lose, they lose a ton of money."

"Exactly," Rick said. "Those are the people who have the greatest incentive to settle. And if they're represented by someone like Shiff,

Marie Callahan's sorry excuse for an attorney, their own lawyer is going to push for a settlement."

So, maybe we have the wrong witnesses," I said. "They're all sympathetic and live in the area, but Marie Callahan and Margaret are the only ones who had a claim for more than a million dollars."

"That's what I'm thinking," Rick replied. He hooked his thumbs in the pockets of his vest before continuing. "Unfortunately, getting people from outside the area would be a logistical nightmare, not to mention expensive." He was right on both counts. Flying witnesses in from around the country, putting them up in a hotel, and feeding them could cost a bundle. And we had never discussed litigation expenses with Margaret, initially intending to cover them ourselves. Of course, that was back when we assumed the insurance company would pay up as soon as we filed suit, and out-of-pocket costs would be minimal. Having been married to an attorney, she perhaps automatically assumed we would deduct costs from any judgment we won. But perhaps not. And raising the issue now could be awkward.

"We don't necessarily need these people to testify," I told Rick. "But we do need to find out who they are. They're among the two hundred or so people on the list we got from FAIL Insurance, but calling a couple hundred people will take time that we don't have." I thought of our alternatives. "Maybe we let those fine folks at FAIL do the legwork for us."

Rick laughed. "Somehow I don't see them doing that for us."

"No, not willingly, but there might be a way."

36

"Tell him it's a go."

While driving to the office the following morning I devised a plan for getting the information about FAIL's big money settlements that Rick and I had talked about the previous afternoon. I was clearly out of time for using the discovery process to obtain that information, but I was hoping Judge Bloomquist's reasonableness, combined with Augustus Carter's arrogance, would help us obtain what we needed. I was so intent on drafting an appropriate motion in my head that I didn't see the black Lincoln Continental until it pulled in two cars behind me.

Continentals aren't nearly as rare as my carefully restored 1965 Mustang, but they're also not among the most common cars seen on New Jersey roads. The Lincoln looked like the one that had followed me on the day of the snowstorm, but since one Lincoln looks pretty much like every other one, that didn't mean much. Probably just a coincidence. "The world is filled with black Lincolns," I told myself.

Yet every time I changed lanes, the Lincoln did too. It never got close to my Mustang and never did anything threatening. It was just always there every time I checked my mirror, giving me the creepy feeling that I was being followed.

I turned left just as the Beverwyck Road traffic light went from green to yellow. The Lincoln accelerated and followed me through the intersection, confirming my suspicion that it was following me. But when I turned onto the street leading to the parking lot behind our building, the Lincoln continued straight.

"You're getting paranoid, O'Brian," I muttered to myself as I parked the car and walked into our building. "The world is filled with black Lincolns."

Once inside, I filled my coffee cup and began to draft the motion to obtain additional discovery from FAIL Insurance. "Calling it an emergency motion should get the judge's attention," Rick said when he read the finished product. I faxed it to Augustus Carter and Judge Bloomquist, requesting a hearing at the court's earliest convenience. My use of "emergency" paid off an hour later when Judge Bloomquist's secretary called to inform me that the judge would hear my motion the following Monday at ten o'clock.

That task complete, I returned to the issue of Mrs. Anderson's potential payoff. Rick was correct in thinking that I had nothing to lose by asking Jeremy Lin for the identity of the buyer he purported to represent. If he refused to provide that information, we would be no worse off. And if I got lucky, he might say something that would help us figure out why someone would shell out so much money for bonds with only minimal value as collector's items.

I dialed the number Lin had provided and was connected after just one ring. The heavily accented voice at the other end of the line obviously wasn't Lin's.

"Jeremey Lin, please."

"I am very sorry, but Mr. Lin is unavailable," said the anonymous voice, "but I am authorized to speak to you about our proposed transaction."

"And you are?"

Instead of providing a name, he said, "I am fully authorized to speak on behalf of the buyer."

"And who is this buyer?"

"I am afraid that is not something I am authorized to tell you. The buyer wishes to remain anonymous. Surely you can understand why someone spending so much money would wish to remain anonymous."

Actually, I couldn't and said as much, following up with, "As I'm sure you can understand, my client is reluctant to do business with someone she knows nothing about. And as an attorney, I have certain ethical obligations to fulfill, particularly when someone I don't know offers to conduct business using a large quantity of cash."

"I can assure you, Mr. O'Brian, that this transaction is entirely legitimate. We are not offering your client blood money."

The mention of blood money signaled that we had a problem. I told the anonymous voice on the other end of the line that I would consult with my client and call back. Then I walked to the reception area and asked Elaine to call Tony Biffano. "Ask him to get here ASAP and tell him to bring everything." In response to Elaine's puzzled look, I put one finger to my lips, then picked up the legal pad on the reception desk and wrote OFFICE BUGGED. Elaine reached for the phone immediately. Hopefully, Tony would understand what I meant by "bring everything."

Tony showed up forty-five minutes later, wheeling an oversized suitcase. I immediately showed him the legal pad with the OFFICE BUGGED message, and without saying a word, he pulled out a bunch of electronic gizmos and went to work. Half an hour later he walked into my office where Rick, Elaine and I were waiting.

"Everything's clean," he announced. I didn't find any cameras or listening devices anywhere on the premises.

"Then the phones are bugged," I replied.

"Why do you think your phones are bugged?" Tony asked.

"Because Edna Anderson used the phrase 'blood money' when she and I spoke on the phone yesterday. The person I spoke with earlier today used the same term, which you'll have to admit isn't all that common.

Tony looked from me to Rick, who shrugged his shoulders. Rick didn't seem entirely convinced by my argument.

"When I swept the place, I took apart the phones and checked to see if anything didn't look right," Tony said. "Nothing there."

"Are you sure?" I told him about the telephone lineman I had seen outside the office on two different occasions. "Couldn't he have done something outside to tap our phone?"

"Do you hear a dial tone when the phone is on the hook?" Tony asked.

"No," I answered. "I don't think so." I looked at Rick, who responded with a shake of the head.

"How about a pulsating static noise?"

Rick and I both told him no.

"When you talk on the phone, do you hear a lot of static or background noise?" Tony asked next.

"Not that I've noticed."

"Humming or popping sounds?"

"No."

"Does your radio or television squeal when you're on the phone?"

I answered his question with one of my own. "Do you see a radio or television?"

"No," he responded, but I seem to recall seeing one in your conference room."

"No squealing in the conference room," Rick said. From his tone of voice I surmised that he was tired of humoring me. "I think we can safely assume our phones aren't tapped."

I wasn't entirely sure about that, but went along with his assessment. "Fine, no phone taps. I'm just being paranoid."

"Proactive," Tony Biffano corrected. "Nothing wrong with that. Better to be safe than sorry."

Late that afternoon, I received a call from Eddie Rizzo on my now guaranteed bug-free phone. "Yo, counsellor. You given any more thought to my plan for getting into that whacko place where the Anderson guy worked?" Actually, I had given Eddie's nutty plan a lot of thought, but hadn't gotten around to conveying my decision to him. Calling Eddie isn't a high priority item for me. "My friend just found out his contract isn't being renewed, so if you want to do this, you gotta move fast. He won't have access to the place after the first of the year."

I wasn't particularly enthusiastic about Eddie's plan, but it was the only plan I had. "Tell your friend it's a go." Then I left a message for Reynaldo Renoir.

37

"I'd like to think we're usually on the same side."

Two days later, I was sitting in my favorite window booth at the diner across the highway from my office when a taxi pulled up outside. An elderly gentleman with a cane got out and slowly made his way up the stairs. He reappeared inside the diner a moment later, looked around to get his bearings, and then began a slow shuffle in my direction, eventually reaching my table in the time it took me to take two more bites out of my tuna on rye. Instead of continuing his slow-motion trek to an empty table, the elderly man carefully lowered himself into the seat across from me. Only then, when he was just a few feet away, did I realize my uninvited lunch guest was actually Reynaldo Renoir wearing a white wig and a fake beard.

A waitress appeared, topped off my coffee cup and filled the empty cup in front of Reynaldo. "You're a little late for Halloween," I said when the waitress was out of earshot, "but I like the costume. Very convincing."

"You're being watched, and we don't want anyone to know you're talking to us," Reynaldo explained.

"Watched by whom?"

"Chinese intelligence. People connected to Consolidated TranShip."

"Which?"

"Either. Both. We're not sure. All we know is you're being watched."

"Why are you so sure someone is watching me?" I asked.

"We know they're watching you because we're watching them watch you. Remember seeing a black Lincoln when you were driving?"

"That was you?"

"No, my people were in the Chevy keeping an eye on the Lincoln keeping an eye on you."

"I don't remember seeing a Chevy."

"Good. You're not supposed to."

I took another bite from my tuna sandwich and tried to make sense of what Reynaldo was telling me. Given all that had happened, it was entirely possible that I was being followed. But by whom? I asked the obvious question. "Were the people following me Asian?"

"Some were, some weren't," Reynaldo answered, quickly adding, "and some we couldn't get close enough to tell."

I was about to ask Reynaldo if he thought I was in physical danger when he said, "I got a message that you wanted to see me. What for?"

"Two things, actually."

Reynaldo looked around, presumably making sure nobody could overhear our conversation. "I'm listening."

"I'm getting phone calls from my client, Mrs. Anderson. She's pressuring me to move forward with her case against Consolidated TranShip." That statement wasn't entirely accurate. What Mrs. Anderson wanted wasn't a trial date, but closure, answers to what had happened to her husband. At our initial meeting in my office months ago, I had promised her I would get those answers. Thus far I had failed to fulfill that promise.

"And this involves me how?" Reynaldo asked.

"I want to speak to Thompson, the technician from the funeral home." That wasn't really what I wanted, although a sit down with Thompson could prove useful. If Reynaldo refused my request, as I assumed he would, that might make him more amenable to giving me what I really needed as a consolation prize.

Reynaldo's answer was what I expected. "No way."

"Why not?"

"We have him in a safe house under twenty-four-hour guard. We'll need him to testify when we're ready to proceed against whoever killed Mrs. Anderson's husband."

"What do you have to lose?" I asked.

"My case and his life," Reynaldo answered.

"You're being a bit dramatic, aren't you?"

"That funeral home didn't set itself on fire," Reynaldo said. "Remember, you're under surveillance. I don't want you anywhere near the safe house. If Mrs. Anderson wants to find out who killed her husband, the best thing you can do is stay out of this and let us do our job."

Staying out of it wasn't what I had in mind, so I steered the conversation in a different direction. "Ever find out if the funeral home fire was arson?"

"No, we're proceeding on the assumption the fire was deliberately set, but we don't have definitive proof."

"Any idea who torched the place?"

"No."

"Do you know why the FBI took over the investigation from the local cops?"

"No."

The conversation came to a halt when a waitress appeared at our table to re-fill coffee cups. When she left, I told Reynaldo, "There has to be some way I can talk to Thompson without jeopardizing his safety."

"At some point, that might be possible," Reynaldo said, "but not right now." He took another sip of coffee from the re-filled cup, being careful not to get any on the fake beard. Then he asked the question that would get us to the real reason for our meeting. "You said you had two things you wanted to talk about. What's the second?"

"I spoke to Eddie Rizzo a couple days ago," I began.

That was as far as I got before Renaldo cut me off. "Good grief, not him."

"Hear me out." I started to explain Eddie's plan for getting into Consolidated TranShip's heavily guarded facility.

I was just getting to the part about the two doors when Reynaldo asked, "What part of 'stay out of this and let us do our job' do you not understand?"

"If this works," I insisted, "we'll both find out what happened to Ronald Anderson."

"If it works."

"Let me finish before you judge." I continued explaining the admittedly somewhat sketchy plan Eddie Rizzo had come up with.

"Well, what do you think?" I asked when I had finished.

"There are so many problems with this scheme, I don't even know where to begin," Reynaldo answered.

"Such as?"

"For starters, why in the world would you trust anything Eddie Rizzo, of all people, dreamed up? You can't trust Rizzo. For all you know, he's setting you up."

"I don't trust Eddie, not really. But he's been useful in the past, and I can't see where he has anything to gain by setting me up to fail." I paused, thinking about the best way to explain my unusual relationship with Eddie Rizzo. "Eddie values me because of what I've been able to do for him over the years. From time to time he does things that he thinks will help me. It's his way of showing gratitude."

"Guys like Rizzo don't show gratitude," Reynaldo snorted. "They don't do something unless there's a payoff for them."

"The payoff," I explained, "is making it impossible for me to turn him down the next time he comes to me for legal help."

"Maybe," Reynaldo said. I could tell he wasn't really convinced but didn't want to pursue the matter.

"You said you had problems, plural. What else don't you like about this plan?"

"Problem number two: it will tip off the people behind Consolidated TranShip that the Juvenal Bureau is investigating them."

"No, it won't. Your people don't need to identify themselves. In fact, they don't even need to say anything. All they have to do is stand there. And they won't be alone. There'll be plenty of local cops backing them up." That wasn't completely true. Detective Henderson's response to my request was somewhat less than a definitive yes. It began with a suggestion that I had taken leave of my senses, morphed into an accusation that I was trying to get Henderson fired for disobeying the mayor's order to stay away from Consolidated TranShip, and ended with a vague semi-promise: "I'll see what I can do."

Reynaldo hunched forward, leaned his forearms on the table, and looked me square in the eye. "The biggest problem I have with this harebrained plan is the fact that it's dangerous. If you do manage to get in, and I'm not sure you will, there's no guarantee you'll get out. You might very well end up like Ronald Anderson."

"Oh, gee, I didn't know you cared," I said sarcastically.

I expected Reynaldo to tell me that what he cared about was me getting in the way of his investigation. Instead, he said, "You and I aren't likely to ever be best buddies, but I'd like to think we're usually on the same side. And I don't want to see you get yourself killed."

38

"Bringing those thirty-five boxes into court paid off."

The following Monday I found myself in Judge Bloomquist's courtroom to argue my so-called emergency motion. Augustus Carter, accompanied by four associates, was quick to question my use of that term. "Mr. O'Brian is not only attempting to circumvent the Civil Practice Rules, he's attempting to defraud the court by calling this an emergency. There is no emergency, just a last-minute fishing expedition."

Judge Bloomquist looked in my direction. "Response?"

"Your Honor will no doubt remember the thirty-five boxes that I brought into court the first day of trial, before you declared a mistrial because of Mr. Carter's ..." I paused, pretending to search for the right word, eventually concluding with "indiscretion." Out of the corner of my eye I saw Augustus Carter turn bright red, apparently angered that I would think a former federal judge was capable of an indiscretion. It might have been my imagination, but Judge Bloomquist seemed to be having a hard time suppressing a smile. "Those thirty-five boxes," I continued, "were delivered to my office in response to interrogatories served on the defendant. The answers to my interrogatories were scattered throughout those boxes, interspersed with things like the menu for the defendant's cafeteria and memos regarding the company's softball team – things that no reasonable person could consider responsive to my questions. So, not only was the defendant late in making discovery, Mr. Carter and his staff deliberately did so in a way calculated to waste my time and make it impossible for me to request additional discovery within the time specified by the rules."

"What, exactly, are you requesting?" the judge asked.

"I'm requesting the defendant to provide me with the name, address, and phone number of beneficiaries of any policy with a death benefit of one million dollars or more, and who settled for less than the policy's death benefit. These people are part of the two hundred names the defendant provided in response to my original request." I held up one of the computer printouts FAIL Insurance had provided. "The information is on the insurance company's computer. All they have to do is push a few buttons."

"It's not that simple," Augustus Carter snapped. "The computer has to be programmed to sort through all the data and find the specific information Mr. O'Brian is requesting."

"How long will that take?" the judge asked Carter.

"I have no idea," Carter answered. "I'm not a computer expert."

"Perhaps one of your associates knows the answer," the judge replied, making a show of counting the four people with Carter at the counsel table.

"They're attorneys, not computer experts," Carter said. "But the real issue here isn't the amount of time it would take to get that information. The real issue is who should be responsible for obtaining it. Mr. O'Brian is asking us to do his research for him.

That's not our job. He asked for data, which we provided. Now it's up to him to use that data any way he wants."

"A valid point," Judge Bloomquist conceded. He nodded in my direction for a response.

"The defendant failed to make discovery within the time prescribed by the rules. And when they did, instead of providing a single document, they separated each sheet, and scattered those individual sheets among thirty-five boxes of mostly irrelevant paperwork. The time we spent sifting through those boxes just to get these pages," I said, once again waving the one-page computer printout, "is time we could have spent obtaining the information we need to present our case."

Carter started to respond, but I wasn't finished. "The defendant has played games with my client and this court right from the outset. They made Mrs. Woodson jump through hoops and provide information that they already had. They subjected her to an examination under oath, asked for more information, filed a series of frivolous motions, and only then did they decide to deny the claim by asserting that Mr. Woodson's death was caused by an act of war. If that was their position, they should have presented that defense at the outset."

"We have the right to try our case as we see fit," Carter said, "not the way Mr. O'Brian would like us to. But there's another issue here that I would ask the court to consider. The rules of evidence clearly prohibit the introduction of evidence regarding settlement offers or negotiations, which is exactly what Mr. O'Brian is asking for."

Judge Bloomquist looked in my direction. "Response?"

"I believe Mr. Carter is referring to Rule 408, which prohibits the use of a settlement offer to prove liability for, or the amount of, a disputed claim. However, the rule specifically permits that evidence to be used for another purpose. That's the case here.

We intend to use this evidence to show that the defendant routinely refused to pay the death benefit for very large policies to induce beneficiaries to accept less than they were entitled to, and that this was part of a scheme to increase profits. It goes to our contention that the defendant acted in bad faith."

Augustus Carter was livid. "That's an outrageous accusation. There's absolutely no basis for Mr. O'Brian's ridiculous claim."

I cut him off before he could say anything more. "There most certainly is, according to our preliminary research. That's why we need additional discovery."

"I'm in favor of broad discovery," Judge Bloomquist said. "And since this information appears to be readily available, there's no real burden on the defendant to produce it."

That's when Carter made the mistake of telling the judge, "No federal court judge would permit a so-called emergency motion like this, much less ..."

That was as far as my adversary got before an obviously annoyed Judge Bloomquist cut him off. "You're not in federal court, counsellor. You're in the Superior Court of New Jersey, my court. In my courtroom, attorneys are expected to adhere to the rules. And, frankly, I can't think of a rule that would justify answering routine interrogatories with thirty-five boxes of mostly irrelevant paperwork."

The judge gave FAIL Insurance twenty-four hours to provide the information I requested.

Bringing those thirty-five boxes into court paid off.

39

"You're a lawyer, so I figure you're good at bullshitting people."

It wasn't until I was in the truck that I realized just how crazy Eddie Rizzo's plan was. As I laid there, curled up in the dark, I began to count all the things that could go wrong. For starters, although Eddie assured me that the guards at Consolidated TranShip no longer bothered to search his friend's catering truck, there was always the possibility that today would be the day they decided to do an impromptu spot check. Secondly, if we managed to get through the gate, there was still the possibility I would be spotted as I scurried to the door that Eddie had told me would be unlocked. But even if I managed to gain entry to the building, there was no guarantee I could get back to the catering truck before it left. Eddie's friend, Carmine, had assured me he would chat with customers and buy me the time I needed, but there was a limit to how long he could stall. And if he was forced to leave the premises before I got back to my hiding place in the truck, my safety would depend on Reynaldo and Detective Henderson, assuming, of course, that they had done what I asked.

Of course, the entire plan depended on the trustworthiness of Carmine, someone I had met for the first time at a strip mall parking lot about a mile from Consolidated TranShip's facility. By prior arrangement, I waited for him on the sidewalk in front of the bakery, dressed in a pair of jeans and a sweatshirt emblazoned with the logo of my law school alma mater, Rutgers. Despite my casual dress, I must have looked like a suburban lawyer because as Carmine got out of his truck, he greeted me with, "You must be Eddie's lawyer."

I don't particularly want to be known as Eddie's lawyer, but instead of telling Carmine that, I said, "Brendan O'Brian" as we shook hands.

Without another word, he led me around to the driver's side of his catering truck and opened the door to a small compartment that ran along the bottom of the truck. "So, here's the way this works. You hide in here until we get through the gate. I park in my usual spot between the two wings of the U-shaped building. Then, I honk the horn to tell them I'm there, and open up the truck on the passenger's side. People come out of the building through the door on that side of the truck. While everyone's milling around on that side of the truck, you climb out on the driver's side and go into the building through the other door, which will be right in front of you when you get out. You just gotta remember to crouch down when you run to the door so you're hidden by the truck."

He made it sound so easy. "Are you sure that door will be unlocked?"

"Pretty sure," Carmine replied. "The whole place is surrounded by an electric fence, so why worry about locking doors, right? Besides, every once in a while someone comes out that door, so I'm guessing it's unlocked."

His use of "guessing" didn't inspire confidence. My hesitation must have showed because he said, "Look, if the door's locked, you get back in the truck and we leave." He shrugged as though it were no big deal.

But it was a big deal. "What if I run into someone coming out that door? Then what?"

"That's why you wear this," he answered, reaching into the truck cab and withdrawing a white jacket with *Carmine's Catering Services* over the pocket. "You're a lawyer, so I figure you're good at bullshitting people. And like I said, I only see people come out that door once in a while."

I was having second thoughts about Eddie's crazy scheme, but decided it was too late to turn back. So, I put on the white uniform jacket and climbed into the compartment. "What's the light for?" I asked, pointing to a small bulb dangling from a wire taped to the ceiling of the compartment.

"I almost forgot," Carmine answered. "I rigged that up so you'd know when to get out. It's attached to a button on the other side of the truck where I stand to collect money from customers. I'll look through the cab windows to make sure the coast is clear, press the button, the light goes on, you get out, and go inside. Simple." It wasn't simple. Not at all. In fact, it was downright crazy, but I didn't tell him that.

The ride from the strip mall to Consolidated TranShip was terribly uncomfortable. Carmine turned out to be the type of person who drives at full speed before stomping on the brake five feet from a stop sign. Every time he did that my head banged the metal wall of the compartment where I was hiding. The third time the truck stopped, I heard a muffled conversation that told me we had finally arrived at the Consolidated TranShip gatehouse. I held my breath, hoping today wouldn't be the day the armed guards decided to take a closer look at Carmine's truck.

I was in luck. The truck started moving again, only to stop a few moments later. This time, instead of a conversation, I heard a honking horn, the signal that Carmine was in position and open for business.

While I'm not claustrophobic, I'm not overly fond of tight spaces, and the compartment in which I was hiding seemed to be getting smaller with each passing minute. So I was relieved when the light flashed, signaling it was time to find out if the supposedly unlocked door really was unlocked.

I eased out of my hiding spot, looked around, and almost immediately spotted the door about twenty-five feet away. Judging by the sounds I was hearing on the other side of the catering truck, business was good that morning. Fortunately, there was nobody on my side of the vehicle.

Hunched over, I began jogging the twenty-five feet that suddenly seemed longer than a football field. Halfway there, I heard a shout and froze in my tracks. I looked back toward the catering truck, expecting to see an armed guard. But there was nobody there. The shout had apparently originated from the crowd of workers on the other side of Carmine's truck.

Reaching the door, I turned the handle and pulled. The metal door opened with a slight squeal, and I slipped inside. I found myself in a huge warehouse with high ceilings and rows of metal shelving. I stood there for a moment, allowing my eyes to adjust to the dim light filtering through skylights that looked as though they hadn't been cleaned in years.

The place was like the new warehouse club that recently opened in Troy Forge, but dark and eerily quiet. As I wandered down the nearest aisle, instead of seeing shelves filled with consumer goods, I found myself surrounded by weapons, file cabinets, wooden boxes with coded markings, and odd cylinders right out of a science fiction movie. Near the end of the aisle, I spotted a pallet stacked with bundles of foreign currency.

Surrounded by this vast collection of seemingly unconnected

miscellany, I realized what made this plan so crazy. It wasn't the *Mission Impossible* stratagem for getting into the compound, but the fact that I had no idea what I expected to accomplish once I was here. I decided that when I reached the end of the aisle, I'd turn around and return to the catering truck ... assuming it was still there. But when I got to the end of the aisle, I stopped dead in my tracks.

In an open area to my left was a flying saucer like the ones I had seen countless times in low-budget science fiction films. I thought back to Tony Biffano's conversation with Ronald Anderson's after-work drinking buddy. The guy might have been falling down drunk, but his ramblings about a flying saucer weren't the product of an alcohol-fueled imagination.

Moving quickly, but quietly (or so I thought), I crossed the open space to the alien ship. I ran my hand over the smooth surface that appeared to be aluminum, but which was more likely an exotic alloy created from metals not found on Earth.

I worked my way around the curved ship, hoping to find a door or hatch that would allow me to see whatever otherworldly secrets lay hidden inside. But instead of futuristic technology, I found a wooden framework supporting the metal skin. My flying saucer was nothing more than a movie prop.

As I stood there trying to figure out why the CIA would be hiding a fake flying saucer in a suburban New Jersey warehouse, I felt a sharp pain like a bee sting.

40

"I thought I had a deal."

I awoke slumped in a chair, my head pounding and my vision blurred. I tried to rub my eyes, but realized I couldn't because my hands were secured behind me.

"He's awake," a voice said.

"Uncuff him," a female voice instructed.

The pressure I had been feeling on my wrists disappeared. Still groggy, I brought my hands up to my face. As I did, I began to fall forward, but whoever was standing behind me grabbed my shoulders, preventing me from tumbling off the chair. A fist appeared in front of my face. I could tell it was a woman's hand by the slender fingers tipped with manicured pink nails. The hand opened, revealing two tablets. Another hand appeared holding a glass filled with a clear liquid. "Take these," the female voice said. "You'll feel better in a couple minutes."

They looked like ordinary aspirin, but I wasn't taking anything for granted at that point. "What are they?" I managed to say in a hoarse, little voice that didn't sound like me at all.

"They won't hurt you, Mr. O'Brian," the female voice said. "If we wanted to hurt you, we would have already done that. We simply want to have a chat with you, and we need you to be wide-eyed and bushy tailed to do that."

My semi-functioning brain reasoned that anyone who used 'wide-eyed and bushy tailed' couldn't possibly pose a threat, so I swallowed the two tablets, spilling some of the liquid, which turned out to be water, on my Rutgers sweatshirt.

It took a few minutes, but my headache began to subside and my vision started to clear. When I asked my captors, "What exactly did you do to me, and why?" I realized that I had also regained some semblance of an ability to think clearly.

A tall, slender woman who reminded me of an older version of Ayita, the pretty young lady I had met in Dahlonega, stepped in front of me. "The why part is easy," the woman said. "You illegally entered a secure government facility. And what we did to you was administer a mild sedative that will have no long-term effects. You'll be fine momentarily." She moved closer and extended her hand. "Elizabeth Scott."

"I don't usually shake hands with people who drug me, but I make exceptions for senators."

Senator Scott laughed as we shook hands. "What I've heard about you was accurate. You do, indeed, have an odd sense of humor."

"Oddest of the odd. But that doesn't mean I'm foolish enough to come here without backup. You might want to look outside. The people you'll see there know what to do if I don't come out of here in one piece." Actually, the people who I hoped were outside wouldn't do anything but serve as props, much like the phony flying saucer I had been examining just before I was drugged. But the senator and her comrades wouldn't know that. At least, I hoped they wouldn't know that.

"I don't think you'll need the cavalry to ride to your rescue," Senator Scott replied. "If we had wanted you dead, you'd be dead by now. We just want to have a chat with you." She nodded to whomever was standing behind me. "Check it out."

I heard footsteps behind me and started to turn around, but two very strong hands immediately twisted me back to face the senator, who shook her head at my unseen captor. "No need for that. Mr. O'Brian isn't the enemy. In fact, I think he'll discover that we're on the same side." The hands disappeared. The senator returned her attention to me. "Can I get you anything?" She sounded almost friendly.

"Answers to my questions."

"I was thinking more along the lines of coffee or a bottle of water, but I might be able to give you some answers eventually. But first, you have to answer my questions." She removed a photograph from a file folder and handed it to me. "Have you ever seen him before?"

The photo showed an Asian man, probably in his thirties. He could have been the driver of the car that pulled alongside us on our drive from the airport, but I couldn't really be sure. I told her that, hoping that a truthful response might persuade her to answer the questions I had.

"How about him?" the senator asked, holding up another photo. It was another Asian man about the same age, but this guy was smiling broadly.

The smile threw me off. "Without the smile, he could be the passenger in that car. You don't happen to have a photo of him scowling, do you?"

Senator Scott found that amusing. "I'm afraid not. One photograph to a customer."

She showed me a third photo. As in real life, the feature that jumped out was the jagged scar on the cheek. I wasn't sure how much to tell her, so I stalled by answering the senator's question with one of my own. "Who are these guys, and why are you interested in them?"

"The first two are Chinese intelligence agents. The third guy is the poster child for why birthright citizenship is a stupid idea."

I reasoned that if the first two guys were Chinese agents, Lin probably was as well, even though the senator hadn't said that. And that suggested she and the people running the Consolidated TranShip operation, whatever that was, would like to know Lin's whereabouts. So, I told her the truth. "The guy in the third photo is named Jeremy Lin. If you're looking for him, I know how to find him."

That was apparently what Senator Scott wanted to hear. "Get Mr. O'Brian a cup of coffee," she said to someone behind me. "Extra cream, no sugar." The fact that she knew how I like my coffee was a bit unsettling. Two men walked into my field of view. One of them disappeared into the darkness, presumably to get the coffee I hadn't asked for. The second took up a position next to Senator Scott. It was Tom Albright, the man I met at the museum in Dahlonega, Georgia.

"I was right about you," I said to Albright. "You are an actor, and a good one. You actually made me believe you were a film company employee." He smiled. "At least until I saw you in the car chasing the two Chinese guys on I-78." His smile disappeared.

Before I could come up with another snarky comment, a tall male figure emerged from the warehouse shadows. As he got closer, I realized it was the man who introduced himself as Donald Helms, the State Department official who had showed up at Carolyn's apartment. I'm sure Laser Eyes knew I recognized him, but just to be sure, and to yank his chain, I said, "Got fired by the Bureau of Diplomatic Security and ended up here, I see."

He ignored me and addressed the senator. "A dozen local cops and Renoir's crew from the Juvenal Bureau are at the fence." I made a mental note to tell Reynaldo his little-known organization was apparently better known than he realized. "Not sure how O'Brian managed to get Renoir involved, but I'm impressed that he did."

"I don't know Renoir," the senator said.

"A bit of a boy scout, but one of the good guys," Laser Eyes responded. The fact he considered the former Navy SEAL a boy scout suggested Laser Eyes was probably a very dangerous person.

"So what are you saying?" Senator Scott asked. "Read O'Brian in?"

"I'm not making a recommendation. I'm just impressed that O'Brian managed to get Reynaldo to show up here," Laser Eyes answered. I noted that he referred to Reynaldo by his first name. "If you want to read a civilian in, that's your call. But don't blame me if things go south."

Senator Scott stuck her hands in the pockets of her blazer and turned toward Albright. "What do you think, Tom?"

"O'Brian strikes me as the kind of guy who might be more cooperative if he knew the big picture," Albright answered, quickly adding, "but it's your call."

Albright's input seemed to sway her decision. Senator Scott pulled a chair in front of me, sat down and began to tell me about what she referred to as Operation Grand Bargain. "Some people in Washington came up with the brilliant idea that trading with mainland China would turn a communist country into a nation of capitalists so busy enjoying cars and washing machines that they wouldn't have the inclination to cause trouble. The whole 'beat their swords into plowshares' thing. I think by now it should be obvious that their approach, however well-meaning it might have been, hasn't worked. The Chinese have used their newfound wealth from international trade to build their military and threaten their neighbors. And it's just a matter of time before they threaten us militarily, as they already have economically."

"How, exactly, are they threatening us economically?"

"They use their corporations, which are controlled either directly or indirectly by the Chinese Communist Party. These entities steal our technology, manipulate markets, and weaken our economy. We've lost millions of manufacturing jobs to China and now run a trade deficit of about two billion dollars a month."

"A month?"

"A month," she assured me. "Not two billion a year." She paused to let that sink in before continuing. "And because of that, the Chinese are believed to hold at least a quarter of America's four trillion dollars of outstanding debt."

"What do you mean they're believed to hold? Either they own it or they don't."

"With the Chinese government, it's never that simple," she said. "Their government owns our Treasury debt directly, but they also employ intermediaries to buy it. So we're pretty certain their Treasury holdings are at least a trillion dollars, but the actual amount is likely much more. Perhaps double that."

"This is all very interesting, but what does it have to do with the death of Ronald Anderson and all this?" I asked, waving my arms to show I was referring to the entire Consolidated Tran-Ship setup.

"Operation Grand Bargain was set up to quietly acquire the bonds issued by China before the communists took over so we can use them to offset China's Treasury holdings. In one fell swoop we cut our federal debt and give the economy a huge boost. And in the process, we re-set the rules for dealing with communist China."

I laughed. "Wait a minute. We've done the research. Those bonds are basically worthless because of a treaty we signed with the Chinese back in 1979."

"That's what most people think, but that treaty only applied to U.S. nationals, not the U.S. government."

"Somehow I don't think the Chinese are going to see it that way."

"It doesn't matter how the Chinese see it," the senator replied. "We present it to them as a *fait accompli* and there's really nothing they can do about it. Operation Grand Bargain re-sets the rules for dealing with the Chinese. If they don't want to honor their obligations, why should we?"

Senator Scott was either a genius or an idiot, but I wasn't sure which. Rather than pursuing the merits of Operation Grand Bargain, I changed the subject. "But you still haven't explained what all this has to do with Ronald Anderson."

"Mr. Anderson figured out what we were doing," the senator answered, "and decided to buy some bonds for himself. Maybe he thought he could sell them to us for more money, or perhaps he thought when we went public with Operation Grand Bargain, the bonds would become valuable."

Edna Anderson was my client, not her late husband. But even so, I felt a duty to defend him. "Or perhaps he thought he was helping you. Maybe he was buying the bonds intending to turn them over to you."

"We considered that possibility," the senator conceded, "but our investigation suggested that's not what he intended."

"So you shot him?"

Laser Eyes, who had been standing behind Senator Scott, entered the conversation. "No, we didn't shoot him." He was downright indignant.

"I've got this, Don," the senator said over her shoulder. "We don't shoot people, Mr. O'Brian. If we did, you'd be on your way to the morgue instead of sitting here having this conversation. We probably would have fired Mr. Anderson, and might even have prosecuted him, but I assure you we didn't shoot him."

"Then who did?"

My question elicited an awkward silence. Senator Scott leaned back in her chair before looking over her shoulder first toward Helms then toward Albright as though she were seeking input. Albright broke the silence. "Might as well tell him. You've told him everything else."

Senator Scott turned back to me. "Jeremy Lin shot Mr. Anderson."

"Of course he did." It came out sounding even more sarcastic than I intended. "Right after he climbed a ten-foot electrified fence topped with razor wire, in full view of a small army of guys with guns."

The senator flashed a rueful smile. "Actually, Jeremy Lin drove right through the front gate."

"How did he manage that?"

"It was easy. He worked for us." She took a deep breath and continued. "In 1960, Mr. Lin's parents, residents of Hong Kong, visited California, where Jeremy was born, automatically making him a U.S. citizen. Seventeen years later, he attended college in Massachusetts, graduated with honors, and was recruited to work for the government. On the surface, he looked like the ideal candidate. An American citizen with a top-notch academic record who was fluent in both English and Chinese. Only recently did we learn that although his parents lived in Hong Kong, they had close ties to the Chinese Communist Party."

I finished the story for her. "And so did he." Suddenly I understood why she had referred to birthright citizenship as stupid.

"Exactly," the senator replied. "We brought Lin onboard because of his language skills. When he found out about Operation Grand Bargain, he tipped off the Chinese, who began buying as many bonds as they could to minimize the impact of our plan. We think Lin found out that Ronald Anderson had acquired some of the bonds and tried to force him to turn them over."

"And when he wouldn't, Lin killed him?" I asked. "Seems kind of drastic."

"We don't really know what happened, but we plan to find out."

A man appeared out of the darkness, stepped into the circle of light where we were gathered, and handed me a cardboard cup filled with a light brown liquid that I assumed was coffee with extra cream but without sugar. I began to lift the cup to my mouth but stopped. Did the coffee contain anything besides cream?

My hesitation made Senator Scott laugh. "Relax, Mr. O'Brian, it's just coffee. We're on the same side. We both want Mr. Anderson's killer brought to justice."

"Actually I want something more," I said before outlining my own version of a grand bargain. When I finished, Laser Eyes escorted me to an exit and opened the door. I was immediately blinded by the sunlight, my eyes having become accustomed to the gloom of the warehouse. As I stood there waiting for my eyes to adjust, I asked my escort, "What's Uncle Sam doing with a fake flying saucer?"

I didn't get an answer to that question, but I did leave Consolidated TranShip with a deal.

At least, I thought I had a deal.

41

"You won't see us, but we'll be there."

I provided Edna Anderson with a highly sanitized account of my meeting with the people running Consolidated TranShip, including their offer to buy her Chinese bonds for $127,545. "Nice round number," I had said to Senator Scott when she made the offer. According to the senator, that number was a so-called rounding error. In Fed speak, rounding error apparently means the maximum amount that can magically disappear from an account without anyone noticing.

Mrs. Anderson, thankfully, didn't ask about the odd amount of the offer. But she did have lots of other questions, many of which I couldn't answer because of the deal I had made with Senator Scott. There was, however, one question I was quick to answer. When she asked if I thought she should take the $127,545, I told her, "absolutely not," explaining that I was working on a way to get her more than that. She was delighted at the prospect of receiving more money, but reiterated her previous opposition to accepting so-called blood money. I assured her what I hoped to secure for her was best thought of a reward from the government. That wasn't exactly a lie, but neither was it really the truth.

Rick, Reynaldo, and Detective Henderson received a considerably more accurate and far more detailed account of my foray into Consolidated TranShip's facility. Their reactions varied, but all were in agreement when it came to the version of a grand bargain I had negotiated with Senator Scott. All three were opposed, but for different reasons. Henderson argued that I was involving myself in something more properly left to law enforcement, presumably the Troy Forge cops. Reynaldo was miffed because I had delivered Laser Eye's message to "stand down and let us handle this." And Rick was worried that I was putting myself in danger. "You can't trust these people," he said. "You don't know what they'll do."

But having made a deal with the senator, I was determined to hold up my end of our grand bargain. So, with Rick, Reynaldo, and Detective Henderson listening in, I called the phone number Jeremy Lin had given me. When a male voice answered on the second ring, I asked to speak with Jeremy Lin.

"I am very sorry, but Mr. Lin is unavailable," the heavily accented voice informed me. He sounded a lot like Charlie Chan, the Honolulu detective in the 1940s movies. "However, I would be most happy to assist you."

"My client has decided to accept your offer," I said, "and I'm calling to work out the details."

"That is very good," Charlie Chan said. "Please allow me to put you on hold for just a moment while I consult with my associates." Without waiting for me to respond, he put me on hold. We waited in silence for about a minute before the voice returned. "Next Thursday morning, you must be at the Troy Forge industrial park on Route 10 at nine o'clock."

Judges are the only people who get to tell me what I *must* do. So instead of explaining that I would be in court for the re-start of the Woodson case Thursday morning, I said, "That won't work for me."

My push back was met with silence. Charlie Chan apparently wasn't expecting me to object to his directive. He waited for an explanation, but I wasn't about to offer one. So we waited in silence, each attempting to force the other to speak first. I won when Charlie Chan eventually said, "I do not understand. Are you not anxious to complete this transaction?"

"On Thursday morning, I'll be in court," I replied. "Perhaps, instead of instructing me to be somewhere at a particular time, you might want to ask what time would be convenient for me."

"I am most sorry," Charlie Chan replied. "It was not my intention to offend you. I was merely relaying information given to me."

Senator Scott had told me that Jeremy Lin's people would become suspicious if I asked too many questions, but my curiosity got the better of me. "Given to you by whom? I'd like to know who I'm dealing with. And if you're so anxious to buy my client's bonds, why do we have to wait until next Thursday?"

Charlie Chan didn't seem fazed by my questions. "I am afraid the identity of the buyer must remain confidential. And we are talking about a considerable sum of money, so it will take some time to make the necessary arrangements. However, we do not wish to inconvenience you. If you will tell me what time is convenient for you next Thursday, we will accommodate you."

I calculated how long it would take to drive from the courthouse in Morristown to the western end of Troy Forge where the industrial park is located. "I can get there shortly after six o'clock."

"Then let us meet on Thursday at six thirty." Charlie Chan gave me detailed instructions on where to go and what to do when I got there. Then, without bothering to say goodbye, he ended the call.

Laser Eyes appeared at my office door a moment later. He and three of this associates had been monitoring fancy electronic equipment near Elaine's desk. "Did you trace the call?" I asked him.

"No," he said. "Tracing a phone call isn't as easy or as quick as they make it seem on television."

"So, what now?" I asked.

"You keep your appointment next Thursday."

Reynaldo spoke up. "You're not seriously planning to send him in there alone, are you?"

Laser Eyes ignored Reynaldo and directed his answer to me. "You won't be alone. You won't see us, but we'll be there."

42

"What did your late husband do for a living?"

Selecting a jury in real life, a process known as *voir dire*, isn't like it's depicted on television. In New Jersey, attorneys aren't permitted to ask tricky questions in an effort to sway the jury even before the trial has begun. In fact, attorneys don't question prospective jurors at all; the judge does. Some judges, like Judge Bloomquist, permit attorneys to suggest questions to be asked. Others, like Ice Cold Cohen, allow little or no input from the attorneys. The system usually produces a jury panel consisting of people who show no obvious bias and who have no connection to the parties or their attorneys. However, the process is far from perfect. For example, it doesn't prevent empaneling people who don't want to be there. And those people, in my experience, tend to have an ingrained bias against the plaintiff. In their view, if the plaintiff hadn't sued in the first place, there would be no need for a trial, and no reason for the juror, terribly inconvenienced in his or her mind, to spend tedious hours in a courtroom.

The jury for the re-start of the Woodson trial contained just such a person. Juror number five, a 40-something self-employed electrician, who sat with arms crossed in the back row of the jury box, didn't want to be there. He made that clear during Judge Bloomquist's questioning, maintaining that every day he spent in court instead of on the job would cost him money. The judge, explaining that jury duty is an obligation of citizenship, refused to release him. And having run out of preemptory challenges, I had no way to prevent him from being seated.

The proceedings started out much like the first attempt that ended in a mistrial. I delivered an opening statement that was very similar to the one I had used at the first trial, minus any reference to the holidays. Once again, when I said that the treatment Margaret had received from the insurance company wasn't an isolated incident, jurors seemed particularly interested, leaning forward in their seats. All except juror number five, the electrician who didn't want to be there.

Augustus Carter's opening statement was also virtually identical to the one he delivered the last time. When he got to the line about honoring the terms of a contract, juror number five nodded vigorously in agreement.

I assumed Carter had finished his opening statement when he returned to the counsel table. But instead of taking a seat, he picked up a legal pad, consulted it momentarily, and then walked to a position in front of the jury box. "Ladies and gentlemen," he continued, "we frequently underestimate the crucial role that insurance companies play not just in our individual lives, but in the economic life of our country." My adversary spent the next ten minutes giving an impassioned speech worthy of Clarence Darrow. By the time he finished, I was almost convinced the insurance industry was God's greatest gift to humanity. Juror number five looked as though he was about to jump to his feet and give Augustus Carter a standing ovation.

I was so entranced by Carter's soaring rhetoric that I almost didn't hear Judge Bloomquist tell me to call my first witness. I called Margaret Woodson to the stand and posed the customary preliminary questions before asking her to tell the jury about her dealings with Federal American. She spent more than half an hour recounting all the things FAIL Insurance had put her through, from the multiple requests for information the company already had to the examination under oath that was tantamount to an inquisition. "I kept looking around for the guillotine," she told the jury as she described her experience at the EUO. That got a laugh from a couple of the jurors.

"And all of this was in connection with your attempts to collect the death benefit from a life insurance policy your late husband purchased twenty-four years ago, is that correct?" I asked.

"Yes."

"During those twenty-four years, did you ever miss a premium payment?"

"Never."

"Were you ever late making a payment?"

"No, because we set up an automatic payment plan with the bank. The insurance company got paid not just on time, but immediately after they sent the bill."

I finished my examination on that note, hoping to leave the jury with the impression that the sacred insurance contract Carter had told them about in his opening statement was, in fact, a one-way affair, the insurance company receiving money for a quarter century but never giving Margaret anything in return.

"Mr. Carter, cross examine?" the judge asked my adversary.

Carter rose, buttoned his jacket, adjusted his tie and asked Margaret, "What did your late husband do for a living?" It was a question I hadn't expected, but probably should have.

"He was an attorney," she answered.

Carter pointed toward the table where Rick and I were sitting. "In fact, he was a partner in the same firm as Mr. O'Brian and Mr. Santorini, wasn't he?" I considered objecting on the grounds that Scott's employment was irrelevant, but decided that would make it look as though we were attempting to hide something from the jury. That turned out to be a bad decision because Carter, without waiting for Margaret to answer his question, asked another one. "And that firm specializes in suing insurance companies, doesn't it?"

I jumped to my feet. "Objection! Mr. Carter's question is..."

That was a far as I got before an obviously annoyed Judge Bloomquist banged his gavel and said, "Sustained. The jury will disregard counsel's questions, both of them. What Mr. Woodson did for a living is irrelevant."

Telling a jury to disregard something that happens in a courtroom is little more than a formality. Once a juror hears something, he or she isn't likely to disregard it. Carter's army of attorneys knew that, which is why they were all working hard to conceal a smile.

Juror number five didn't even try to conceal his.

During re-direct, Margaret testified that Scott handled primarily divorces cases, but by then the damage had been done. Carter had managed to put us on the defensive, planting the idea in jurors' minds that the insurance company was a victim rather than a predator.

43

"He would never do that."

It was a bit early for a break, but a tired looking Judge Bloomquist granted my request for a brief recess. "I think Carter is digging himself a deeper hole with the judge," Rick said as we stood outside the courtroom. "I've known Ken for years, and he doesn't go for that sort of thing."

"I'm more concerned with how that little tactic played with the jury," I replied.

"You have to admit, it's a clever strategy."

Rick was right, it was a clever strategy, although I wasn't willing to admit that out loud.

Tony Biffano, who had been sitting in the public gallery with our next witnesses, joined us. "Mrs. Comstock is up next," I told him. "Is she ready to testify?"

"Ready as she'll ever be," Tony replied.

"That doesn't sound very reassuring. We've gone over her testimony more than once. What's the problem?"

"Rehearsing in your office is one thing. Testifying in court is something else," Tony explained. "I think she's a bit nervous, but she'll be okay."

A few minutes later, back in the courtroom, Helen Comstock, a petite woman whose oversized handbag made her look even smaller than she actually was, took the witness stand and proved Tony right – at least initially. Mrs. Comstock was still grieving over the death of her husband a year earlier. I had an uneasy feeling she would be joining him in the great beyond sooner rather than later, the victim of a broken heart.

I asked Rick to conduct the direct examination, explaining that he seemed to have established a rapport with Mrs. Comstock during the trial preparation sessions at our office. My real reason, however, was to introduce Rick to trial work by giving him what I thought would be an easy task.

Rick got through the usual preliminary questions without incident. But then he asked Helen Comstock, "You're a widow, aren't you?"

Augustus Carter jumped to his feet. "Objection. Leading the witness." Realizing Rick wasn't a seasoned trial attorney, Carter no doubt objected just to rattle him. It was a ridiculous objection. Although technically a leading question, it was the kind that never draws an objection from opposing counsel.

Judge Bloomquist seemed less than happy with Carter's gamesmanship. Instead of ruling on the objection, he said to Rick, "Just ask her if she's a widow."

Rick rephrased the question and Mrs. Comstock answered, "Yes, my husband died in an auto accident last year."

"Did your husband have a life insurance policy with the defendant, Federal American International Lines Insurance?"

"Yes," she answered.

"How much was the policy's death benefit?"

"Five hundred thousand dollars."

"After your husband died, did you file a claim with the defendant?"

"Yes."

"Did you receive five hundred thousand dollars from the defendant?"

As we had instructed her to do, Mrs. Comstock looked directly at the jury as she answered. "No, I did not."

"Did you receive any money at all from the defendant?" Rick asked.

Still looking at the jury box, she answered slowly, spitting out one word at a time for emphasis. "Not even *half* that amount."

"And why is that?" Rick asked.

"The insurance company said the policy didn't pay if my husband committed suicide, but that they would give me two hundred thousand dollars if I signed a paper promising not to sue them. I think they called it a release."

Rick moved to a spot in front of the jury box and made eye contact with the jurors in the front row before asking, "Mrs. Comstock, did your husband commit suicide?"

Mrs. Comstock, who had kept her composure up to that point, broke down and started to cry. "No," she managed to get out between sobs. "He would never do that."

Judge Bloomquist handed her a box of tissues. "Do you need a minute?"

"No, I'll be fine," she replied. "I'm sorry."

"No need to apologize," Judge Bloomquist said.

I looked over to the jury box and saw that everyone, even juror number five, seemed to be moved by Mrs. Comstock's display of grief. I signaled Rick to continue.

Rick patted Mrs. Comstock's arm the same way Carolyn had patted mine that day in Georgia, and asked her in a gentle voice, "How did your husband die?"

"An auto accident. He lost control of the car and had a head on collision with a truck. The insurance company said he did it on purpose, that it was suicide. But I know it wasn't. Fred was a devout Catholic. He never would have taken his own life."

"Did anyone from the insurance company ever tell you why the company considered your husband's death a suicide?"

"Yes, that man," Mrs. Comstock replied, pointing toward the public gallery. "The man in the blue suit with the red tie."

Rick turned to see where she was pointing. "Let the record show the witness is pointing to Mr. Harry Sporn," Rick said, "the defendant's vice president in charge of a so-called Special Investigative Unit." Turning back to the witness stand, he asked, "Did Mr. Sporn tell you why the company considered your husband's death a suicide instead of an auto accident?"

Mrs. Comstock looked directly at the jury before answering. "He told me Fred wasn't wearing a seatbelt, and that was proof that he intended to commit suicide. I thought that explanation was ridiculous, but I was still in shock from Fred's death and I needed money. So I took the two hundred thousand dollars instead of fighting the company in court for who knows how long. I realize now that was a mistake."

44

"What did Fred sign?"

When Rick finished his examination of Mrs. Comstock, Judge Bloomquist decided to take an early lunch break. "I'm a bit under the weather," the judge announced. "So, when we return from lunch, Mr. Carter will conduct his cross-examination of the witness, and then we'll adjourn for the day." He banged his gavel and hurried off the bench to his chambers.

After the lunch recess, an obviously unwell Judge Bloomquist took the bench, box of tissues in hand, and the trial resumed with the cross-examination of Helen Comstock. Augustus Carter stood, adjusted his tie, buttoned his suit jacket, and approached the witness stand. But instead of asking a question, Carter addressed the judge. "If Your Honor isn't feeling well, the defense would have no objection to an adjournment."

Realizing Carter was just playing to the jury, the judge dismissed the offer with a wave of his hand. "Get on with it."

Carter acknowledged with a nod before turning his attention to Mrs. Comstock. "On behalf of Federal American, please accept my condolences on the death of your husband."

"I'd rather accept a check for the three hundred thousand

dollars your client owes me," she replied. Several jurors were amused by her reply – a good sign.

But then things starting going downhill.

"Did your late husband suffer from high blood pressure and elevated cholesterol?" Carter asked.

"Yes," she replied, confirming what she had told us when we first interviewed her. "But so do a lot of people," she added. "Besides, he was taking medication to control both conditions."

"How about diabetes?" Carter asked. "Did your husband have diabetes?"

"No, he didn't" Mrs. Comstock answered.

"Are you sure?"

"Absolutely." She was adamant, almost offended that Carter would doubt her.

Carter returned to the counsel table where one of his associates handed him a document. "Isn't it true that two months before your husband died, he gave up drinking beer?"

"Yes, that's right."

"And at that time he also stopped eating dessert?"

"Well, he was getting a little thick around the middle," Mrs. Comstock admitted, somewhat sheepishly. That elicited a smile from two jurors, who seemed to be fighting a similar battle.

Carter scanned the document his associate had just handed him before rolling it up and walking back to the witness stand. "That might well be, but isn't it true that two months before he died, your husband had an appointment with a doctor named Ronald Davidson?"

Mrs. Comstock appeared to be surprised. "Well, yes, now that you mention it, he did see Dr. Davidson about then," she said slowly, before adding, "but he had been seeing Dr. Davidson for many years."

"But at that particular appointment, didn't Dr. Davidson diagnose your husband with diabetes? And isn't that the real reason he gave up alcohol and sweets?"

"No," Mrs. Comstock insisted.

"Are you sure?"

I got to my feet and was about to object when Mrs. Comstock asked my adversary, "Are you calling me a liar?"

"No, ma'am, not at all," Carter answered. "And if you thought that, I apologize. That was not my intent. I know you've been through a lot and I don't mean to add to your pain." Most members of the jury appeared to think Carter was being sincere. I doubted that, but decided that objecting wouldn't help our case, so I sat down. "All I'm suggesting," Carter continued, "is that you might not know as much about your husband's health as you think you do."

I considered objecting, but before I could get to my feet, Carter shifted gears and asked, "Where was your husband going on the day he died?"

During our sessions in the office, we had told Mrs. Comstock that attorneys sometimes change topics suddenly to confuse a witness. Despite the warning, she seemed unprepared for the question. "I'm not sure I remember," she answered.

"Take your time," Carter said gently. "I know testifying in court can be unnerving." My dealings with Augustus Carter convinced me he was an unprincipled, win-at-any-cost attorney, but he was doing a good job of hiding his true nature from the jury.

After thinking for a moment, Mrs. Comstock came up with an answer. "He was running errands."

"Do you remember what kind of errands?" Carter asked, still using a soothing voice.

"I seem to recall he went to the grocery store and the hardware store." That was consistent with what she had told us.

Carter walked to the counsel table where one of his associates handed him a document. Once again, he scanned it, rolled it up, and returned to a position in front of the witness stand. "Did you and your late husband ever have any dealings with an establishment called Loving Memories Funeral Home?"

"Where's he going with this?" Rick whispered. "She never mentioned anything about a funeral home."

"Not sure," I answered. "But I think we need to find out." I got to my feet. "Sidebar, Your Honor?"

Judge Bloomquist motioned us to the side of the bench farthest away from the witness stand and the jury box. "Judge," I began, "this is the second time Mr. Carter has used an undisclosed document to suggest facts that are not in evidence."

"I'm not suggesting anything," Carter told the judge. "I simply asked the witness if she and her husband ever had any dealings with a particular establishment. It's a simple yes or no question."

"It's not the question that's the problem," I replied. "It's the rolled-up piece of paper he looks at before asking the question. He's suggesting to the jury that he has documentary evidence involving the witness and a funeral home, evidence that hasn't been revealed to us."

"You never asked for it," Carter interjected.

"The same is true of his questions relating to Dr. Davidson," I continued, ignoring Carter's interruption.

"Now you've piqued my curiosity," the judge said. "Let me see that document," he instructed my adversary.

"Judge, this is attorney work product. It's not subject to discovery."

Judge Bloomquist wasn't about to be dissuaded. "It might not be discoverable to opposing counsel, but I'm not opposing counsel. I'm the judge, remember? Hand it over."

Carter complied, a bit too quickly, I realized in retrospect.

A few seconds after beginning his review of the document, the judge said, "Well, this is interesting."

"Indeed it is," Carter replied. "Signed the day he died."

Judge Bloomquist handed the document to me, but before I could take it from him, Carter said, "I thought we had agreed it wasn't discoverable."

"If you intend to introduce this in evidence, as I assume you do, Mr. O'Brian has the right to see it."

When I read the document, I came up with half a dozen reasons why it shouldn't be admitted into evidence, including the contention that Carter was engaging in what the judge had previously referred to as trial by ambush. My arguments fell on deaf ears. "We're here in search of the truth," the judge told me, "and that document has probative value that outweighs any detriment to the plaintiff. You'll have an opportunity to deal with it on re-direct."

The sidebar conference concluded, Augustus Carter continued with his cross-examination of Mrs. Comstock. "Please tell the jury of any dealings you and your husband had with Loving Memories Funeral Home." The solicitous tone was now gone.

Mrs. Comstock had never told us anything about a funeral home, so we had never prepared her for Carter's question. "Well," she began, "at one point we had attended a presentation they have about pre-planning final arrangements." She seemed embarrassed. The reason for her embarrassment became obvious when she elaborated. "The seminar was at a local restaurant, and the funeral home gave everyone who attended a nice steak dinner."

"Did you ever sign a contract with the funeral home?" Carter asked.

"No."

"Did your husband?"

"No."

"Would you recognize your husband's signature if you saw it?" Carter asked.

"Yes, of course," Mrs. Comstock answered.

Carter folded the document he was holding so only the bottom of the page was visible. He showed it to Mrs. Comstock and pointed to a spot on the page. "Is that your husband's signature?"

"Yes, that's Fred's signature," she answered.

"And is the date next to your husband's signature the same day that he died?"

Mrs. Comstock was now thoroughly confused. "Yes, it is." She looked from the document to Carter. "What did Fred sign?"

He unfolded the document and handed it to Mrs. Comstock. She looked at it and gasped. "Oh, Lord."

"Please tell the jury what your husband signed just half an hour before he died," Carter instructed.

Mrs. Comstock couldn't do that. In fact, she couldn't do anything but stare at the document in her hands. So, Carter answered his own question. "Half an hour before steering his car into the path of an oncoming truck, Fred Comstock signed a contract with a funeral home to have his body cremated."

I jumped to my feet to object, but the reaction of virtually every juror told me I was too late. They had all bought into Carter's theory that Fred Comstock had committed suicide. My adversary had transformed Federal American from corporate villain shortchanging a grieving widow to a world-class humanitarian that gave her two hundred thousand dollars to which she wasn't really entitled.

45

"If the Chinese are watching me, won't they see me talking to you?"

Augustus Carter left the courtroom, followed by his entourage of associates, all looking quite pleased with the way the day's proceedings had gone. Rick and I were anything but pleased, and Margaret Woodson was in a panic. "We could actually lose this case," she told me over and over. I tried to allay her concerns by reminding her that we had three additional witnesses, including Marie Callahan, who I considered the strongest of the three. I had originally intended to call Mrs. Callahan last, but decided to have her testify first thing in the morning in an effort to overcome Mrs. Comstock's disappointing performance.

Leaving Tony Biffano to make the necessary arrangements for Mrs. Callahan to be at the courthouse in the morning, Rick and I drove back to the office. We rode in silence for most of the trip back to Troy Forge. I spent the time reviewing the instructions I had received for the meeting in the industrial park that evening. Rick must have been thinking about the Woodson case because as we turned onto Route 46, he said, "That was a sneaky, underhanded way for Carter to convince the jury of something that's probably not true." I told him he was right. I didn't, however, tell him that had I been in Carter's shoes, I probably would have done the same thing. I also declined to point out that his use of "probably" meant we might have made a mistake selecting Helen Comstock as one of our four witnesses.

Back at the office, I changed into jeans and a flannel shirt, and ate a tuna sandwich as I prepared for Marie Callahan's testimony in the morning. At quarter to six, as I was getting ready to leave for my rendezvous with some unknown Chinese bond buyer, Rick appeared at my office door. "You sure you want to go through with this?" he asked. "This could be dangerous."

"Couldn't be more dangerous than sneaking into Consolidated TranShip in a catering truck, and that worked out okay."

Rick wasn't about to give up. "I still don't think this is a good idea."

"I never said it was a good idea, but I promised Edna Anderson I'd get as much as I could for her bonds, and this seems the best way to do that. Besides, I made a deal with Senator Scott and I intend to hold up my end of our so-called grand bargain." I ended the conversation by reminding Rick that Laser Eyes assured us his people would be watching my back, even though I wouldn't see them.

Light snow had been forecast for the evening, and although the sky looked threatening, the snow had not yet begun to fall as I began the drive to the Troy Forge Industrial Park on the western edge of town. More than three times larger than the Railhead Park where the Consolidated TranShip facility is located, the Troy Forge Industrial Park has three separate entrances off of Route 10. Once inside the industrial park, drivers are confronted with a road network that looks as though it had been designed by a team of confused drunks trying to find their way home. It's easy to get lost even in broad daylight. I assumed my mysterious Chinese buyer had chosen this location to make it easy to spot anyone who might be following me.

As I entered the industrial park, I switched on a flashlight so I could read the directions I had written on a legal pad during my phone conversation with the mystery buyer's agent. At the first intersection, I turned left, followed by two rights, left at the stop sign, another right, and a final left at an intersection with four-way stop signs. I followed that road to the cul-de-sac visible from the intersection, backed my Mustang up to the guard rail at the end of the pavement and waited, a briefcase filled with old Chinese bonds on the seat next to me.

Six-thirty came and went without a sign of my supposed buyer, so I decided to get out of the car and stretch my legs. As I opened the door, the rag that filled the gap at the top of the window dropped to the ground. I got out, picked it up and tossed it on the front seat. Rick was right; I should take the car to the dealer and get the window fixed.

Standing in the dark, deep in the industrial park, away from the highway, the only sound I could hear was the hushed gurgle of the stream behind me. I scanned the street, both sides of which were lined with warehouse buildings, all the same height and all with flat roofs. Visions of Chinese snipers with night vision goggles popped into my head. I started to shiver, perhaps from the cold or perhaps because it suddenly dawned on me how dangerous this so-called transaction could become. What was to stop the Chinese from shooting me and taking the bonds, instead of paying for them? After all, Wu had pulled a gun on Carolyn when she caught him rummaging through the dresser in her apartment.

"O'Brian, don't turn around." The vaguely familiar voice came from the darkness behind me.

"Who's there?"

"Tom Albright. You're under surveillance, so don't turn around or do anything to let them know I'm here."

"How do you know I'm under surveillance?"

"Because we have them under surveillance." Visions of CIA snipers targeting Chinese snipers popped into my head.

"I don't see anyone," I said, not specifying whether I was referring to the Chinese or Albright's colleagues.

"You might not see them, but they're there," Albright replied. "On the roof of the first building on your left."

"Who? The Chinese or us?" The words had left my mouth before I realized "us" was a bit presumptuous, implying that I was part of Albright's crew. Despite our so-called grand bargain, I'm pretty certain Albright and his people thought of me as live bait rather than a member of the team.

"Chinese intelligence," Albright answered.

"Where are your guys?"

"Don't worry; they're there. You just can't see them, and neither can the Chinese."

"If the Chinese are watching me, won't they see me talking to you?"

There was a moment of hesitation before he answered. "We don't think their technology is that sophisticated."

"But you're not sure?"

"No, not a hundred percent," Albright replied, annoyance creeping into his voice. "So just listen and don't talk."

I stood in silence for a couple minutes. The snow began falling more heavily, and the temperature dropped. I stomped my feet and swung my arms in an effort to keep warm. Albright must have sensed my discomfort because he said, "Let's see if we can draw them out. Put the briefcase on the hood of your car and open it up so they can see the bonds."

I did as he instructed, thinking if the Chinese were able to see the bonds, they probably saw me talking to Albright. They might not have seen him, but they must have known he was there.

Checking my watch, I saw that it had been five minutes since I had displayed the bonds on the Mustang's hood. I brushed a light coating of snow off the yellowed parchment and waited. Another five minutes passed, then another and another. I was about to suggest to Albright that we call it a night and go home when a panel truck entered the intersection with the four-way stop signs. The truck stopped in the middle of the intersection as though the driver was deciding what to do. Instead of turning, the truck continued straight and disappeared into the night. A moment later, Albright said, "The Chinese are moving out. You can head home."

46

"I wasn't sure what
to make of that one."

With the bond-filled briefcase still on the seat beside me, I drove to my house in Mountain Springs, continuously checking my rearview mirror. I had visions of Chinese agents running me off the road and taking the bonds.

I arrived home without incident, but hit the brakes as I pulled into the circular driveway in front of the house. There was smoke coming from the chimney and an unfamiliar vehicle parked in the drive leading to a detached garage in the rear of the property. Were Chinese intelligence agents waiting for me? Was their plan all along to lure Laser Eyes and his people to the industrial park while they waited for me in my own home?

As I sat in the Mustang deciding what to do, the front door of the house opened and a male figure appeared on the porch. In the dim lighting I couldn't tell who it was, but he was too tall to be Jeremy Lin. The figure motioned for me to come inside before retreating into the house and closing the door.

Reasoning that Chinese intelligence agents would be more likely to lie in wait in a darkened room than light a fire in the fireplace, I went inside.

"I started a fire to take the chill off," a voice said from the living room as I closed the front door and crossed the entry hall. "Hope you don't mind." The words were the same as those Reynaldo Renoir had used the night I returned from Georgia in late October, but it wasn't Reynaldo's voice.

Entering the living room, I found Laser Eyes sitting in a chair by the fireplace.

"What are you doing here?" I asked.

"I'm here in case our Chinese friends show up in the middle of the night for the bonds they didn't buy earlier this evening."

"Do you think they'd do that?"

"Don't know," my uninvited visitor answered, "but I'll stay here tonight, just in case."

I walked to the bar in the corner of the room and poured myself a glass of Jameson. "Join me?" I asked my personal bodyguard for the night.

"I'd love to," Laser Eyes said, "but I'm on duty. If you get visitors in the middle of the night, you're going to want me wide eyed and bushy tailed."

I couldn't help myself; I laughed.

"Did I say something funny?"

"Senator Scott can get away with using 'wide eyed and bushy tailed,' but it just doesn't sound right coming from a gun-toting CIA agent, or whatever it is you actually are."

"Hang out with people long enough and you start picking up their speech," he replied, neither confirming nor denying his CIA connection.

I sat down in the other chair by the fireplace and sipped my glass of Irish whiskey. "So tell me, did I screw things up at the industrial park?"

Laser Eyes seemed surprised by my question. "Why would you think that?"

I told him about the possibility that the Chinese could see me speaking to Albright. "If that's the case, it's on Albright, not you. Tom wasn't supposed to contact you, just be ready in case you ran into trouble."

We spent the next half hour in conversation that turned out to be both interesting and cordial. At one point, I asked his opinion of Senator Scott and her so-called grand bargain. "I have no idea whether or not it will work," he replied, "but I give her a lot of credit for trying. She's one of the few people in Washington who believes in America first, last and always. Too many of the D.C. crowd like to think of themselves as citizens of the world."

"Yeah, it's pretty clear she's not a big fan of the Chinese," I said in response to his appraisal of the senator.

"She has no beef with Chinese people in general," Helms replied, "but she's absolutely convinced the Chinese Communist Party is a menace to the free world."

"Are you?"

"If it isn't now, it will be at some point in the near future. At the rate we're going, it's just a matter of time before the Chinese corner the market for drugs, electronics, and a bunch of other things. Then the communists will have us over a barrel." He got up and tossed another log on the fire. "I have to assume you agree, otherwise you wouldn't be on board with what we're doing." What I was on board with was getting Edna Anderson as much as possible for her bonds, but I didn't say that.

Near the end of our conversation I said, "I gather that you and Reynaldo Renoir are buddies."

"Colleagues, not buddies," he replied. "In our business, you don't make friends. Just colleagues." I thought I detected a note of sadness in his voice.

"Back in the warehouse you referred to him as a boy scout. Why's that?"

Helms thought for a moment before replying. "Let's just say that Reynaldo has difficulty accepting the fact that sometimes good people have to do bad things for the greater good." I started to ask what he meant by that, but he cut me off. "Just leave it at that."

I finished my glass of Jameson and debated whether or not to have another. Since I had court in the morning, and wanted to review my notes for Marie Callahan's testimony before going to sleep, I passed on the Jameson and announced that I was going to turn in. "One question before I head upstairs. Is Donald Helms your real name or is that a CIA alias?"

He laughed. "You've been watching too many spy movies. Yes, it's my real name, but people call me Don, not Donald."

"In that case, good night, Don, and thanks. Help yourself to anything you find in the kitchen."

When I came downstairs the following morning, Helms was nowhere to be found, but he did leave me a note on a chair by the front door. The note contained three neatly numbered items. The first advised me that an agent named Fischer was sitting in a car in front of the house to keep an eye on things. That was comforting. The second told me to hurry or I'd be late for court. That was not only true, but proof that gun-toting CIA agents can have a sense of humor. The third was a message that Helms asked me to pass on to Reynaldo.

I wasn't sure what to make of that one.

47

"That's just wrong."

When I arrived at Judge Bloomquist's courtroom, Rick and Elaine were already there, speaking with two of the three witnesses scheduled to testify that day.

"Anybody seen Tony and Marie Callahan?" I asked as I approached the group.

"He's probably in the Nook giving her the Tony talk," Elaine said, referring to the little speech Tony Biffano gives to nervous witnesses to calm them down before they testify.

The Nook is a term local attorneys use for a section of corridor that begins just past the entrance to Judge Bloomquist's courtroom and leads to a dead end. Nobody knows why it exists. The leading theory is that this twenty-foot section of corridor was used to access a storage room that was eliminated when the building was renovated. Regardless of how it came to be, the Nook is a quiet alcove to hold a private conversation in a busy and otherwise noisy building.

Elaine left to find Tony and our first witness for the day's proceedings while Rick and I gave last minute instructions to Charles Farmer and Sofia Hernandez, who would testify after

Mrs. Callahan. I had just finished answering a question for Mr. Farmer when Augustus Carter and his small army of insurance company attorneys entered the courtroom. They were followed by Harry Sporn and half a dozen men in suits, each carrying a briefcase. It was like a small parade, no doubt intended to intimidate my witnesses.

Several members of Carter's team seemed especially pleased with themselves. "They're too happy by half," Rick whispered. "What do they know that we don't?"

Before I had time to respond to Rick's question, the jurors filed into the jury box, and Judge Bloomquist took the bench. Yesterday, the judge looked a mite peaked, as my grandmother would have said, but today he was clearly ill, most likely suffering from either a severe cold or the flu. "Call your first witness, Mr. O'Brian," the judge said, skipping the usual preliminaries.

"I believe she's in the hall, Your Honor. My assistant went to get her." For some reason, several of Augustus Carter's assistants found that amusing.

Judge Bloomquist blew his nose. This was followed by a coughing fit. When the coughing stopped, the judge said, "Times a wasting, Mr. O'Brian. Call a different witness."

Not wanting to irritate the judge, I called Charles Farmer to the witness stand. Small and wiry, with oversized glasses, Mr. Farmer was a slightly healthier looking version of Thompson, the funeral home technician who was now in Reynaldo Renoir's protective custody. An accountant by training, as well as disposition, Farmer was precise and well organized. At our first meeting he came prepared with every letter he had received from Federal American, as well as copies of his letters to the insurer, all neatly arranged in chronological order in an expanding file folder.

After the usual preliminary questions, I asked if he had ever had any dealings with the defendant.

"Yes," he answered, "my wife, Anna, and I had an accidental death policy that was supposed to pay fifty thousand dollars if either one of us died in an accident."

"Is your wife deceased?"

"Anna died about nine months ago. She had gone to the grocery store, and on her way home she was involved in an auto accident. She died in the ambulance on the way to the hospital."

"Did you file a claim with the defendant?"

"I did, about a month after Anna's death."

"Did the company send you a check for fifty thousand dollars in response to that letter?"

Mr. Farmer laughed. "No, they sent me a letter telling me they needed a copy of Anna's birth certificate. I assumed that was a mistake and they meant they needed a copy of the death certificate, which I had already sent them. So, I called and talked with a woman in the claims department who told me that they needed her birth certificate to process the claim. I pointed out that my wife had obviously been born, otherwise she couldn't have died, but the woman insisted they needed the birth certificate."

"Did she tell you why?"

"Company policy."

"Did you send the defendant a copy of your wife's birth certificate?" I asked.

"It took me over a week to get a copy," Farmer answered, explaining that his wife had been born out of state. "But as soon as I had it, I sent it to the insurance company by certified mail."

"And then they sent you a check?" I asked, knowing full well that they hadn't.

"Oh, no," Mr. Farmer said. "After two weeks went by, I called the company. The woman I spoke to the first time wasn't available, but another person, a gentleman this time, told me that the company needed a copy of Anna's birth certificate. I told him I had mailed that two weeks earlier, but he claimed they didn't have it."

"What did you do then?" I asked.

"Fortunately, I had gotten two copies of Anna's birth certificate, just in case. So, I drove to the insurance company's office in Newark and gave them the second copy." At that point my milquetoast witness became downright pugnacious. "And I made them give me a receipt to prove I had delivered it. At that point it became clear to me that I couldn't trust these people."

Farmer spent the next twenty minutes detailing all the letters he received from Federal American in the following months, each demanding more information or claiming not to have something he had already sent them. Each letter was entered into evidence and handed to the jury to inspect. Jurors initially seemed to find the situation humorous, understandable in view of some of the oddball things the insurance company requested. But by the time we got to the fifteenth letter, no one in the jury box was amused, not even juror number five, the self-employed electrician who didn't want to be there. In fact, several jurors were casting hostile glances at the row of well-dressed insurance executives seated behind Augustus Carter and his associates.

"So, after you responded to all of these letters, did the insurance company finally send you a check for fifty thousand dollars?" I asked.

"No, they sent me one more letter," Mr. Farmer said. "Nine months after Anna died, and after busting my chops asking for all that information, I got a letter from the company's Special Investigative Unit informing me that my claim was denied." Every juror leaned forward, anxious to hear the reason for the company's denial. "Federal American told me that the driver of the other vehicle, in an act of road rage, deliberately caused the accident. And since Anna's death wasn't accidental, and we had an accidental death policy, the company didn't owe me anything."

"Did they tell you how they came to that conclusion?" I asked the now obviously agitated witness.

"No, never," he answered. "I asked, but I never got an explanation."

There was murmuring from the jury box as well as the public gallery. I'm reasonably certain I heard one of the jurors, a middle-aged woman in the front row, tell the man next to her, "That's just wrong."

I waited a moment for things to settle down. "One last question, Mr. Farmer. Did you ever receive any money at all from the defendant?"

"After I got the letter denying the claim, I went to see an attorney. Well, two different attorneys, actually. Each one wanted a retainer of, I think it was five thousand dollars. I didn't have the money, so when the insurance company sent a final letter offering to pay me twenty-five thousand dollars to settle my claim, I accepted." He thought for a moment before adding, "I wish I hadn't done that."

48

"I believe it's called the reasonable expectation rule."

Judge Bloomquist, who seemed to be getting steadily sicker, called for a recess after Mr. Farmer testified. Carter and his entourage filed out of the courtroom with Harry Sporn and his well-dressed associates close behind. Rick and I remained at the counsel table, and Elaine joined us. "I can't find Tony or Marie Callahan anywhere in the courthouse," she reported. "I looked everywhere."

I went out to the Nook and tried to reach Tony on my cell phone, but ended up leaving a message when he didn't answer.

"This is strange," I said to Rick when I returned to the counsel table. "Something must be wrong. It's not like Tony to do a disappearing act." Elaine left the courtroom with instructions to continue calling Tony until she reached him. Biff knows how to take care of himself, so there was little reason to worry about his safety. But given all that had happened, I worried anyway.

The judge returned to the bench a few minutes later, looking no better than he had at the start of the recess, and the trial continued with Augustus Carter's cross-examination of Mr. Farmer.

Carter began with the soothing, solicitous tone he had used when speaking to Mrs. Comstock, assuring the witness that everyone at Federal American was sorry about the tragic, untimely death of his wife. Charles Farmer didn't respond verbally, but met Carter's comment with an icy stare. Two of the jurors exchanged glances, smiled, and shook their head. Carter's mendacity was obvious.

Carter abruptly shifted from consoling to interrogating. "Did you read the insurance contract when you purchased it?"

"Yes," Mr. Farmer answered.

"So you knew it only covered death caused by an accident, is that correct?"

I had prepared Mr. Farmer for that question, and he responded just as I had instructed him to. "I knew it covered death caused by what the average person would think of as an accident. In my wife's case, a collision with another car." His answer caused several of the jurors to nod in agreement. In addition to remembering my instructions, Farmer remembered my explanation of the legal concept behind his answer. "I believe it's called the reasonable expectation rule. Words in an insurance policy are interpreted to mean what the average person reasonably expects them to mean. And the average person ..."

That was as far as the witness got before Carter cut him off. "I thought you were an accountant, Mr. Farmer. But you obviously must have a law degree as well since you seem to know so much about the law." My adversary's condescending attitude didn't go over well with the jury. Even juror number five appeared annoyed at Carter's attempt to belittle Mr. Farmer.

I hadn't prepared Farmer for that question, he handled it deftly. "No, I'm not an attorney," he told Carter, "but Mr. O'Brian explained the law to me, which is why I can't understand how your client gets away with cheating its policyholders by not paying perfectly valid claims."

Augustus Carter was livid. "I move to strike the witness' unsolicited commentary from the record," he told the judge.

I decided to fan the flames. "All Mr. Farmer did was answer counsel's question. If Mr. Carter doesn't want an honest answer to a question, he shouldn't ask the question."

The judge waived me back to my seat before telling Mr. Farmer, "Just answer the question that's asked; don't editorialize." Then he turned his attention to Carter. "Motion denied. Ask another question."

Carter was clearly unhappy, but he did what the judge instructed him to do, in the process, doing a little editorializing of his own. "According to your testimony, Federal American gave you twenty-five thousand dollars, even though the company didn't owe you anything. Who did ..."

I interrupted before my adversary could continue. "That wasn't Mr. Farmer's testimony. He never said that the defendant didn't owe him anything. What he said was ..."

It was Carter's turn to interrupt me. "I'll rephrase the question."

"Good idea," Judge Bloomquist said. "And this time make it an actual question."

"Who at Federal American did you deal with after you received the letter denying your claim?"

"That man," the witness said, pointing toward Harry Sporn who was sitting directly behind the five attorneys accompanying Augustus Carter that day. "Harry Sporn, the man who signed the letter from the Special Investigative Unit."

"Did you know that prior to joining Federal American, Mr. Sporn was a prosecutor in Hudson County?" Carter asked.

Farmer answered with a question of his own. "How would I know that?"

"Did you have any contact with Mr. Sporn prior to the discussions that led to the twenty-five-thousand-dollar payment you received from Federal American?"

"No, up until then, I never laid eyes on the man." Farmer looked to where Sporn was sitting before adding, "And I hope I never see him again."

"Who is Frances Wakefield?" Carter asked next.

Mr. Farmer hesitated, apparently as surprised by the question as I was. "My late wife's sister," he answered hesitantly.

Carter walked to the defendant's counsel table where one of his associates handed him a document.

"Where's Carter going with this?" Rick whispered.

"No idea," I replied. "But I'm not going to let him continue playing the mysterious document game."

I stood up to object, but before I could say anything, Carter handed the document back to his associate and returned to the witness stand. "Is it true that Ms. Wakefield was prosecuted for shoplifting in Hudson County in September of 1982?"

It suddenly became clear why Carter had wanted the jury to know that Sporn had been a prosecutor in Hudson County before joining Federal American. I started to stand up, but Farmer answered the question before I could object. "I believe that's correct," he said, adding, "but I'm not sure of the date. It was a long time ago."

Carter plunged ahead. "You were very fond of Ms. Wakefield, your sister-in-law, weren't you?"

"What are you implying?" the witness asked.

"I'm not implying anything. I'm asking a question."

Perhaps sensing that my adversary was setting a trap, Farmer's answer was carefully worded. "My sister-in-law and I were on good terms."

"How about Mr. Sporn? Were you on good terms with him before he authorized Federal American to give you twenty-five thousand dollars?"

The question unleashed months of pent up anger and frustration. "Your client didn't *give* me twenty-five thousand dollars. Those bastards *took* twenty-five thousand dollars. And before he helped screw me out of that money, I had never met Harry Sporn."

Carter turned back to the defendant's counsel table, a smirk on his face disarmingly similar to Harry Sporn's predatory smile. In response to a slight nod, one of his minions unfolded an easel and positioned it so whatever was to be displayed on it would be visible to the judge, jurors, and the witness. Another assistant, an extremely cute young lady with blond hair, retrieved a poster-sized photo that had been leaning against the railing behind the counsel table. As she handed it to Carter, I got a good look at the photo and realized I couldn't allow the jury to see it.

"Objection," I said, getting to my feet. "Sidebar, judge?"

Judge Bloomquist motioned us to the far side of the bench where the jury wouldn't be able to overhear our conversation. "The jury can't be allowed to see that," I began, nodding toward the poster-sized photo Augustus Carter was holding. "It's prejudicial and immaterial."

"Let me see it," the judge told Carter, who complied by holding the photo so the three of us could see it, but the jury couldn't. It was a grainy black and white shot of Charles Farmer, Harry Sporn, and a woman who I assumed was Frances Wakefield, Farmer's sister-in-law. They were standing in front of what looked like the Hudson County Courthouse. An obviously outraged Farmer was literally no more than a few inches from Sporn's face, his right arm raised as though he intended to pummel Sporn, who I later discovered had been assigned to prosecute Frances Wakefield.

We spent several minutes arguing whether or not the jury should be allowed to see the photo, the argument growing progressively louder and more heated. Judge Bloomquist eventually decided that the jury could see the photo, pointing out that Mr. Farmer would have an opportunity to explain it on re-direct.

The jury's reaction to the photo was mixed. A few seemed to find Farmer's actions offensive. Other seemed to shrug it off. On re-direct Mr. Farmer managed to get in a parting shot at the head of FAIL's Special Investigative Unit, telling jurors, "Mr. Sporn doesn't seem to believe in win/win situations. For him to win, he has to make the other person lose."

49

"What the heck
are you doing in Florida?"

When I finished my re-direct examination of Charles Farmer, Judge Bloomquist recessed for lunch. I used the time to run a few errands before grabbing a quick bite to eat at the coffee shop across from the courthouse.

Rick was in the Nook talking on his cell phone when I got back to the courthouse. "Florida? What the heck are you doing in Florida?" he was saying. When he saw me, he told the person on the other end of the line, "Hold on. Brendan's here." He handed the phone to me.

Tony Biffano's familiar voice came on the line, and I listened as he recounted a story that sounded like something dreamed up by a Hollywood script writer. When he finished, I told him, "Whatever happens, I need you in court Monday morning, with or without."

"I can't believe what Tony told me about Marie Callahan," I said to Rick after I ended the call. "Monday is going to be a three-ring circus."

"We have a more immediate problem," he replied, motioning for me to follow him as he left the Nook.

We walked to one of the attorney conference rooms on the other side of the courthouse where Elaine was carrying on an animated conversation in Spanish with Sofia Hernandez, our next witness. I only know three Spanish words – taco, siesta, and sombrero – so I had no idea what was being said. Despite my admittedly limited linguistic abilities, I could tell that Mrs. Hernandez was upset.

"What's going on?" I asked Elaine.

"Two immigration agents showed up at her apartment this morning," Elaine answered. "And she thinks she saw them again in the hallway outside Judge Bloomquist's courtroom." It suddenly became clear why we were in a conference room on the other side of the building, as far away from the judge's courtroom as possible.

It was somewhat less clear why immigration agents would be a problem for Mrs. Hernandez. Like all our witnesses, we had checked into her background to ensure there was nothing that would come out at trial and undermine her testimony. Of course, we hadn't known about Charles Farmer's altercation with Harry Sporn, so perhaps there was room for improvement in how we vetted our witnesses.

"Are you telling me we have an immigration issue?" My question wasn't directed to anyone in particular, allowing either Elaine or Mrs. Hernandez to respond. Each looked at the other before Mrs. Hernandez answered.

"I don't want trouble," she said. "I promise that I testify, but I cannot." She got up, gathered her coat and purse, and headed for the door, stopping long enough to say, "I am very sorry."

I started to follow her, but Rick grabbed my arm. "Let her go." He was right, of course. In her agitated state, Sofia Hernandez wouldn't be a very effective witness. And Augustus Carter would destroy her on cross-examination.

The loss of Mrs. Hernandez as a witness would hurt us. In addition to being a way to connect with our two Hispanic jurors, she had a compelling story to tell. After her husband was killed in a botched robbery attempt, she filed a claim with FAIL Insurance for the hundred-thousand-dollar death benefit under an insurance policy the couple had bought two years earlier. After months of delay, the insurance company denied her claim on the ground that an autopsy on her husband's body revealed he had hepatitis, a pre-existing condition that he had failed to disclose when applying for the policy. Mrs. Hernandez told us repeatedly that neither she nor her late husband knew he had hepatitis. In dire need of money, she accepted a thirty-five-thousand-dollar settlement from FAIL instead of the policy's hundred-thousand-dollar death benefit.

"What now?" Rick asked.

"Now we ask the judge for a continuance until Monday."

An obviously ill Judge Bloomquist was more than happy to grant my request.

50

"This time we meet somewhere more convenient."

"Do you really think Carter sicced INS on Mrs. Hernandez?" Rick asked as he, Elaine and I walked to my car parked in the lot behind Macy's. "Even for him, that seems a bit extreme."

"After what we just learned about Marie Callahan, I don't think there's any limit to what Parker, Cole, Landy & Long will do to win a case."

The sky that had been blue when we arrived at the courthouse that morning was now gray. The temperature had dropped and the wind had picked up, making even the short walk to the parking lot uncomfortable.

Elaine continued to Macy's while Rick and I hurried to my car to get out of the cold. I had just started the Mustang when my cell phone rang. There are only three people who have that number. Rick was sitting next to me, so it wasn't him. I could see Elaine as she walked to the back entrance to Macy's, and she wasn't calling me. So I knew the caller must be Tony Biffano, hopefully calling with an update about Marie Callahan.

"Biff, what's up?" I said into the phone.

"Good afternoon, Mr. O'Brian. I'm afraid this isn't Biff, whomever that might be." I recognized the voice just before the caller identified himself. "This is Jeremy Lin. We spoke previously about the bonds your client wishes to sell."

Instead of asking Lin how he had gotten my cell phone number, I said, "You never showed up at the industrial park last night. What happened?"

"The buyer I represent is very security conscious," Lin replied. "You were seen talking to someone, but there was no one visible. That made my buyer's people nervous." Albright had obviously under-estimated Chinese surveillance equipment.

"Your buyer's people are very observant, but not as observant as they should be. Had they looked more carefully, they would have seen my car window was open a few inches, and I was talking to my partner, Rick Santorini, who was sitting in the car."

Lin began talking to someone in what I assume was Chinese. The conversation ended, and Lin went from suspicious to contrite, or at least that's what he wanted me to think. "I am very sorry for the misunderstanding, Mr. O'Brian. My buyer is still interested in purchasing Mrs. Anderson's bonds, and would like me to set up an appointment."

"Fine," I said. "But I'm not freezing my ass off sitting in a car in an industrial park after dark. This time we meet somewhere more convenient, and at a reasonable hour."

"What do you propose?" Lin asked. He was still acting conciliatory. I took that to mean that his mysterious buyer really wanted those bonds.

"Meet me tomorrow at noon at The New Amsterdam Inn on Route 10. It's at the western end of Troy Forge. Do you know the place?"

"Yes, I'm familiar with it," Lin replied, "but I'm not sure that's a good place to transact business."

"No, The New Amsterdam Inn is perfect," I insisted. "We'll just be two businessmen meeting for lunch. I'll have the bonds in a briefcase. You bring an envelope with the check. After lunch, you walk out with the briefcase and leave the envelope with me. Heck, I'll even spring for lunch."

There was another conversation in Chinese, after which Jeremy Lin said, "Very well, I will meet you at noon tomorrow." Then he hung up without saying goodbye.

I called Don Helms and told him what I had arranged.

Then I called Reynaldo and gave him the same information. I concluded that call by reading from the note Helms had left at my house the previous night. "Tell Reynaldo we know Tom Albright is one of his guys."

51

"Probably happened while you were examining the dead fly in the candle."

I arrived at The New Amsterdam Inn just before noon and was shown to a quiet corner table, the same one Margaret Woodson and I had occupied in September when I promised she would soon be getting a check from FAIL Insurance. In fact, it's the table I always ask for when I come to the restaurant. Sitting at "my" table gives me home court advantage in my dealings with whomever is dining with me. It also provides an unobstructed view of the entire room.

With the bond-filled briefcase on the floor by my left foot, I scanned the room to see if I could identify the agents Don Helms assured me would be there. He had told me I wouldn't be able to spot his people, but I was determined to prove him wrong. I quickly ruled out the elderly couple directly across from me, reasoning that the CIA, or whatever agency Helms worked for, would want agents capable of outrunning their Chinese counterparts. On the other hand, the walker near their table could simply be a prop, and the couple might be in disguise.

The one Reynaldo wore that day at the diner across from my office was pretty darned convincing.

The thirty-something couple at a nearby table also didn't seem like secret agent material. Although they looked perfectly capable of chasing bad guys, they were sure to be slowed down by the two little kids with them. The elderly couple's walker might be a prop, but I was pretty certain the children weren't.

The most likely person to be an agent was the middle-aged man sitting alone at the corner table on the opposite side of the room. His mustache reminded me of Boris Badanov, the cartoon character I remembered from my youth. Boris had been finishing dessert when I entered the restaurant, meaning he was now fully nourished and ready to jump into action. A real-world version of the cartoon Natasha, complete with tight-fitting dress, entered the room a moment later. Boris jumped into action, but catching Chinese spies wasn't the sort of action he had in mind. He tossed his napkin on the table, stood up, wrapped his arm around Natasha's tiny waist and guided her out of the room. Based on the body language, I surmised they were heading to the no-tell motel a mile away.

I was so intent on playing spot the spy that I didn't see the man wearing an ill-fitting red vest appear at my table until I heard the sound of water being poured into my glass. I thanked him, and he moved on to nearby tables, repeating the process at each one.

I continued surveying the other diners in the room, and eventually came to the unsettling conclusion that none of them were likely to be working for the CIA or any other government alphabet agency. Either Helms had been less than honest or he had another way to keep an eye on things. I looked for surveillance cameras, but didn't see any. I examined the candle in the middle of the table, thinking it might contain a miniature camera or a recording device. I discovered a dead fly, but no electronics of any kind. The lamp hanging over the table also appeared to be just a lamp. Next I scrutinized the small flower-filled vase next to the candle. But when I caught a waiter giving me the evil eye, I put the flowers back in the vase and decided I'd just have to take Helms at his word.

Checking my watch, I was surprised to see that my detailed examination of the dining room and its patrons had taken twenty minutes. I had promised Jeremy Lin that I would buy lunch, but neglected to mention that my promise was only good for fifteen minutes. And since he was late and I was hungry, I decided it was time to order a tuna on rye. But before I could get the waiter's attention, Reynaldo appeared at the dining room's arched entryway and motioned for me.

After retrieving the briefcase by my foot, I followed Reynaldo outside. Helms, Albright, and about a dozen other sunglass-wearing, gun-toting law enforcement types were gathered in the parking lot. Some were standing near a sedan with heavily tinted windows and a metal barrier separating the back seat from the one in front. There was someone in the back seat, but because of the tinted windows I couldn't tell who it was.

The remaining agents were standing by the open tailgate of a Buick Roadmaster station wagon examining the contents of a briefcase that matched the one I carried. When I got closer, I saw that the briefcase contained Chinese bonds like the ones I was hoping to sell to Jeremy Lin for a lot more money than they were actually worth.

"Put your briefcase up there next to its twin and let's see if I was right," Helms said, pointing to the station wagon.

I did as he asked, and one of the agents, a guy Helms referred to as Agent Robin, opened the briefcase to reveal stacks of neatly bound hundred-dollar bills.

"I win," Helms said to Reynaldo, who responded by forking over twenty bucks.

"Wasn't expecting that," Reynaldo said. "I thought they'd leave a briefcase filled with newspaper just to piss him off."

"Yeah, but from their point of view, this is better," Helms replied. "This way they can piss off both O'Brian and Anderson's widow at the same time."

I looked from Helms to Reynaldo. "One of you want to explain what's going on here?"

"They switched briefcases when you weren't looking," Helms replied.

"How could they have done that?" I protested. "That briefcase was on the floor next to my foot the whole time."

"Probably happened while you were examining the dead fly in the candle," Helms said. His tone of voice suggested he wasn't particularly impressed by my secret agent skills. He confirmed his displeasure by not answering my question.

When I realized he wasn't going to explain how the switch occurred, I asked, "Why leave all that money? Why not just take the bonds and leave nothing?"

"Payback for getting in their way," Helms answered. "Plus, it helps further their goal of undermining our currency and our economy."

"How, exactly, does leaving me a briefcase filled with hundred-dollar bills do that?"

"Go, ahead, you tell him," Helms said to Reynaldo. "Secret Service is part of the Treasury Department, so it's more ironic coming from you."

"Shortly after depositing that money in your trust account and writing a check to Mrs. Anderson, the Secret Service would show up at your office and either haul you in for questioning or maybe even arrest you on the spot," Reynaldo said.

"Depositing money in a bank, even a large sum like this, isn't a crime" I said, pointing to the briefcase filled with cash.

"It is when the money is counterfeit," Reynaldo replied.

52

"Carter himself seemed surprised."

"I'm still unclear why the Chinese left you a briefcase filled with counterfeit money instead of just taking the bonds and leaving nothing," Rick said as he, Margaret Woodson, and I sat in Judge Bloomquist's empty courtroom Monday morning.

"I asked the same question," I replied. "According to Helms and Reynaldo, the Chinese figured I'd do one of two things. I'd either deposit the cash in our trust account and write a check to Mrs. Anderson or I'd split the cash with her. If I wrote her a check, it would bounce once the bank realized the money was counterfeit. She files an ethics complaint and I'm in hot water with the bar association as well as the Feds, and we have one pissed off client to boot. If I split the cash, as soon as either of us spends it or deposits it, the Feds find out and the Secret Service investigates. Either way, Jeremy Lin and his accomplices get the perverse satisfaction of knowing they caused us grief."

"Pretty diabolical," Rick said. "Did Helms tell you how they managed to get the briefcase without you seeing it happen?"

Helms never told me that, but I suspected it happened when one of the kids at a nearby table spilled his milk, causing a minor disturbance that diverted everyone's attention. I was about to share my theory with Rick when our conversation was terminated by the arrival of Augustus Carter, Harry Sporn, and a small army of insurance company executives and attorneys.

Tony Biffano entered a moment later, signaled "no" with a nod of his head. He had just taken a seat in the first row of the public gallery when Judge Bloomquist took the bench, a box of tissues in hand. The court officer headed for the door by the jury box to summon the jurors but froze in his tracks when he heard me tell the judge, "Your Honor, before we seat the jury, there's a serious matter of witness tampering that I need to bring to the court's attention."

Out of the corner of my eye, I saw two members of Augustus Carter's legal team exchange glances. Interestingly, Carter himself seemed surprised.

"Witness tampering is a serious allegation," the judge said. "I hope you have some solid evidence to back that up."

"Mr. Biffano, my investigator, is in the courtroom and is prepared to provide testimony that I'm quite certain Your Honor is going to want to hear."

"Very well, let's hear it," the judge instructed.

Tony took the witness stand and testified about his recent trip to Florida. "When I went to the home of Marie Callahan, who was scheduled to testify for the plaintiff, she and her children weren't home. However, her mother, who moved in after the death of Mrs. Callahan's husband, was there. She told me...."

That was as far as Tony got before Augustus Carter objected. "Hearsay, Your Honor. If Mrs. Callahan's mother has relevant information about this case, she should be the one testifying, not Mr. Biffano."

"There's no jury, so I don't think we need to worry about hearsay," a very tired looking Judge Bloomquist said. "Objection overruled."

Tony continued with his testimony. "Mrs. Callahan's mother told me that Mrs. Callahan had received a letter informing her that she had won an all-expense-paid trip to Disney World for herself and her children. She didn't remember entering any contest, so she called the phone number in the letter and was told she had been randomly selected. The person she spoke with assured her the contest was legitimate. Later that day, a messenger arrived at her home with airplane tickets and other documents."

"Hearsay upon hearsay," Augustus Carter said, once again getting to his feet. "Now we have testimony from some unnamed person in a phone conversation with Mrs. Callahan as told to Mr. Biffano by Mrs. Callahan's mother."

"Yes, technically, it probably is," the judge said, "but again, there's no jury." The judge blew his nose before turning his attention to me. "Continue, but hurry up and get to the punch line."

I nodded for Tony to continue. "I flew to Florida and went to the Disney security office to see if there was some way they could track her down in the park. Unfortunately, there are so many people at Disney World that finding a particular person is darn near impossible."

"So, what did you do then?" I asked.

"I went to the hotel where they were supposed to be staying, thinking I'd see her when she returned at the end of the day."

"Did you?" I asked.

"No. As it turns out, she had never been at the hotel mentioned in the prize notification letter. When she and the children arrived in Florida, the outfit that arranged her travel plans took them to a different hotel, telling Mrs. Callahan that she was getting upgraded accommodations."

"How did you find out about the hotel change?"

"Mrs. Callahan's mother told me when I called to see if she had heard from her daughter."

"More hearsay," Carter muttered. It was loud enough for Judge Bloomquist to hear, but the judge ignored the comment.

"Did you ever manage to locate Mrs. Callahan?" I asked Tony.

"No," he answered.

Carter took the bait. "Your Honor," he bellowed, "all this proves is that Mr. O'Brian's witness went on vacation instead of coming here to testify. It doesn't even begin to support counsel's unfounded and unprofessional accusation of witness tampering."

"Oh, but it does," I assured the judge. "A couple more questions and everything will become clear."

"Get on with it," Judge Bloomquist instructed.

"Can you tell us the name of the company that gave Mrs. Callahan the Disney trip?" I asked Tony.

"No," he answered.

"Why not?"

"Because the letter Mrs. Callahan received came from the company's representative, not directly from the company."

"Do you have that letter with you?"

"I do," Tony answered, withdrawing a document from his pocket and holding it up for everyone to see.

"What is the name of the company's representative."

Tony unfolded the letter he was holding, turned in the witness stand so he could look directly at Judge Bloomquist, and held the letter up so the judge could see it. "The law firm of Parker, Cole, Landy and Long – Mr. Carter's firm."

53

"You'll do more than just look into it."

"I think I have the flu or maybe the world's worst cold," Judge Bloomquist said as we entered his chambers. "So keep your distance. You don't want to get what I've got."

Instead of sitting across from the judge at his desk, Rick, Augustus Carter, and I remained standing at the back of the room.

The judge took a sip of tea and blew his nose before continuing. "This is either the tallest tall tale I've heard in all my years on the bench or it's the most brazen stunt ever attempted in my court."

I spoke up before Carter had a chance to respond. "I can assure you, judge, that every word of Mr. Biffano's testimony is true. When Mrs. Callahan returns from Florida, I'm sure she'll corroborate his testimony and provide details."

"What can you tell me about this letter, Mr. Carter?" Judge Bloomquist asked, pushing the letter across his desk toward us.

Carter picked the letter up and started to read it. Without waiting for him to finish, the judge asked, "That is your firm's letterhead, isn't it, Mr. Carter?"

I expected my adversary to tell the judge the letter was a forgery that I had created or to suggest that the stationery had been stolen. Instead, he told the judge, "It would appear to be," before quickly adding, "but this is the first time I've seen this letter. I didn't send it or authorize anyone else to send it. In fact, to the best of my knowledge, Gordon Duckworth, the person who signed the letter, doesn't work at Parker Cole. And the phone number the letter tells Mrs. Callahan to call isn't one of our numbers."

"No," the judge agreed. "It's probably a cell phone owned by the person calling himself Gordon Duckworth."

"I can assure you that I had nothing to do with this," Carter told the judge. "But you have my word that I'll look into this and take appropriate action when I find out who sent the letter."

"You'll do more than look into it," the judge replied. "You'll find out who sent the letter and report back to me. You've got exactly two days."

I wasn't entirely sure what the judge's reference to two days meant, so to push for the interpretation I wanted I said, "I'm not sure Mrs. Callahan will be back by then. I'd like to request a longer continuance than that."

"No continuance, Mr. O'Brian," the judge replied. "Two days is how long Mr. Carter has to straighten all this out to my satisfaction before I make an ethics complaint to the bar association. You have other witnesses you can call so there's no need for a continuance. Besides, the most important issue in this case is whether or not the war risk exclusion in the insurance contract applies in this situation. Your missing witness wasn't going to address that issue."

I started to object, but the judge cut me off. "We'll start promptly at one o'clock. Be ready to go then. Now get out of here so I can get some rest."

As we entered the hallway outside the judge's chambers Carter said, "Bloomquist looks awful." It was the first thing on which he and I could agree.

54

"Are you familiar with the consulting firm of Frankel, Baldwin & Ingram?"

It was a Herculean effort, but we managed to get all thirty-five boxes of discovery material to Judge Bloomquist's courtroom before court resumed at one o'clock.

Minutes after we arrived, Augustus Carter walked into the courtroom, accompanied not by his usual entourage of well-dressed and most likely well-paid associates. For the afternoon session the former federal judge had only two people with him. One was Harold Lamb, the attorney who appeared at the motion hearing in November. The second was a young lady who didn't look old enough to be out of high school, much less a member of the bar.

Harry Sporn sauntered in after Carter and took his usual seat in the front row of the public gallery directly behind the defendant's counsel table. He was accompanied by just two insurance company executives rather than the half dozen who had attended previous sessions. The older of the two was Thornton Bell, the CEO of FAIL Insurance. A descendant of Alexander Graham Bell, inventor of the telephone, Thornton Bell had a quiet, grandfatherly demeanor that served him well when testifying before congressional committees. I guessed the younger man was Bell's assistant.

"What's Bell doing here?" Rick whispered. It was the first time the company's CEO had shown up at the trial.

"Not sure," I replied. "If he's here to testify, he's early. We won't finish with Sporn this afternoon."

The jury filed in, Judge Bloomquist took the bench, and the afternoon session began with my direct examination of Harry Sporn. After the usual preliminary questions, I asked, "Before joining Federal American International Lines Insurance, were you a prosecutor in Hudson County?"

"Yes," Sporn answered. The jury already knew that because of Charles Farmer's testimony on Friday, but I wanted to make sure they remembered that Sporn had a legal background.

"And as someone with legal experience, you're familiar with the discovery process in litigation, are you not?"

"Correct," Sporn answered.

"Please tell the jury what discovery is."

Augustus Carter got to his feet. "Relevance? This isn't a law school classroom, and Mr. Sporn isn't ..."

The judge waved Carter back to his seat and instructed Sporn to answer the question.

"Discovery is the process that allows each side to obtain information in the possession of the other party," Sporn answered.

"And information supplied by each party has to be truthful, correct?"

"Correct," Sporn answered.

"You're a vice president of Federal American, the defendant, are you not?"

"Correct," Sporn answered, once again sticking with a one-word response.

"As a vice president, do you see policy manuals, studies, and other documents relating to the company's operation?"

"Usually."

Out of the corner of my eye, I watched Carter and Thornton Bell as I asked the next question. "For example, if there were a study done by a consultant on how to increase company profits, would you see that document?" Bell whispered something to his assistant.

"I assume I would," Sporn answered.

Rick got up and walked to the thirty-five numbered boxes stacked on the far side of the courtroom.

I pointed to Rick. "In response to my request for information, the discovery process you told us about a moment ago, you delivered the thirty-five boxes of material my partner is standing next to." It wasn't a question, so Sporn didn't have to respond, and he didn't.

"One of the things I asked for were copies of memos or other writings from outside consultants relating to your company's policies, official or unofficial, regarding the payment, negotiation, or denial of claims. Did you provide that information?"

"I assume we did," Sporn said. "But we had staff compile that information, so I have no personal knowledge of any particular document."

"Are you familiar with the consulting firm of Frankel, Baldwin & Ingram?" As I asked that question, Rick opened the box with a large "18" on the side and made a show of looking through it, although both of us knew the document he wanted was right in the front where he had put it.

"I might have heard of them," Sporn answered just as Rick withdrew the copy of the memo the cute redhead had slipped into a copy of *Sports Illustrated* the day Margaret and I went to the insurance company's office in Newark.

"Yes, I'm sure you have," I responded. "It's a nationally known firm that does a lot of work for insurance companies, including Federal American, the defendant." As I crossed the well of the court to retrieve the memo from Rick, Thornton Bell leaned over the railing and whispered something to Augustus Carter. Carter turned in his seat and a hushed conversation ensured.

"Something you'd care to share with the class?" Judge Bloomquist asked Carter, displaying for a brief moment the sense of humor that had disappeared as his illness progressed.

Before Carter could respond to the judge, I asked Sporn, "Are you familiar with a Frankel, Baldwin & Ingram memo to your company entitled *Maximizing Profits By Minimizing Claims Payouts?*

Carter jumped to his feet. "Don't answer that," he instructed Sporn. Turning his attention to the judge, my adversary said, "Your Honor, I respectfully request a short recess to consult with my client."

Perhaps sensing that we had reached a crucial point in the trial that could lead to a settlement, Judge Bloomquist granted Carter's request.

55

"Why such an odd amount?"

Thornton Bell and his assistant hurried out of the courtroom even before Judge Bloomquist had left the bench. I followed at a discrete distance. In the hallway just outside the courtroom, I overhead Bell tell his assistant, "Make that call to Parker."

I pulled my cell phone out of my pocket and fiddled with it as though I were planning to make a call. Augustus Carter emerged from the courtroom a moment later, and he and Bell headed for the Nook. Once they rounded the corner and were out of sight, I walked to a spot where I could overhear their conversation. I got there just in time to hear Bell tell Carter, "My assistant is on the phone with Cornelius Parker, who is about to become as unhappy as I am. Parker will be calling you momentarily. I strongly suggest you listen carefully to what he says."

Realizing the one-sided conversation was about to end, I quickly walked away from the Nook, put my cell phone up to my ear and began to carry on what I hoped would be a convincing conversation with the non-existent person on the other end of the call. The ruse worked. Bell passed me and disappeared down the hallway toward the courthouse exit without any indication that he knew I had overheard what he said to Augustus Carter.

I retraced my steps to my eavesdropping spot outside the Nook where I listened to Carter's side of a phone conversation. Based on the former federal judge's obsequious tone, I was certain he was talking to Cornelius Parker, his firm's founding partner. "I have no idea how they got it," he was telling Parker, quickly adding, "if, in fact, they did. O'Brian is known for bluffing." There was a pause, after which Carter said, "Yes, you're probably right. The fact that they know it exists means they probably have it." There was another pause during which I heard footsteps. I turned around, expecting to find someone approaching, but that stretch of hallway was deserted. I realized the footsteps I was hearing were Carter's, who was pacing while talking to his firm's founding partner.

"I have no idea," Carter said next. "I absolutely did not send that contest letter, and never authorized anyone else to send it." After a short pause, Carter said, "I might have said that the Callahan woman was their best witness, but I never suggested the Disney trip or anything like it." The pacing stopped. "I have my suspicions, but don't have any solid evidence, at least not yet." The pacing resumed. "Yes, I realize supervision is part of my job."

There was a long pause, and I thought the conversation had ended, but then Carter said, "They told us to do what?" There was another pause, shorter this time, followed by Carter asking, "Why would they get involved in this? They have nothing to do with the case." Carter waited, apparently receiving an answer to his question, before adding, "Yes, I realize the party is one of our most important clients, but I don't understand why they would tell us to do that. And why such an odd amount?" Carter started pacing again, listening to whatever explanation Cornelius Parker was providing. "Yes, I've got it. Yes, those exact words. I understand."

This was followed by "yes, sir" and "no, sir" and "I understand, sir" and "I agree completely, sir" more times than I could count. Carter was apparently receiving a tongue lashing from his superior.

"I'll take care of it and call you immediately," he finally said. "But just one last question, if I may, sir. What if O'Brian wants punitive damages?" Although I couldn't hear Parker's answer to the question, Carter's response told me all I needed to know. "Out of my bonus? That hardly seems fair."

The string of expletives I heard next told me that Carter had finished the call with Cornelius Parker. Putting my cell phone to my ear, I walked back toward the courtroom, trying to appear casual as I carried on yet another phony conversation.

"Mr. O'Brian, a word please." I turned to find Augustus Carter heading in my direction, giving no indication that he realized I had overheard his conversation with Parker. I made a show of terminating my non-existent conversation just as Carter reached where I was standing. "I underestimated you, O'Brian. You apparently have friends in high places." He waited for me to respond to his statement. When I didn't, he continued. "I've been authorized to settle this matter by paying your client the full amount of the policy's death benefit, with interest from the date of her husband's death. I've also been authorized to pay your firm a fee in the amount of $127,545."

"That's an odd amount," I replied, echoing the words I had spoken to Senator Scott when she mentioned that sum during our conversation at Consolidated TranShip.

"I quite agree," Carter replied. "I was told to tell you that it's a rounding error, part of a grand bargain. I have no idea what that means, but apparently you do."

I did, but instead of telling him that, I said, "The legal fee is fine, but there's not going to be a settlement unless your client is willing to pay punitive damages."

"You need to take my offer to your client," Carter said. "You've won. Be happy with that. If we go back in that courtroom, you don't know what's going to happen."

Having overheard his conversation with Cornelius Parker, I knew Carter was bluffing. "No settlement without punitive damages."

I turned around and walked away. I hadn't gone more than ten feet before Carter stopped me. "Wait. What kind of money are you looking for?"

"The amount of your annual bonus," I wanted to say. But since I couldn't let on that I had overheard his phone call, I pulled a number out of thin air. "Three hundred thousand."

"That's absurd."

Instead of responding verbally, I shrugged my shoulders and once again walked away.

"Wait a minute," Carter said.

I stopped and turned to face him. "Three hundred is my first, last and only offer."

Apparently resigning himself to the three hundred thousand, Carter said, "Fine," sounding like a petulant child.

"Have one of your associates tell the judge we want to put a settlement on the record." It felt good to issue a command to a self-important former federal judge.

Carter slunk away like a wounded animal and disappeared into the courtroom, brushing past Rick and Margaret, who had been observing the impromptu negotiations.

"You win," I told Margaret when I got to where they were standing. "You get the full death benefit, plus interest. You also get three hundred thousand dollars in punitive damages."

"Two hundred thousand," she corrected me. "You get a third of the punitive damages. That was our deal."

"I think we can waive our fee in your case," Rick said.

Margaret shook her head. "No, a deal's a deal."

Rick looked at me to back him up, but, instead, I agreed with Margaret. "A deal's a deal."

"Why didn't you waive our fee on the punitive damages award?" Rick asked during our drive back to the office. "After all, we picked up $127,545 from FAIL. Not a bad payday."

"No, a pretty good payday," I replied, "but $227,545 is an even better payday."

Rick gave me a look that I interpreted to mean, *I can't believe you said that.*

When I explained my plan for the money, Rick neither agreed nor disagreed. He just reiterated his earlier argument that real estate closings would generate a steady cash flow for the firm.

56

"I had no idea."

The week after the Woodson case concluded, I drove to Rizzo's Ritzy Rememorables in Dover to buy an item I had seen in the display window when Rick and I went there in search of information about Ronald Anderson.

I was in luck. The item I sought was still there, surrounded by the same bizarre collection of old magazines, rusting tools, and jewelry of doubtful provenance.

The interior was also the same as I remembered, from the dirty tile floor to the even dirtier Grateful Dead T-shirt on Gordy, Eddie Rizzo's overweight, balding cousin running the place. Gordy didn't show any signs of recognizing me, and I didn't bother to jog his memory. Shopkeepers who pull a gun on me aren't on my list of people to befriend.

After completing my purchase, I drove to Edna Anderson's house. I had called ahead, so I wasn't surprised when she opened the door even before the doorbell stopped chiming.

"Mr. O'Brian," she said. "It's good to see you. Please come in. How are you?"

A pot of coffee and two cups awaited us in the living room. "When I was in your office, I remember you drinking coffee, so I made a fresh pot." She poured us each a cup and we exchanged pleasantries for a few minutes. Finally, she couldn't contain her curiosity any longer. "When you called, you said you had information about Ronnie."

"I do," I answered. "Much of what I learned has come from my contacts in the federal government, and because of national security issues, I can't provide as much detail as I'd like." That wasn't an entirely accurate statement. There were certain things that Helms and Senator Scott told me I shouldn't reveal, but I came up with the national security angle to avoid having to tell Mrs. Anderson anything that might put her late husband in an unflattering light. The woman had been through a lot, and there was no reason to increase her suffering.

I took another sip of coffee before beginning my prepared speech. "Your husband was involved in a top-secret project for the federal government, the details of which I can't reveal. That project is still ongoing, and if it's successful, it will make headlines around the world. All I can tell you is that your husband died a hero in the line of duty."

"Oh, my," Mrs. Anderson said. "I had no idea."

"While I can't tell you what your husband was doing," I continued, "I can assure you that he was a crucial part of the project." Helms had told me that Ronald Anderson's job was moving items around the Consolidated TranShip facility, so "crucial" might have been a bit of an exaggeration.

I handed her the folded American flag encased in a triangular, glass-faced oak display case that I had bought at Rizzo's Ritzy Rememorables. "On behalf of a grateful nation, please accept this as an enduring reminder of your husband's faithful devotion to duty." Senator Scott hadn't authorized me to make the presentation, but I don't think she would have objected.

In retrospect, I think Edna Anderson was more impressed by my unauthorized flag ceremony than the check for $227,545 that I handed her on my way out the door.

Epilogue

Judge Bloomquist's health took a turn for the worse, and shortly after the Woodson trial concluded, he was admitted to Morristown Memorial Hospital with an advanced case of pneumonia. He died three days later.

Senator Scott also died, but under conditions considerably more mysterious. On a sunny morning in April, she boarded her private plane at a small airport outside Atlanta for what was supposed to have been a routine trip to Washington, D.C. The trip proved to be anything but routine, however. Shortly after takeoff, her plane crashed, killing everyone on board. The National Transportation Safety Board arrived on the scene to determine the cause of the crash, but their investigation came to a sudden halt when FBI agents appeared and took control. The FBI released a report two weeks later concluding that the crash was caused by tainted fuel that made the plane's engine malfunction. Interestingly, a local television reporter named Lytle discovered that all planes at that airport were fueled from the same source, and that no other plane experienced a similar problem. Lytle's revelation became national news, but was soon forgotten when the media turned its collective attention to the death of former president Richard Nixon.

A week after the senator's plane crashed, I drove to the Consolidated TranShip facility to ask Helms about Operation Grand

Bargain. The ten-foot electrified fence was gone, as was the guard house, allowing me to drive right up to the padlocked building. I looked through a window and saw nothing but an empty warehouse.

Helms wasn't the only one to do a disappearing act. When I called the number for Axberg Novelty Products on the business card that Reynaldo had given me, I got a recording that the number was no longer in service. Likewise, I have no idea what happened to Thompson, the funeral home employee who had been in Reynaldo's protective custody, or Jeremy Lin, the Chinese intelligence agent. I'm hoping Thompson is in the federal witness protection program, living a quiet life in a town somewhere far from Troy Forge. I'm guessing Lin is back in communist China.

In June, Carolyn, my former secretary, married Professor Chad, who teaches biology, not Medieval poetry. The ceremony took place in the back yard of Carolyn's sister's house in Dahlonega, Georgia. Rick and Elaine told me it was a beautiful ceremony.

I'll have to take their word for it.

I wasn't invited.

A Note from the Author

The characters, events and organizations in this book are the product of my over-active imagination. Any similarity to actual events, organizations and persons, living or dead, is purely coincidental, with the following exceptions:

The cases and court rules are real, including *Pickett v. Lloyd's*, which O'Brian tells Margaret Woodson about in chapter 2. The *Pickett* ruling, decided several months before the story takes place, made it difficult to prove an insurer's bad faith under New Jersey law. The task has been made easier, however, by more recent cases, such as *Bello v. Merrimack Mutual Fire Ins. Co.*

The witnesses who testify for the plaintiff are fictional, but their situations are based on real cases. Likewise, the reasons for avoiding payment articulated by Augustus Carter throughout the story (*e.g.*, concrete dust is the same thing as smoke) are also derived from actual cases.

The jury selection process explained in chapter 42 (*i.e.,* questioning by the judge rather than attorneys) is the way juries have been selected in New Jersey since 1969. In *State v. Manley*, decided by the New Jersey supreme court that year, the court pointed out that allowing attorneys to question prospective jurors results in attorneys seeking "a jury as favorable to the party's point of view as indoctrination through the medium of questions on assumed facts and rules of law can accomplish."

Although the consulting firm of Frankel, Baldwin & Ingram is fictitious, the memo that O'Brian obtains in chapter 5 and uses in court in chapter 54 is based on a real study done for a major insurance company by a nationally known consulting firm. Like its fictional counterpart, the real-world memo suggested that the insurance company could increase profits by minimizing claims payouts.

The Chinese bonds that play an important role in the story are very real. In the early years of the 20th century, the Chinese government issued a massive amount of sovereign debt that was purchased by governments, financial institutions, and individual investors around the world. When the communists took control of China, they repudiated that debt, a clear violation of well-settled international law. The 1979 treaty that Rick explains to O'Brian in chapter 13 is also real. However, I took liberties with the wording of that agreement. The actual treaty refers to "claims of the United States and its nationals." Such wording would seem to preclude a real-world equivalent of Senator Scott's Operation Grand Bargain if the U.S. government were to adhere to the literal terms of the agreement. Of course, as Senator Scott asks in chapter 40, if the Chinese don't want to honor their obligations, why should we? As Rick explains in chapter 4, British bondholders received payment when the U.K. government threatened to close that country's financial markets to China in 1987. Details about the fascinating subject of unpaid Chinese bonds can be found on the website of the American Bondholders Foundation (https://www.americanbondholdersfoundation.com).

If you enjoyed this book, please tell others and consider posting a review on Amazon. Favorable reviews and word of mouth are the best ways for independent authors to gain readers.

Contact the author at kerwinbook@icloud.com

GREY SQUIRREL PRESS

Made in the USA
Columbia, SC
28 July 2020